"If you like Paris, swords as old as time, a soul-deep love story, and wild adventure, then *The Deepest Edge* is for you."
                                            —Catherine Coulter

Pierced . . .

"Go." Jian-Shan didn't have time to argue with the child, so he gave her another small push toward the house. The sound of a gasp nearby made him step between it and Lily, automatically shielding her with his body.

Someone, a woman, appeared from behind one of the garden stones. His mouth tightened as he recognized her—the fallen angel who had tried to see him at his office and followed his limo.

Why is she running?

He anticipated her path, then saw the dark figure of the man she was running from. The man removed something from his coat. Jian-Shan immediately reached down and jerked the small revolver from its ankle holster, and had it in his hand a heartbeat before the woman reached him.

She hurtled forward, her dark eyes wide, her arm reaching out as if to stop him. "Look out!"

Something struck her, driving her forward into him. Steel pierced his flesh as he caught her. Time stopped as they stood together, her terrified gaze locked on her hand where it lay pinned against his chest.

He clamped his left arm around her narrow waist and targeted the man in the coat. "Han!"

His bodyguard ran out of the house, saw Jian-Shan, then scooped Lily up in his arms and dropped behind one of the boulders to take cover.

THE
DEEPEST
EDGE

Jessica Hall

A SIGNET BOOK

SIGNET
Published by New American Library, a division of
Penguin Putnam Inc., 375 Hudson Street,
New York, New York 10014, U.S.A.
Penguin Books Ltd, 80 Strand,
London WC2R ORL, England
Penguin Books Australia Ltd, 250 Camberwell Road,
Camberwell, Victoria 3124, Australia
Penguin Books Canada Ltd, 10 Alcorn Avenue,
Toronto, Ontario, Canada M4V 3B2
Penguin Books (N.Z.) Ltd, Cnr. Rosedale and Airborne Roads,
Albany, Auckland 1310, New Zealand

Penguin Books Ltd, Registered Offices:
Harmondsworth, Middlesex, England

First published by Signet, an imprint of New American Library,
a division of Penguin Putnam Inc.

First Printing, February 2003
10 9 8 7 6 5 4 3 2 1

 REGISTERED TRADEMARK—MARCA REGISTRADA

Printed in the United States of America

PUBLISHER'S NOTE
This is a work of fiction. Names, characters, places, and incidents either are
the product of the author's imagination or are used fictitiously, and any
resemblance to actual persons, living or dead, business establishments,
events, or locales is entirely coincidental.

BOOKS ARE AVAILABLE AT QUANTITY DISCOUNTS WHEN USED TO PROMOTE PRODUCTS
OR SERVICES. FOR INFORMATION PLEASE WRITE TO PREMIUM MARKETING DIVISION,
PENGUIN PUTNAM INC., 375 HUDSON STREET, NEW YORK, NEW YORK 10014.

To Cecilia Oh
With much love and thanks

Chapter 1

As soon as he saw her appear on the wall of video screens, he forgot about the sword in his hands. Security cameras two floors below his office tracked her as she passed through the double glass doors, crossed the white marble floor, and stopped in front of the lobby reception desk. Every movement she made was like a subtle invitation.

Watch me.

Without looking away from the monitor, T'ang Jian-Shan took the three-foot-long Masamune blade he had been examining and replaced it in its sheath.

At first glance, nothing about the woman necessarily demanded his attention. Of average height and slender build, she presented no apparent physical challenge to his security guards. The slim briefcase she carried wasn't handcuffed to her wrist. The low-heeled pumps on her feet matched her unremarkable, conservative jacket and skirt. Everything about her said "businesswoman."

Everything but the way she moved.

Her stride was easy, fluid, without hesitation—as if she was so intent on her target that nothing else mattered. She was like the sword in his hands and the way it glided through the air—just before it sliced through skin and muscle and bone.

Is she a businesswoman, or a weapon?

He reached out and pressed the zoom switch to enlarge her image. She was not beautiful, and her exotic features and bone structure hinted that more than Caucasian blood ran in her veins. Other than a narrow watch and small gold hoops in her earlobes, she wore no jewelry. Not that she needed more.

She wears her hair and her skin like jewels.

When she turned slightly to speak to the receptionist, light played over the sophisticated coil of pale hair at the back of her head and chased the movements of her gleaming lips. She'd used dark lipstick to camouflage the full curves of her mouth, but like her body, it too sent a message.

Would you like a taste?

As if sensing the camera, the woman removed her sunglasses, exposing the full impact of her striking face. Long lashes swept up, revealing unusual eyes—so dark that he could not see the pupils within the irises. They glittered above her prominent cheekbones and slightly crooked nose like *kurozuishou* cabochons set into an alabaster Noh mask.

Her lips said *come to me*, but her eyes added *if you dare*.

He felt the allure of that challenge but ignored it. An ordinary businesswoman didn't have clever eyes and the mouth of a fallen angel. At least, not in his business.

"Han." The black-and-white screens didn't reveal the precise color of her fair hair or midnight eyes, which annoyed him. "This gaijin, do you recognize her?"

His bodyguard lumbered over to loom beside him, and inspected the close-up image of her face. "No, I have not seen her before, *kei*."

He touched a switch to zoom out as his business manager, Madelaine Pierport, appeared in front of the woman at the reception desk. The visitor switched the briefcase from her right hand to her left before shaking Madelaine's hand.

He pushed the sword case across the desk. "Put the Masamune in the car, if you would."

"*Hai.*" Han retrieved the case and departed.

He waited until the door closed before he enabled the audio. A low, sultry voice came over the speakers, as close and warm as a caress.

"—letters of introduction," she was telling Madelaine. "I'd be happy to leave them with you."

An American. Who desired an introduction. How interesting.

He'd hired Madelaine for her competence at handling the public as well as the many brokers, buyers, and collectors he dealt with, and she'd never disappointed him.

Nor did she now. "Mademoiselle, I regret I cannot be of assistance." She made a small gesture with one of her slim ringed hands. "The owner does not accept unsolicited offers or invitations."

That much was true. Jian-Shan did the offering and inviting, or not at all. Yet he was briefly tempted to call down and have the American brought to him. All it required was the press of a single button on the security console, and his guards would escort her directly to his office. Whether she wanted to come to him or not.

Maybe that is what she wants.

The uninvited visitor didn't give up that easily. "Then I'd like to make an appointment to speak with him personally. Today, if possible."

Madelaine produced a small, pitying smile. "Monsieur T'ang also does not accept unsolicited appointments."

"Surely Mr. T'ang has a free moment or two." She looked around the lobby, assessing everything. "I'm the only person here."

His hand went to the security console as Madelaine continued to deny the visitor any access to him.

"I'm sorry for making a fuss. It's just imperative that I speak with him." Oddly, the American sounded both exasperated and amused. "Can you at least tell me if he received the letter I wrote to him, regarding our proposal for the fall exhibition? I'm a curator with the New Orleans Museum of Art and Antiquities."

His hand stopped, and moved away from the button.

Madelaine shook her head. "Again, I must disappoint you, mademoiselle." She turned to the receptionist. "Lisette, would you call a taxi for the mademoiselle, please?"

He knew his business manager would have thrown away the American's proposal, along with the rest of the unsolicited mail sent to him each month. He sensed movement, and looked up to see the office door open.

"*Sumimasen, kei.*" His bodyguard nodded toward the corridor. "The car is ready."

"Thank you, Han." He rose from his desk and closed his briefcase, but continued to watch the screen.

"Mr. T'ang does not exhibit his collection in public," his business manager was saying to the American curator. "The White Tiger *zaibatsu* is a private conservatory society, devoted solely to the identification and preservation of priceless Asian antiquities."

"I know; I do the same thing on the other side of the ocean." She glanced toward the security guards for a moment. "You're positive there's no other way I can reach Mr. T'ang?"

Han tensed at the sound of her voice. "This gaijin is an American."

"Yes." Discipline demanded that he stop playing voyeur, so he reached over and switched off the monitors. "It does not matter. She is leaving."

Valence St. Charles had absolutely no intention of leaving Paris.

From the moment her cab from the airport had entered the city last night, she'd been enchanted. The city was much larger than she had imagined, and bejeweled with light and sound and color. She would be sightseeing whether she wanted to or not, for there were astonishing sights at the turn of every corner, from the ornate architecture of many different eras to the charm of tulip gardens blooming in carefully tended parks.

She had rolled down her window to hear something of the city's sounds. Beyond the rushing cars and beeping horns, music spilled from open doorways and windows—she caught snatches of everything from the obligatory "La Vie en Rose" to

American jazz. People walking dogs strolled along the sidewalks, and their pets' barks added sharp staccato notes to the mix. And everywhere people gathered, voices rose and fell in the familiar, melodic rhythms of French.

Eighteen hours later, the beauty of Paris had not faded, but some of its charm had. Probably because Val had not expected to be so completely stonewalled by one inhabitant in particular.

"Again, I must disappoint you, mademoiselle." T'ang's business manager, Madelaine Pierport, turned to the receptionist. "Lisette, would you call a taxi for the mademoiselle, please?"

The hell with the taxi, I want five minutes alone with T'ang Jian-Shan. She'd tried to coax the French-woman into making an exception for her, until she made it obvious that a private meeting between Val and her boss wouldn't happen until hell hosted the Winter Olympics.

"Well, thank you for your time." Val handed the woman her business card. "I wrote the number of my hotel on the back. If you would mention to Mr. T'ang that I've traveled all this way to Paris specifi-cally to see him, I would appreciate it."

"I'm sure you would." The tip of Madelaine's high-bridged nose elevated another notch, and she held the card the way she would a piece of contam-inated trash. "Enjoy your visit to my country, mademoiselle."

Val kept a straight face until she strode out of the building, and then allowed herself to scowl. "'Enjoy your visit to my country.' Ha. That sounded more like 'Go jump in the Seine.'"

She paused outside on the narrow sidewalk to

lift her face toward the pastel blue and pink sky. After being stuck in the artificial environments of the airplane, taxis, her hotel, and T'ang's building, she enjoyed feeling the sun on her skin. The thought of abandoning her task to explore Paris and enjoy herself became far too tempting.

Getting here was half the battle. I can't give up now.

T'ang was her immediate problem. Someone else might give her permission to examine the White Tiger swords, but as the owner, only he could consent to exhibit the entire collection in another country. The book she was writing depended on the swords themselves, but her continued employment centered on getting him to approve the loan of them to her museum. And she had gambled everything to get here—not only her job, but her professional reputation and possibly her entire career.

If I could just talk to him for five minutes.

His business manager's Doberman-like attitude eliminated any hope of seeing the owner at his offices. She would simply have to find another way to get to T'ang and speak to him about the swords. Then if he said no, she'd call it quits and do some sight-seeing.

Not like I'll have to hurry home.

As a taxi pulled up to the curb, the sound of another, smoother engine made Val turn. A limousine with dark-tinted windows pulled out from behind T'ang's building and waited to edge into the frantic flow of morning traffic. The license plate was unremarkable, but a small black square with a white Chinese symbol was stuck to the inside of the back window.

The man himself, perhaps?

She yanked open the door of the battered cab and slid inside. "Can you follow that limousine?" she asked as she climbed in.

"De quoi parlez-vous?" The heavyset driver lifted his cap and glanced back at her. "What limousine, mademoiselle?"

"The one right . . . there." Val peered through the windshield, but the big black car had vanished. *"Oh, merde."*

She thought for a moment. If T'ang wouldn't see her without an invitation, she'd have to get one. Perhaps one of the other members of his society would be willing to assist her. She took her personal data organizer from her briefcase and checked her list.

"Would you please take me to 27 rue de l'Observatoire, to le Galerie du Dragon Rouge?"

"Mais oui, mademoiselle."

On the way to the gallery, Val rehearsed a short speech in her head. The antiquities dealers in any major city were inevitably a very tight-knit, reserved group who didn't welcome outsiders. The fact that all of the Asian dealers in Paris had formed their own inner circle within the market in the White Tiger *zaibatsu* also didn't bode well.

Her obnoxious boss had been quick to point that out, along with every flaw in her plan, in no uncertain terms.

"You don't understand these Orientals, Val." Drake Scribner III clipped the end of a thin cigar and lit it, puffing until the tip glowed. "First of all, they hate women, especially the ones who don't stay at home, cooking and having babies."

"I'm well aware of the traditional Asian male's

attitude toward women's roles in society, Mr. Scribner." She produced a patient smile. "But I'm a foreigner—a gaijin—so I think they'll show a little more tolerance toward me."

"Well, then there's the other thing: you know as well as I do that T'ang went public with the White Tiger blades only last month. The minute he did, every museum curator in the world—excuse my language—got a big old hard-on for those swords." He regarded her through the exhaled smoke. "You're going to have to do something real special to push to the head of the line, with all those folks waiting to . . . romance the man."

Val wondered if Scribner knew how tiring his phony "Southern Poor Boy Makes Good" routine was. While he enjoyed making people believe he'd overcome poverty to make his own fortune and place in society, she knew from staff gossip that his family had moved to New Orleans from Cleveland, where his grandfather had made a fortune in the aluminum siding business. Drake himself had been educated at Harvard and hadn't done an honest day's work since.

Scribner was also a Neanderthal-class chauvinist with the libido to match, but a woman found that out ten seconds after meeting him.

"The Glasgow Museum of Weaponry was happy to lend us their fifteenth-century claymores for the summer," she reminded him, her voice as patient as she could make it. "If you remember, that collection had never left Scotland before."

"I admit, Glasgow was a touchdown." Scribner blew more smoke in a thin stream across his desk, which was littered with college football memorabilia from his short and largely unsuccessful stint as a second-string lineman at Harvard. "But that's what I'm saying—it's yesterday's news, Val. I've got a fall exhibition coming up and three senators making speeches. I need a draw."

What he meant was, *What are you going to do for me today?*

The acrid smoke made her eyes water, and she blinked. "The largest private collection of Nagatoki swords in existence is definitely a draw, sir. Collectors and scholars from all over the world will come to see them."

He brushed a bit of ash from the sleeve of his white suit. "You thinking of offering this Chinaman the same services you gave them Scots?"

Scribner made it sound as if she'd traded oral sex for the claymores. "The Glasgow Museum was delighted to get my research. With it, they were able to positively correlate clan ownership for twenty previously unidentified blades." She removed a file from her briefcase. "What I'm offering T'ang is much more significant. It will change everything that has been assumed about the forging of Nagatoki blades. It's all outlined here."

"I've already read it." Her boss casually waved a hand. "You know, I never pegged you as a closet feminist. In any case, you should drop this whole idea before it gets you into some serious trouble."

She was used to tolerating his patronizing attitude, but this was pushing her patience past even her limits. "My theory has nothing to do with the feminist movement. It's a valid explanation for a lot of inconsistencies with the Nagatoki blades."

"There was no sword described in T'ang's collection like the one you seem to think is so important. Which one was it? The bird blade?"

"Lady Kameko called it the phoenix blade."

He waved a hand. "Bird, phoenix, chicken, doesn't matter. According to what I read, he ain't got one of them."

"We don't know that. Mr. T'ang didn't list a complete description of all the Nagatoki swords in the press release."

"Or it's more of that pure wishful thinking you seem to indulge in." His gaze flickered down to her breasts as he produced a mock sad expression. "All you've got here, honey, is some spectacular speculation. That's it. And in this field, proof is the meat and potatoes. Unless you get the evidence to back it up, you won't change shit."

"Examining T'ang's collection will give me all the proof I need." She placed the file on his desk. "He owns more of them than any other collector in the world. According to Lady Kameko's journals, the phoenix symbol will be etched on at least ten of them. Those blades, combined with the key phoenix sword, will reveal the name of the true sword maker."

"And if you unwrap those hilts and find not a single little bird on fire? What then?" He chuffed out a laugh. "Oh, honey, just give it up. You've got a better chance of finding and digging up another Tutankhamen than validating this theory of yours."

"I'll prove it." She got to her feet. "And I'd appreciate it, sir, if you wouldn't call me 'honey.'"

He smirked. "I reckon you think it's demeaning, and unprofessional."

"The same way you would if someone went

around calling you a prick," she said without thinking.

"No one would be that stupid, would they?" Scribner rolled the cigar between his fingers. "You know, it occurs to me that I've put up with a lot from you, *Ms. St. Charles.* I think it's high time I draw the line now. I'm not wasting museum funds on a fairy tale that my junior curator's been telling herself so she can go to Paris and do some shopping."

And that summed up precisely what Scribner thought of women: they were good only for sex, wild-goose chases, and shopping. He had more in common with the traditional Asian male attitude than he realized.

"I never expected you to pay for it." Val kept her tone even. "I'll cover the trip myself and use my vacation time. If I'm right, and T'ang agrees to loan us the White Tiger swords, then you can refund my expenses. If he doesn't, you lose nothing."

Scribner considered that. "I guess I've got no choice, then. All right, I'll let you go on your little crusade. You have a real good time, but just remember one thing. I've got twenty girls just panting in the wings, watching your job. Girls who would be more than grateful for the promotion."

What he meant was he'd replace her with the redheaded graduate student who worked in the restoration rooms. The same one who giggled incessantly whenever Scribner surreptitiously squeezed her youthful backside. "I understand, sir."

"Good. I'll give you a week to pull it off. If T'ang turns you down"—he smiled around the cigar—

"stay in Paris and enjoy yourself. Won't be any reason for you to hurry back at all."

Val's thoughts snapped back to the present as the taxi came to a stop in front of a row of antique stores.

"Ici, mademoiselle."

"Mademoiselle Pierport called this morning," Shikoro said in Japanese as she brought the tray of tea to his desk and gracefully folded back one sleeve of her kimono before pouring. "Madam Chen also wishes to speak to you regarding a recent acquisition."

"Thank you, Shikoro." Jian-Shan glanced at the open doorway. "Has Lily had lunch yet?"

"Han is in the kitchen with her now, catching her peas." The middle-aged woman smiled. "Her aim improves each day."

"I will take her out in the garden when she is finished eating." He sipped his tea. "You should not allow her to pelt your husband with her food."

"They make a game of it." When she noticed his expression, she sobered and bowed. "Of course, it will be as you wish, *senpai.*"

As he dialed Madam Chen's number at her gallery, Jian-Shan thought about the American woman again. Her image had never really left his mind. All morning she had hovered at the fringes, looking through the black-and-white screen at him, as if she knew he was studying her from the other side.

Watch me.

He had not felt such a strong response to a woman in years, not since meeting Karen for the first time at his father's home in Beijing.

As the only son of T'ang Po, head of the Shan-

dian tong, Jian-Shan had been carefully trained
from birth to serve his father and to one day take
over his vast global crime organization. He had
met Senator Colfax during the American's visit to
China, but politicians seduced by his father's
money were not uncommon. The senator's wife, on
the other hand, was a singularly lovely and fragile-
looking blonde, and he had been drawn to her the
first time he had looked into her large, haunted
eyes. Jian-Shan might never have guessed what put
the shadows in Karen Colfax's eyes had he not
stumbled onto her secret late one night.

The smell of perfume and the sound of weeping
had drawn him to his father's garden, where he
discovered the source of both. "Are you well,
Madam Colfax?"

She had tried to run away, but he had seen the
blood on her face and stopped her. Someone had
struck her, for her lip had split and a bruise surrounded her right eye. He knew exactly how hard
the blows would have been to do that. He had
done the same and worse to any number of enemies of his tong.

That someone dared do it to an honored guest in
his father's house enraged him. "Who did this to
you?"

"No," she pleaded. "I'm fine. I just . . . I just fell,
and . . . and . . ." She stopped and flinched as he
touched her face, checking for broken bones, then
dropped her head against his chest and simply
sobbed.

He had taken her inside, to calm her down and
wash the blood from her face. Even after she
stopped crying, she refused to tell him who had

beaten her, still insisting she had fallen and hurt herself. Only when she begged him not to tell her husband did he realize it had been the senator who had used his fists on her. From the degree of terror she displayed, Jian-Shan suspected it was not the first time he had beaten her either.

"You will have to wear dark glasses tomorrow, Madam Colfax," he told her, wishing her husband was not so important to his father. A man who abused his woman didn't deserve to breathe. "And you must know he will not stop."

Judging by her shudder, she knew. "Thank you for helping me. I'm very sorry about this."

He gently pressed a finger against her swollen lips. "If you need help again, come to me."

That had been the beginning.

Then he touched the scar on his throat and remembered the day a year later, when he had tried to leave China the first time. That day, he had stared down three feet of razor sharp steel into his father's furious eyes.

Make no mistake, my son. Your hands belong to the tong, but your soul belongs to me. You will do as I tell you, whatever I tell you to do. Forget about that American whore.

T'ang Po had subsequently ordered his bodyguards to beat Jian-Shan until he lost consciousness. When he came to, he had pretended to defer to his father, until he could steal what he needed to make his second escape attempt successful.

There were still moments when Jian-Shan perversely wished he had listened to his father. If he had, Karen might still be alive.

With some effort, he shifted his focus from his

past mistakes to his present plan. He couldn't afford to make a mistake, not this late in the game. Not when he was this close to achieving everything he had lived for since Lily was born.

He had brought the swords to France and hidden them. He had sent a message to the tong, informing them that he would never return, a direct challenge to his father's authority. All he had to do was wait for T'ang Po to take the bait.

He took out a contact list for the members of the White Tiger society and dialed the first number. "Yohto Tenaka, please."

Three hours later Val sat down at a small table and kicked off her shoes. Tourists and city workers crowded the busy outdoor café, but she ignored them as she stretched out her tired legs and contemplated her cramping toes.

Since when did I become the Ugly American?

As she'd gone from shop to shop, she'd discovered two things: the Chinese and Japanese dealers who dominated the Asian antiquities market all sported the same white-on-black Chinese-character sticker in their shop windows. None of them would talk to her the moment she mentioned Jian-Shan.

"All I'd like to do is meet the man," she told one elderly Japanese woman, who only shook her head and pointed to the door.

"Is there some function Mr. T'ang attends regularly?" she asked another dealer. "Perhaps you could direct me—"

Before she could finish, the man erupted into furious Chinese and literally marched her out to the street.

Word passed down the row of shops, judging by the increasingly hostile reception she got. Doors were slammed in her face. Shades were pulled down. CLOSED signs were slapped in windows. No one was going to help her; that was evident. Not that that was anything new. Yet, in a strange way, she admired T'ang's society. Commanding that type of blind loyalty took some doing—what sort of man was he?

You want to find out, you'd better track him down your own way.

She considered privately advertising that she had a Nagatoki blade for sale, but undoubtedly a middleman would be sent to check it out. Once T'ang learned she had no sword, the doors would only slam in her face that much harder.

There's no other way. I've got to go to him.

As a kid in New Orleans, Val had learned how to dodge a lot of people: welfare officers, social workers, even the shopkeepers who suspected she'd stolen from them. The French Quarter was a veritable rabbit warren of side streets and niches that she had memorized, until she had dozens of safe places to go to ground. Even experienced beat cops policing the tourist district had been hard-pressed to find her.

She'd also learned a few other tricks in the process.

"Mademoiselle?" A dark-haired waiter with a beaky nose appeared at her elbow, hovering with the kind of patient indignation that only a true Parisian could pull off. "You wish to order something?"

"Café noir, s'il vous plaît." Ignoring his bad mood, she gave him a smile to melt stone. "Monsieur, tell me something. If I showed up at your house on a

motorcycle and knocked on your door, would you slam it in my face?"

"*Non, mademoiselle*," he said, his expression becoming even more pained. "My wife would, but only after she stabbed me in the heart with a butcher knife."

She tilted her head back and laughed. "I guess I won't follow you home, then."

His lips twitched with reluctant admiration. "*Merci beaucoup*, mademoiselle."

In a more expensive restaurant a few blocks from where Val sat drinking black coffee and plotting, another visitor contemplated his assignment. There were a few benefits to working in Paris, the assassin thought as he finished his superb meal. The people were obnoxious and the traffic ridiculous, but the food was incomparable.

An immaculately dressed waiter appeared two seconds after he took the last bite of his chicken and truffles. "Monsieur?"

"I will have café au lait and *la patisserie chocolat*," he said.

The waiter removed his plate and refilled his glass with pale wine. "Very good, monsieur."

As he waited for the dessert course to be served, his digital cell phone rang. Several other patrons of the restaurant eyed him with clear disapproval as he answered it. The French considered eating well a religion, and taking a phone call at the table was cognate to shouting in church.

The assassin personally thought the French could spend less time stuffing themselves in their culinary shrines and more getting some much-needed exercise. *"Oui."*

"You have located the swords?"

"I have some leads." He sipped his wine and suppressed a small belch. "Your impatience will not bring a speedy end to my task."

"I am not paying you to sit and gorge yourself on overpriced mushrooms."

"A man has to eat." The assassin allowed his gaze to casually sweep the interior, and in one corner he spotted a man studying a menu intently. "I will contact you when I have more information."

"There was a young American woman who visited the shops today, asking about Jian-Shan. She left a card with the name Valence St. Charles and an address for a museum in New Orleans. Find her and learn if she knows anything." The caller abruptly hung up.

The assassin rose from his table and wandered through the restaurant to the small corridor leading to the rest rooms. Across from the men's facilities was a stack of boxes around an open doorway. A quick glance inside revealed a crowded supply closet. At the sound of footsteps, he crouched behind the boxes.

When the assassin returned to his table several minutes later, he found the waiter waiting with his coffee and dessert. "Ah, I must forgo the pleasure. Here." He dropped a handful of notes on the table and left.

When required to do so, the assassin could work both quickly and efficiently. Within four hours of the call from his informant, he knew where the young American woman was staying and why she had come to Paris. Now all he had to do was stake out her hotel, follow her when she left, and discover if she knew where T'ang Jian-Shan was hiding the White Tiger swords.

As for the waiter, the assassin's generous tip more than made up for his criminal neglect of the best patisserie in the city, and for another customer who had somehow slipped out without paying his bill. He gave no further thought to the two men until later that evening, when the plumber, who had been summoned to fix one of the toilets, ran out of the men's room shouting for someone to summon the police.

The waiter found his missing customer in one of the stalls, which had a handwritten OUT OF ORDER sign hung on the door. The man had been propped on top of the toilet, with his lower legs and feet tucked inside the bowl.

The thin wire used to strangle him still remained around his neck.

Renting the motorcycle and buying the outerwear she needed created another set of challenges, but Val was able to charm her way through the process. She found that, much like their counterparts across the Atlantic, even the gloomiest of Parisian shop owners could be mellowed by a smile and some mild flirtation. Within a few hours she donned her new leather jacket and helmet and drove the rented Ducati to an alley across from the White Tiger *zaibatsu* building, where she parked next to a public phone booth.

Now, where is that big black limo, Mr. T'ang?

Her surveillance proved fruitless on the first day. Toward the end of the second, when she was idly considering calling Scribner and telling him to hire the little redhead he wanted to chase around his desk, the long black limousine abruptly appeared and parked behind T'ang's building.

From her position, she saw only an enormous Asian man dressed in a plain dark suit emerge from the driver's side. *Probably the bodyguard*, she thought, and watched as he disappeared.

She heard a second door slam, then she climbed off the motorcycle and went to the phone. "*Bonjour*, White Tiger *zaibatsu*," the receptionist said.

"I have a delivery for a Mr. T'ang," Val said in her best fake Parisian accent. "Our courier will arrive at his office in five minutes. Is he there to sign for it?"

"Monsieur T'ang does not come to this office."

"His man—the big fellow—I have delivered to him before. Is he available?"

"Mr. Han just arrived. Shall I transfer you?"

"*Non, merci*," she said, and hung up the phone, then walked out to look at the limo in the alley. *So you send Mr. Han to collect whatever you need from the office.*

The bodyguard didn't stay very long. Val had waited only thirty minutes before she heard a door shut and saw the oversized driver walk around the back of the car and climb in behind the wheel. As the limo departed, she started the motorcycle's engine and pulled down the visor on her helmet.

Now let's see where you go from here, cher.

As Han maneuvered the long vehicle through traffic, Val tried to keep two cars between them. When they left the business district, she dropped back even farther, pacing the car from different lanes, always keeping a low profile. Then a truck stopped suddenly to avoid a taxi speeding through a red light, and traffic came to a complete halt.

She flipped up her helmet's dark visor to see what was wrong, and someone in the back of the limo opened the black-tinted window and leaned out to do the same thing. Then he turned and saw her. He was wearing shades, so she couldn't see his eyes; she got only a quick glimpse of his face before he retreated and closed the window.

There were two men in the car?

The impact of that brief glance sizzled through her—it was almost as if he'd recognized her. But she was positive she had never seen him before. *And he can't be T'ang, he's too young. He wouldn't ride in the back unless he were family. Could he be a son?*

The limo driver suddenly turned out and eased through an impossibly narrow gap to make the corner.

No, no, not now.

She pulled her visor down and followed, weaving around the gridlocked cars to get to the corner. The limo was already four blocks away and traveling at high speed, moving in and out of traffic. Val tried to catch up, but lost the vehicle as it disappeared into a network of streets and alleys behind some auto and body shops. She ended up stopping at a curb and wrenching off her helmet.

"Damn it!"

A trio of mechanics working in the open bay of a garage gave her a disapproving look, until she threw up her hands and yelled, "What is it with you men?"

"Women, mademoiselle," one of them told her. "It is always the women." The three broke into laughter, and after a moment she joined in.

Chapter 2

Val returned to the alley for the remainder of the day, but the limo never reappeared. It also remained missing on the next day. On the third, however, it pulled in again behind the building. She didn't hesitate, but left the motorcycle and crossed the street as soon as the driver entered the building alone. Through the clear front windshield of the limo, she could see that the vehicle was empty.

Not sneaking along for the ride anymore, Mr. T'ang? I'll still find you.

Her stroll across the street included a check for security cameras on the exterior of the building. The only one she saw was angled toward the driver's side of the vehicle. Still moving as if out for a walk, Val ducked under the camera, then dropped and rolled beneath the limo. She had to inch her way to the back of the vehicle, where she pulled herself out and up to a crouch behind the trunk.

The key lock proved as simple to pick as the ones from her childhood. The pins depressed easily, one by one, until the inside latch released. She caught the edge of the trunk and slowly eased it up until there was enough space for her to crawl in. Once inside, she looped a finger through the trunk latch and pulled it down far enough to make it appear closed without actually locking herself in the trunk.

Now let's see where you take me.

The driver climbed into the limo a short time later and drove away from the building. The ride was long, and Val peered through the gap, trying to see where they were going. The driver was clever; he drove through the rows of auto shops and then quickly backtracked. He even pulled in at a busy limousine service shop, where there were more than a dozen cars identical to his moving in and out of the back lot, and parked for several minutes with the motor running.

As if he knows someone could be following him and is trying to catch them. It was impossible to see if anyone was; Val's view of the street was limited to a small gap.

Finally the limo left the lot and traveled to an exclusive residential street near the Champs Elysee. Many of the stately homes there were surrounded by privacy fences, and what she hoped was T'ang's was no exception. She eyed the high masonry wall with its electronic gate as the limo drove inside; then she pulled the trunk lid down to make it appear closed.

Definitely no trespassing here.

It was so easy it bordered on ridiculous.

On the first day the assassin had followed Valence St. Charles, he'd achieved nothing. In fact, given her talent for surveillance, he began to wonder if the American girl's identity was a complete facade and he was actually dealing with a professional colleague. He revised his opinion when he easily slipped into her hotel suite and tagged her clothing with a small tracer.

On the second day, his reluctant admiration returned as he observed her slipping into the trunk of the limousine. Now that was street-smart American ingenuity at work, he thought as he filed away the idea for future assignments.

Following the tracer signal led him through a rabbit warren of streets, but he was able to remain some distance behind so as not to alarm the driver or the girl. Valence St. Charles's cheeky move led him directly to T'ang's safe house, which he had been trying to find for three weeks.

He called in to his employer, and gave him an updated report. When he was finished, he added, "I should wait until dark, then go in to find the swords. I can kill him as he sleeps."

"No. They will not be there; he only pretends to keep them close at hand." His employer snorted. "Hoping to lure me to him."

The assassin suppressed a sigh. Although his employer was extremely wealthy, he suspected he was also seriously unbalanced, especially where Jian-Shan was concerned. "Then what do you wish me to do, sir?"

"Disable my son and bring him to me."

Val waited until she heard the limo's door open and close, then allowed a few more minutes for T'ang's driver to enter the house before she raised the trunk hatch again and climbed out.

The limo was parked in a garage, the door closed behind it. Two doors were visible at the other end.

Better he finds me in the yard than in the house. Val quickly moved across the garage and slipped out into the back. There she found herself standing in the middle of a large, serene Asian garden.

Unlike traditional Western gardeners, the Japanese preferred shrubs and trees to flowering plants, so everything was cool and green. Sweeping expanses of white sand, carefully raked with long stretches of curving lines, imitated ocean waves as they swirled through the yard.

Interesting rocks studded the sand, most of them round and ranging in size from riverbed pebbles to half-ton boulders. Small circular patches of mossy grass grew around the stones, also the result of meticulous attention. Four weathered stone lanterns were placed at strategic points along the sand sweeps. Above her head, feathery ferns hung in baskets suspended from the branches of willow and cherry trees. It was as if she had stepped through a door to another part of the world.

All this place needs is a little bottle labeled DRINK ME *in Japanese.*

She didn't see any residents of Wonderland or Tokyo, but toward the center of the yard was a large, bright green turtle filled with some of the same white sand. A bucket and shovel sat beside it, waiting for a child to come along.

Maybe he has a granddaughter.

Movement nearby made her crouch down behind one of the boulders, and then she heard a little girl laugh.

*   *   *

"Lily-san is eager to go to her turtle," Shikoro said.

Unobserved by Han or his wife, Jian-Shan watched from the doorway. His daughter wriggled in her high chair as his housekeeper wiped the small face and hands clean.

"Lily-san is eager to do everything but put her food in her mouth," his dignified bodyguard said as he carefully removed several smashed peas from his immaculate jacket, hands, and face. The former sumo wrestler bent over to regard the child. "You will dig only inside your turtle today, Lily-san. *Hai?*"

She showed him all six tiny pearls of her teeth. "*Hai.*"

Jian-Shan had suspected that the recent addition of the garish plastic turtle to Han's otherwise flawless *karesansai* garden had been to protect his carefully tended sand from Lily's busy toy spade.

"I will take her." He moved into the kitchen and removed the little girl from her high chair and set her down on the floor. "Come, Lily."

He had gotten into the habit of supervising the child while she played in the garden. Shikoro cared for Lily virtually twenty-four hours a day, and she deserved an hour of peace in the afternoon. Sometimes he would watch her antics from one of the low stone meditation benches, but today he felt restless and decided to repeat his morning tai chi exercises.

Someone is close.

He scanned the garden but saw nothing. No one knew the location of the house; he and Han had made sure of that.

Will it never end?

The serenity of losing himself in the Cloud Hands exercise helped for a brief time, until Lily called to him. She often chattered her infantile nonsense, so he paid no attention to her until her insistent hands tugged at his trousers. He halted and frowned down at her.

Judging by her wordless urgency, she wanted him to look in her sandbox. To see yet another hole she had dug. "No, Lily. Go and play."

Her bottom lip trembled, but she obeyed him and slowly walked back to climb into the turtle. Her behavior was improving, for the most part. They had gone through a period last month when any refusal would cause her to launch into a loud, tearful tantrum. However, she had soon learned that such displays of temper resulted in her being whisked off to the nursery by Shikoro at once.

She will learn to control herself. As I learned.

Sand scraped against stone, and Jian-Shan went still. He scanned the entire garden, but saw no sign of an intruder. Again, the sensation of being watched made him focus sharply on his surroundings. No movement. No sound. The only scent he could detect was the warm, sensual blend of sun and roses.

Only there were no roses in his garden.

Get Lily inside.

He went to the child, who gazed up at him with obvious confusion. He didn't wait for her to climb out, but lifted her small body from the sandbox and gave her a push toward the door to the house. "Go inside, child."

"Da?" She looked puzzled.

"Go to Shikoro, Lily. Now, hurry."

*   *   *

Val didn't recognize the child, but the man who followed her into the garden was the same one who had been in the backseat of the limo that first day she had followed it. Judging by the plain clothes, the Asian cast of his eyes, and the cat-quiet way he moved, he was probably another bodyguard. But why would a crotchety old sword collector have two bodyguards and a blond toddler living in his house?

Maybe she belongs to one of the other servants.

Careful not to make any noise, she crept closer and looked around the stone lantern. The little girl had jumped into the green plastic turtle sandbox and was busily digging her way to China. Her determination made Val smile for a moment.

Quit admiring the kid, she told herself. *You've got to figure out how to get past her and the bodyguard and into the house without getting arrested.*

She turned her attention to the bodyguard, who was unbuttoning his collar. A quick breath escaped her lips as he pulled his shirt over his head and revealed half the muscles he owned.

Oh, Lord. Keanu Reeves, eat your heart out.

The bodyguard moved to a small, circular patch of grass at the edge of one of the sand swirls and began what looked like a solo dance to unheard music. Gleaming muscles flexed and stretched as he pivoted, then began bringing his hands up to pass in front of his face. The deliberate movements reminded her of martial arts, although everything he did was in slow motion.

What is that? Karate? Kung fu?

The child called to the bodyguard, who ignored her. Val's lips quirked as she watched the little girl stand up, brush sand from the front of her romper with a casual swipe, then make an urgent, wordless sound at her baby-sitter—just like the mew of a kitten.

I know just how you feel, chaton—*what's a girl got to do to get a little attention in this town?*

The bodyguard paid no attention to her, until the child grabbed his pant leg and made another, louder sound. With a slight frown, he stopped and bent down to speak to her, too low for Val to hear. Whatever he said, the answer was no. The toddler let go of his trousers and dragged her feet as she returned to the sandbox, while the bodyguard resumed his exercises.

Val felt like walking over there and slapping him. *Would it have killed you to go look at it for her?*

She shifted her weight, and inadvertently dragged some sand over a flat stone beneath her shoe.

He stopped his elegant dance and instantly turned to stare in her direction. Val ducked back behind the boulder and prayed he hadn't seen her.

God, what would he do if he did see me?

She'd been so focused on getting to T'ang that she hadn't given any thought to the consequences of what she was doing. How could she explain her presence if the bodyguard found her skulking around behind the stones in T'ang's garden? Would he simply assume she was a thief, trying to get into the house? Would he call the police, or do something worse?

This was really not a good idea, Val.

After a few moments she dared to glance up at where the bodyguard was standing. He had abandoned his practice and was helping the child out of the sandbox. There was a strange set to his features, almost as if he was angry, but he didn't look in her direction again.

Whew. Close one.

The seriousness of her situation sank in at last, and she decided to give up what had been a rather foolhardy idea to begin with. The smart thing to do now would be to leave while she still could and return another day. Now that she knew where he lived, she could approach him using more conventional methods.

I could deliver something. Not flowers. More rocks, maybe?

As she rose from her hiding place, Val felt the hair on the back of her neck prickle. Another man was standing a few yards away from her, with his back to her. His coat collar was turned up, and he wore a wide-brimmed hat.

Where did he come from?

Why was he standing there like that, watching them? Seemed a little odd. He looked almost poised for something. His feet were spread apart. His hat was tilted back, but it still hid his face. Without realizing it, Val started moving toward him. Her curious gaze followed his arm down to where he had thrust it into his coat pocket, from which he now took a thin, gleaming blade.

She stopped looking, turned, and ran.

"Go." Jian-Shan didn't have time to argue with the child, so he gave her another small push toward the house. The sound of a gasp nearby made him step between it and Lily, automatically shielding her with his body.

Someone, a woman, appeared from behind one of the garden stones. His mouth tightened as he recognized her—the fallen angel who had tried to see him at his office and followed his limo.

Why is she running?

He anticipated her path, then saw the dark figure of the man she was running from. The man removed something from his coat. Jian-Shan immediately reached down and jerked the small revolver from its ankle holster, and had it in his hand a heartbeat before the woman reached him.

She hurtled forward, her dark eyes wide, her arm reaching out as if to stop him. "Look out!"

Something struck her, driving her forward into him. Steel pierced his flesh as he caught her. Time stopped as they stood together, her terrified gaze locked on her hand where it lay pinned against his chest.

He clamped his left arm around her narrow waist and targeted the man in the coat. "Han!"

His bodyguard ran out of the house, saw Jian-Shan, then scooped Lily up in his arms and dropped behind one of the boulders to take cover.

Warm wetness running down her arm confused her. It didn't make sense—then it did. The man in the coat and hat had been trying to kill the bodyguard. She'd gotten in the way, although just not soon enough.

She stared at her hand, which wouldn't move. Mon Dieu, *it went through both of us.*

The bodyguard had shouted something, and

now he held her with one arm. Shock made everything grow dim and distant, and a strange fizzling
sound crackled in her ears. His face, so close to
hers, blurred.

That man tried to kill him. Right in front of the baby.

The hard arm around her waist wouldn't let her
fall. Instead, the bodyguard guided her down until
they were both on their knees. The cool, fine sand
felt strange against her hot skin.

Long black hair touched her face as the man bent
down to look at the blade buried in her hand. He
took her wrist with his fingers and held it. "Don't
move."

"I won't." She couldn't. "Can you get it out?"

"Yes." His voice changed, became gentler. "Hold
on to me."

She swallowed and clutched his other shoulder.
He grabbed the hilt of the knife that had gone
through her hand and into his chest, and with one
quick jerk, he pulled it out of both of them.

The pain hit her then, driving all the air out of
her lungs. Blood streamed down her arm and his
chest to mingle between them.

"Thank you," Val heard herself say, before she
slumped forward in a dead faint.

Jian-Shan kept the unconscious woman upright
with one arm and tossed away the dagger. He saw
no sign of the assassin, but that meant nothing. Another glance told him Han had already taken Lily
back into the house. Then he noticed that blood
running from her hand and his shoulder had begun
to stain the white sand between them.

He eased her down on her back long enough to

take a handkerchief from his trouser pocket. After he wrapped it around her hand, he applied direct pressure to both sides of the wound.

Everything you touch dies.

Jian-Shan pushed aside outrage and guilt and lifted her into his arms. His own wound was insignificant, but the blade had penetrated her palm completely. Carrying her limp body to the house, he kicked the door open. "Han!"

His bodyguard stood just inside, armed with a revolver and a machine gun. "I am here, *kei.*"

He kept his hand clamped around hers, stanching the flow. "Lily?"

"She is safe, with Shikoro in the nursery."

"Check the property." He strode through the kitchen. "If you find anyone, bring him to me alive."

Jian-Shan went directly to his bedroom, where he carefully placed the woman on his bed. She looked smaller there, and too still and white. Quickly he extended her arm, removed the makeshift bandage and examined the wound again. The blade had gone between the second and third tendons, but careful inspection revealed no broken bones. The penetrating wound bled freely, and other dark drops pelted her skin as blood dripped from his shoulder onto her arm.

Cold rage collected inside him, a silent, lethal whirlwind of ice. *Whoever did this will suffer for it.*

After he swiftly checked her for other wounds, he tore a wide swatch of linen from one of the sheets to make a temporary pressure dressing for her hand. Only when she was bandaged did he go to the mirror to examine and dress his own wound.

It would have been much worse had she not reached out to try to stop the blade.

Why did she do it? What woman would put herself between a knife and a stranger?

A discreet sound behind him made him turn. "Was there any trace of him?"

"None, *kei*." Han came to him, then glanced at the bed. "You both are in need of medical attention."

He couldn't risk taking her to a hospital, and he knew only one doctor he could trust—the man who had delivered his daughter. "Send for Toyotomi. Tell him to come directly here and to bring what he needs for minor surgery."

"You have had no contact with him since Karen-san . . ." The big man faltered and looked at the floor. "Of course. I will call him at once."

"We will need extra men to guard the property until we can relocate. Contact Raven." Jian-Shan thought for a moment. "The woman dropped her bag in the garden. There is also the knife. Bring them to me."

Val opened her eyes to darkness. She was lying in her bed. Soft, cool linen sheets covered her. She could smell something sweet, blended with something more exotic. Like roses in an herb garden. The flower scent came from her own perfume, but the herbs . . .

Where am I?

She would have sat up, but she realized she was naked. No, not entirely. Only to the waist. Her left arm was in a fabric sling, and a thick gauze bandage covered her entire hand. Beneath it, something throbbed with deep, steady pain.

How did I do this?

Reaching up to touch the bandage made the pain swell and radiate up her arm and into her chest like a thousand tiny, hot blades.

The knife. The man in the garden.

A light snapped on, and a dark-haired man appeared at the side of the bed. "Ms. St. Charles?"

Why is this guy in my room? Then Val glanced around and realized she wasn't in a hospital room.

The man turned his head and muttered something else, in another language she didn't understand.

He didn't sound French or American, or even Asian. He sounded a little British. His voice was softer and deeper than she'd thought it would be. Sort of a low, melodic purr. The shadow of a beard darkened his jawline, and his straight black hair had been pulled back from his angular face and braided into a long queue. When he looked down at her again, she realized he had very thick, straight eyelashes that softened the eastern inner fold of his upper eyelids.

An Asian guy with a British accent. Okay. She wanted to ask about a million questions, but her tongue felt like a stick of chalk. She could only manage a simple "Where am I?"

"This is my home. Here." He brought a clear glass tumbler to her and helped her hold it with her good hand as she sipped from it.

"Thanks." The soft light from the one lamp cast shadows over his face, making it hard to read his expression. "*Le chaton*—I mean, the little girl—she is all right?"

"Yes." He looked puzzled. "*Parlez vous français?*"

She smiled. "*Oui, est-ce que c'est interdit?*"

"No, of course not—I speak fluent English and French." He tilted his head. "You, however, have a very odd accent."

"It's New Orleans French." She glanced around the room again. "The little girl wasn't hurt, was she?"

"No, my daughter is unharmed."

That darling little blond kitten is his daughter? Her eyes moved to his shoulder. "And you? You're okay?"

"My wound is minor, thanks to your swift intervention." His exotic black eyes never left hers as he pressed one of his long, cool hands to her brow. There it was again—that scent. Like herbs. *His* scent. "How do you feel?"

"A little silly. I've never fainted before in my life." Val clutched the sheet to her breasts, then carefully slid up on the mattress until she could assume a semi-sitting position. She lifted the sling and stared at her heavily bandaged hand. "How bad is it?"

"The knife penetrated your palm completely and nicked one of the tendons. Otherwise, it was a remarkably clean wound." He adjusted the support of the thick pillows behind her, and even brushed a lock of her hair from her cheek. The contact made her skin tingle. "My physician says it will be some weeks before you regain full use of the hand."

His physician. His daughter. His home. *Bodyguards must do better than I thought.*

Val exhaled slowly and closed her eyes. The last time she'd felt this light-headed was after a double shift of waiting tables at a blues bar during Mardi Gras. "I can't believe that man threw a knife at you—and I'm sorry, I know I shouldn't have been on the property in the first place."

"Don't apologize, Ms. St. Charles. You saved my life, and possibly my daughter's as well."

She looked up and gave him a foolish grin. "I did, didn't I?" Her head wobbled, and she stabilized it with her good hand. "*Dieu*, what's the matter with me?"

"I have injected you with morphine for the pain, mademoiselle." A shorter, heavier Japanese man appeared on the other side of the bed. "It will cause you to feel disoriented for several hours."

"This is Dr. Toyotomi, my personal physician."

The doctor gave her a short bow. His bald head and round, frowning face reminded Val of a sad billiard ball.

"Your *personal* physician." She checked out the room again, and her practiced eye noted several startlingly good antique pieces. "Just how much money do bodyguards make, anyway?"

"I am not a bodyguard."

"Oh. Well, that explains it." *Right.* She watched the doctor take her pulse. "Shouldn't we be doing this in a hospital?"

Toyotomi exchanged a glance with the man who wasn't a bodyguard. "You should rest now."

The morphine hadn't fogged her head *that* much. "I'll rest later, at the hospital. I'd like to know what happened out there."

Le chaton's father bent closer, blocking the light

from the lamp. "This man who threw the knife, what did he look like?"

"I don't know. I didn't really see his face." She slowly moved her head from side to side, consciously trying to overcome the disorienting effect of the drug. "He was wearing a hat and had his collar up. What happened? Was he some kind of burglar? Are the police looking for him?"

His black eyes narrowed. "You are certain you don't remember what he looks like, Ms. St. Charles?"

Why was he asking her all these questions? Why weren't the police here to do it? How did he know her name? Maybe she should ask a few questions of her own. "Yes, I'm sure. Why did he throw that knife at you? So he could get to Mr. T'ang?"

He straightened. "I am T'ang Jian-Shan."

"Get out of town." She laughed, but when she saw he was serious, she stopped. "Really? *You're* the owner of the White Tiger collection?" He inclined his head. "But you're not a crotchety old man!"

"I regret that I disappoint you."

"I'm not—" She caught herself before she blurted out something really inane. "I'm sorry. That didn't come out right. I meant—I just assumed that you were older."

The senior citizen she'd been anticipating meeting couldn't be more than thirty-five or forty, at the most. And he hadn't answered her questions about the police or the killer. Panic set in and cleared more of the haziness from her mind. What kind of man was he, to have people sneaking onto his property to knife him?

I don't think I want to know. It's time I go to a nice, safe emergency room.

"I should leave now." Val tried to roll over onto her uninjured side, but her limbs didn't want to cooperate. "Um, maybe you could help me?"

Jian-Shan didn't help when he reached down and held her still by gripping her waist. "You are in no condition to leave now. Even if you were, I could not allow it. It is not safe."

He was right. She was so dizzy she wouldn't make it as far as the floor, much less the door. Then the rest of what he said finally registered. "Why isn't it safe? I haven't done anything wrong."

The two men exchanged another silent look before Jian-Shan's shrewd eyes moved to her face.

She abruptly recalled what she had been doing in his garden. "Okay, I was trespassing. I admit it. But that man was after you, Mr. T'ang, not me. I just got myself and my hand in the way."

"For which I am considerably in your debt." His grip eased, and Val saw the doctor doing something to the tube of the IV running into her arm. "However, the man who attacked me cannot afford the risk of you identifying him. You are in serious danger, Ms. St. Charles."

"You mean he's going to come after me?" When he nodded, the silliness she'd felt evaporated, and she swallowed against a surge of bile. "But I don't know him—I didn't even see his face."

Jian-Shan's voice gentled. "He does not know that."

"I can't believe this is happening to me." Val stared up at him, convinced that nearly all of it was his fault. "All I wanted was an appointment to speak with you. If you'd given me five minutes, none of this would have happened."

"True." He touched his own bandaged shoulder. "Yet had I granted you an interview, I would likely be dead now."

"Don't try and make me feel better. You're the reason I've got a knife-throwing maniac after me." Her eyelids drooped. "No job is worth this. I want . . ."

What she got was another plunge into darkness.

Jian-Shan watched Val's eyes close as the additional morphine Dr. Toyotomi had injected into her IV took effect. Her breathing went slow and shallow as she slid into a drug-induced slumber.

"She appears to be in excellent health, Mr. T'ang."

"Yes." He reached out and touched her cool brow. No fever yet. He hoped that the antibiotics Toyotomi had previously administered would ward off an infection.

"You took Lily and left the hospital so suddenly after Karen's death," the physician said, mild censure coloring his words. "I had expected to see you before now."

"*Kei.*"

Jian-Shan looked over his shoulder, almost relieved at the interruption. "What is it?"

His bodyguard brought him a file with half a dozen sheets of paper in it. "The report you requested."

"Thank you, Han." To Toyotomi he said, "We will speak later. Watch her closely for me, Doctor."

Han accompanied Jian-Shan as he walked out of

the bedroom and began to skim through the file. "Raven found no connection with Shandian?"

"None at this time. The fingerprints we sent verified the gaijin's identity. Her name is Valence St. Charles, and she is a junior curator with the New Orleans Museum of Art and Antiquities."

Details from the report made him frown. "She has a police record in New Orleans as well?"

"A juvenile record. No adult arrests or convictions."

"Have Raven obtain a copy of it."

Jian-Shan automatically went to the room he used as his study and nodded absently when Han offered to prepare tea. He read quickly through the remainder of the reports. When his bodyguard returned, he closed the file. "What are your thoughts about Ms. St. Charles?"

"She is an ideal candidate for tong membership," Han said as he prepared the pot. "Most of their recruits are orphaned, poor, and friendless. And she has already been in trouble with the law."

"That may be."

Han set a black porcelain cup in front of him and poured fragrant, steaming green tea in it. "A curator's dossier can be easily falsified. You have done as much yourself, *kei*."

He had, to smuggle the swords out of China and into France. "If she falsified it, she went to a great deal of trouble to make it appear authentic." A long list of former employers took up two pages alone. "According to these dates, before she was hired at the museum, she worked at least two jobs every day for the past nine years."

"Given her appearance, I doubt very much that

is true. Shandian operatives go to great lengths to make themselves appear harmless on paper," Han reminded him.

Jian-Shan sipped his tea as he considered this. "True." Another paragraph caught his eye. "She was found abandoned as an infant, and yet emancipated by the state by the time she was sixteen."

His bodyguard looked puzzled. "Emancipated, master?"

"It is a legal term. It means the authorities recognized her ability to live independent of family and support herself on her own income."

Han shook his head. "Americans have no filial piety."

The rest of the report on Valence St. Charles contained more contradictions. She maintained modest balances in her checking and savings accounts, yet paid high insurance rates for an expensive sports car. Her wardrobe, too, indicated that her taste often exceeded her income; the blouse he had been forced to cut off her was made of high-quality silk. Yet if the details of the background report could be believed, she had practically enslaved herself to pursue an education and a career in a fickle and demanding field in which only a precious few ever enjoyed real success.

She could be exactly what she appeared to be—an impulsive young woman in a foreign land who had put her own life in danger to save that of a complete stranger. If that was the case, it still didn't explain how she had gotten into the garden without tripping any of the perimeter alarms.

However suspicious the circumstances, he still felt the tug of deeply ingrained tradition. What she'd done could not be recompensed. She had taken a knife meant for him, saving his life and almost certainly Lily's. Her actions imposed an uncomfortably heavy debt on him—one he might never be able to repay. He glanced at his bodyguard.

"You are thinking of when you found me," Han said as he warmed Jian-Shan's tea. He was an expert at reading his employer's thoughts. "You know Americans do not consider self-sacrifice to be a life debt."

"I know." He rose to his feet. "You were able to contact Raven?"

"Yes, she is bringing the additional guards herself. *Kei* . . ."

He knew what his bodyguard was going to say. Taking care of the American, keeping her in the house, was madness. Yet until he knew more about her, and how much danger she had placed herself in by saving him, he could not let her go. "The situation remains under our control, Han. Let me know when Raven arrives."

Chapter 3

Val knew she was sleeping, and dreaming, but nothing made sense—she was alone, surrounded by a circle of flying knives that kept getting closer with every pass, and yet she couldn't get away, couldn't wake up, couldn't escape the flashing, deadly blades. She tried to lift her arms up to cover her head, but they were paralyzed, like the rest of her body. All she could do was cringe and close her eyes and wait for the cold bite of steel to slice into her flesh.

"Please." She hated the sound of her own voice begging, and the hot streaks of the tears spilling down her face. She had never cried or begged, not even when she'd lived on the street. But she felt so alone, so abandoned. "Please, make them stop."

"Do not cry." Warm, strong hands touched her face. "Open your eyes. Look at me. You are safe here."

It was the man from the garden. She couldn't quite remember his name, only that it sounded lyrical, like poetry. Like him.

Something she'd read once echoed in her mind. *If*

I am dreaming, let me never awake. If I am awake, let me never sleep.

"The knives," she whispered. "I'm afraid of them."

For a moment his expression seemed angry. Then the grim lines disappeared, and his fingers combed a tangle of hair back from her cheek. "I will not let them hurt you."

"Thank you." She tried to focus on the robe he wore, but it blurred and changed into a sleek white pelt with jagged black stripes. "You're the white tiger."

He muttered something about "fever" and "drugs" as he pressed a cool, damp cloth against her burning forehead.

"I came to Paris to find you." She turned her head, trying to bury her face in the soothing cloth. "I need you so much."

Long black hair fell forward, hiding his face from her. "Why?"

"You're all I've ever needed." One part of her knew she was jabbering, talking nonsense, and yet another was sure he was the key to something important. She had to make him understand. "You know secrets, don't you?"

He lifted the hot, clinging sheet away from her and replaced it with one that was dry and cool. "Everyone has secrets, Valence."

"Not like this one." She managed to catch his hand with hers. "Please, help me. Help me to show them."

"Who are they?" He threaded his cool fingers through hers. "Tell me what you need to show them."

She squinted at him. The black-and-white pelt was stretching and growing, and his face was changing, becoming narrower and more feline. His dark eyes turned white-blue and stared at her without blinking.

Blind eyes. Nagatoki's eyes.

"The secret you're hiding, *cher.*" Val felt better now. There was something comforting in knowing that Nagatoki himself was watching over her, even if he had turned into a big, snowy cat. Now all she had to do was convince him to tell her about Lady Kameko. "The truth about your wife—help me tell them what she did for you."

The huge white tiger drew back. "What do you know about my wife?"

"She told me." She felt so hot, so tired now. Didn't he know what his wife had written about him, in her journals? "She risked her life for you, didn't she?"

Before the darkness dragged her away from the dream, she thought she heard his low voice whisper one last time.

"She died for me."

"It says here in my brochure five million people come to the Musée National du Grand Louvre each year," the American tourist woman said, separating each French word into slow, Southern-accented syllables. She popped a strip of chewing gum into her mouth and glanced at her husband. "This place is going to be packed, honey."

The assassin, who had been obliged to stand beside them on the bus for fifteen minutes, idly considered strangling her with one of her sagging bra straps.

"I *told* you," the husband said in an aggrieved

tone. "We should've gone to England. At least there I could get a decent beer with dinner."

"The travel agent said this Louvre place is one of the most important museums in the world." She chewed her gum for a moment. "It's got countless treasures."

"The Louvre has become essentially a modern cultural theme park," a more educated tourist sitting across the aisle from the couple said. "It's the Disney World of art and architecture."

"Hear that?" The wife poked her husband as the hotel bus slowed to a stop outside the museum complex. "We just might get to see Mickey."

Each day thousands of tourists walked through the infamous glass pyramid commissioned by President François Mitterrand to explore the museum and the sixty thousand square meters it devoted to seven permanent collections of some thirty thousand individual exhibits. They were carefully watched over by the eighteen hundred employees in forty different professions, from administrative and academic workers to the eagle-eyed security staff.

Few people visiting the museum knew that the staggering numbers of art and antiquities on display constituted only five percent of the treasures owned by the Louvre, or that running the great museum cost more than 652 million francs a year.

The assassin didn't follow the group from his bus. Disdaining the main entrance, he entered the museum via the Richelieu arcade between the rue de Rivoli and Cour Napoleon and made his way to the basement level, where Greek, Etruscan, and Roman antiquities were kept on permanent display. Several guides were already there, conducting tours in six different languages, and the assassin joined the English-speaking group in room three.

"Ladies and gentlemen, here we have the *Torso of Miletus*—Greek, marble, one hundred thirty-two centimeters in height, sculpted sometime between 480 and 470 B.C." The tour guide took a step to one side so photographs could be taken.

At the back of the group, the assassin lifted his camera and snapped a shot.

An older man moved to stand beside him. "One of my men is lying in a Paris morgue," he murmured, as if commenting on the weather.

"Archaeologists hail the *Torso of Miletus* as a milestone in the development of Greek sculpture," the guide continued. She frowned as she noticed the two men at the back. "Traces of burns on the marble substantiate claims that it was created before the Persians attacked Asia Minor in 490 B.C."

"You have my sympathy." The assassin adjusted his lens. "A pity your employee was not more . . . cautious while performing his duties."

"This is one of the first works to display the *contrapposto*"—the guide pointed to the lower half of the sculpture—"where the body's stance is on one leg, leaving the other free to be moved in a variety of positions to imitate true motion."

"A pity you were not as proficient with my son."

The assassin advanced the film roll in his camera. "Regrettably, the young woman got in my way. It will not happen again."

"It has already been proven that this sculpture was damaged and restored in antiquity, and became a fixture on the main facade of the theater in Miletus." The guide held up a finger. "However, there are also disputes that it is, in fact, authentically Greek in origin."

"Is she still alive?"

The second man took another photo. "Not for long."

"Looking at this torso fills us with strong emotions, particularly when you consider what Rainer Maria Rilke wrote in his sonnet 'The Archaic Torso of Apollo' while he served as secretary to the great French sculptor Auguste Rodin—'*There's no place therein which fails to see you. Change your way of living.*'"That caused some murmurs, and the guide smiled. "Now, if you will follow me, we will move on to the Coptic Egypt Antiquities room."

The two men remained behind as the group left. "It will interest you to know there was also a child present."

"A child?" The older man's voice sharpened. "Male? Female? How old?"

"Female, perhaps a year old. A fair-haired Caucasian." The second lowered his camera and advanced the film. It amused him to add, "With her father's blue eyes."

"The whore's brat." The first man sounded savagely pleased. "Kill the child and the woman who interfered, but bring my son to me."

It was not the first time he had been ordered to murder a child, and it would not be the last. As for the wounded woman, he was almost positive she had seen his face. Regardless of his employer's orders, she had to die. "That will require another hundred thousand in addition to my original fee."

"Agreed. One more thing: assure that my son

sees both of them die, or you will make this torso look beautiful when I am done with you."

The assassin lowered his camera and contemplated the headless, armless, legless, castrated sculpture. "Yes, Mr. T'ang."

If there was an art to killing, the Japanese had perfected it in their swords.

The White Tiger collection included more than twenty *chokuto* and *warabite-tachi* blades, some of which were over a thousand years old. Yet it was the relatively new Kunisada *katana* sword that Jian-Shan preferred to use for his daily practice—perhaps because damaging a sword that was only three hundred years old, unlike the other relics his family had amassed over the centuries, would not bring the wrath of the Shinto gods down on his head.

I have done enough to displease the gods.

Following the discipline of *iaido*—the art of drawing the blade—compelled him to clear his mind. To kill with a single blow required not only a sword of incomparable craftsmanship but also concentration paired with serenity, and decades of practice. Something an American could hardly comprehend.

I will not think about her.

He barely felt the weight of the *montsuki* and *hakana*, the white and black silk garments he had donned, or the protective pad he had wrapped around his left knee. Automatically he made his *rei*, though there was no opponent present who required a bow, and slowly he drew his sword from the scabbard tucked into the obi around his waist. His movements would have been the same if he had occupied the Central Tokyo Arena for an exhibition match before the heads of state.

No thought. No self. Only the sword.

He went immediately into the standing attack of the *shinobu*, the "loyal retainer" movement used in areas with many obstructions. The *katana* descended as he made the obligatory "ground tap" to warn the imaginary enemy he was attacking from behind to turn around.

The image of Valence running toward him, arms outstretched, the black crystal of her *kurozuishou* eyes stark in her white face, her unpainted lips parted as she called to him, too late. And then the flash of the knife piercing through her, into him.

Only a coward attacks from behind without warning. Only a craven coward assaults an unarmed woman.

A moment later he lifted the sword, stepped forward, and brought it down with much greater force. If the assassin had been standing in front of him, the downward stroke would have cut his body cleanly in two.

You're all I've ever needed.

Jian-Shan flipped the blade from side to side—another, unconscious movement used by swordsmen to shake off blood—then resheathed it and stared at the empty space before him. He had not achieved the no-mind, no-self serenity he needed for his practice. The memory of Valence's hand against his chest would not leave him. Nor would the slowly building fury from knowing his father had once more struck a blow against him through a helpless woman. A woman who had no reason to bleed for him.

*He will try again. Even if she is everything Raven's
report indicates, I cannot let her go.*

He found he could not complete the other three
standing sets he had planned, so he put away the
katana and headed for his bedroom.

He turned on the light and saw that Val remained
unconscious from the morphine. As he stood over
her, he stripped off the voluminous *montsuki* and
used it to rub the sweat from his chest.

Finally he asked her the question that had been
annoying him all day. "Why did you do it?"

She didn't move.

He checked her IV, then the small pulse point beneath her jaw. The curve of her breast brushed the
underside of his arm, and he abruptly removed his
hand.

What had she called him? *Cher?*

He hadn't liked it. Who was this woman, to be calling him her dear one? She knew nothing about him.

Please, help me. Help me to show them.

Or did she?

His hand strayed to her again as he traced the
delicate curve of her cheek and felt her red-gold
hair against his skin. It felt dense, but incongru-
ously as fine and soft as Lily's. He tucked one
flame-colored strand behind her ear, then circled
his fingertips against her scalp.

Val stirred, and a sigh escaped her lips. One corner of her mouth lifted, as if she were dreaming of
something pleasing.

Was she waking? "Ms. St. Charles?"

She moved restlessly, causing the sheet tucked
over her breasts to slip down.

Slowly his hand left her hair as he reached down

and pulled the sheet back in place. He got to his
feet and strode away from her to stand at the window. There, he stared out into the night. His hands
gripped the moldings until his knuckles paled.

No.

It was understandable. A rudimentary attraction.
After all, he had removed her blouse, and a man
did not even partially undress a woman without
some sexual speculation. Jian-Shan saw himself
bending over her again. His hands, drawing the
sheet away from her slender limbs. His eyes, inspecting every inch of her skin.

And if he touched her, he would—

"*Kei.*"

Denying himself the pleasure of putting his
hands on her made Jian-Shan's voice flinty. "What
is it?"

"Miss Raven has arrived. The men are in place,
and she is waiting to speak to you in your study."

"I'll be with her in a moment." Jian-Shan turned
from the window. "Contact Kalen Grady for me on
the safe line. Put him through to me directly."

Han stared at him. "*General* Kalen Grady?"

"You heard me. Do it now."

Jian-Shan found Raven lounging on one of the
leather-covered armchairs near his desk. Her long
legs were draped over one arm, her neck cushioned
on the other. She had kicked off her shoes, and one
bare foot swung lazily as she thumbed through the
latest issue of *Vogue.*

"What do you think, Handsome?" She gave him
an impish grin as she held up the magazine. It displayed a collage of images from her latest photo
shoot. In this one, Jian-Shan saw, his friend wore a

series of chic bathing suits. One appeared to be assembled from nothing but small scallop shells and some snarled jute cord.

In China, wearing such an outfit would have gotten her arrested. "You look like a topless German tourist on the Côte d'Azur."

As friends, they made an odd couple, but besides Han and Shikoro there was no one Jian-Shan trusted more.

She stretched. "You're such a prude, Jay. I'm glad I never fell in love with you. You'd have made me wear a veil in public."

"That is what Muslim men do. Chinese men make you bind your feet so you can't run away."

"Just as bad. So"—she tossed aside the magazine and yawned—"why did you ruin my afternoon nap and make me round up half a dozen guys who cost way too much money?"

"Someone tried to kill me in the garden today."

"What?" The teasing look disappeared as she jumped up from the chair. "Damn it, Jay, I *told* you this sword deal was a really lousy idea!"

"Han has been very careful. However, we did not anticipate this." He took out the tracer he had found in Val's jacket and handed it to her.

Raven turned it over on her palm and whistled softly. "This cost a nice chunk of change. Who carried it in?"

He sat down at his desk. "The woman you investigated was also in the garden. She stepped in front of the assassin as he threw a knife. I have her here now."

"You kept the museum lady? *Here?*"

"I believe she saw his face. Or he thinks she did." He pulled a file from his desk and handed it to her.

"This is a list of my father's contacts who currently reside in Paris. One or more of them could be involved as procurers."

She scanned the page and groaned. "Jesus, Jay, there's a good twenty names here." Raven squinted for a moment. "The chairman of—your dad owns *him*, too?"

"He owns whomever he can buy. I need you to eliminate all of them." He turned to gaze through the window at the garden. "The assassin is a professional, top quality. He didn't panic when he hit the girl instead of me. He would have retrieved the knife and tried again had I not drawn my own weapon."

She nodded and closed the folder. "I need a day, maybe two. Security on the Euroweb is getting harder to crack now. In the meantime, get out of here. Stay at my villa in Provence," she added. "It has everything, and the nearest neighbor is ten miles away. No one will bother you."

That solved one of his immediate problems. "Yes, that would be convenient. Thank you, Sarah."

"Don't thank me." She scowled at him. "Even if I feel like smacking you sometimes, I owe you."

"If there was a debt, you've more than repaid it." A light blinked on the console at his hand. "Excuse me for a moment. This will be General Grady."

"That's my cue to get lost." As she picked up her bag, she glanced at the phone, and a note of flat hostility entered her voice. "Send the cold-blooded bastard my love, will you?" She sauntered out of the room.

He pressed a button to activate the speakerphone. "General. Thank you for your prompt response."

"Save it," Kalen Grady replied in a testy voice. "Are you ready to come in now?"

Jian-Shan knew how much the general had hated offering him political asylum in the U.S. Grady had gone to great lengths to acquire the encoded microdisk that Jian-Shan had stolen from the Shandian tong, as it contained detailed information on every aspect of T'ang Po's illegal activities. However, the general subsequently discovered he could not decrypt the code—not without the help of Jian-Shan, who had encrypted it. Hence the offer.

Yet the Americans had not come through soon enough, and after Karen died Jian-Shan saw no reason to help the man who might have been able to save her life. "Regrettably, I must again decline."

"Then why the hell are you calling me?"

"An American woman was wounded this afternoon at my home." Jian-Shan briefly described the attempted assassination. "The hit was meant for me."

"Pity she didn't duck in time. What hospital is she in?"

"She saw the face of the man who has a contract on me," Jian-Shan said. "Until the situation is resolved, she will remain in my safekeeping."

"Short of body shields, are you, T'ang?"

Jian Shan's hands became fists, but his voice remained expressionless. "If I release her, she'll be dead within an hour."

"If she's a U.S. citizen, she's not your problem. Give me an address, and one of my people can pick her up within the hour."

"No." He leaned forward. "However, I will consider releasing her in exchange for T'ang Po."

Grady laughed. "You've got balls, T'ang. If I had your father, I wouldn't be wasting my time talking to you."

"Very well, General." Unconsciously relieved, he sat back in his chair. "We will remain at this stalemate, and the woman will stay with me."

"If you think you're going to play her, the way you did with Karen Colfax—"

"Do not speak about my wife." He matched the general's harsh tone. "As for the American, she is under my protection. Once the assassin has been eliminated, I will have Raven return her to you, unharmed."

"Send someone else; Raven isn't welcome on American soil. As for you, you'd better keep her safe, or I'll personally hunt you down." Grady slammed his phone into its cradle with a crash.

There were no more nightmares, and no more men with lyrical names who turned into tigers. When Val finally opened her eyes, she was alone. Sunshine streamed through gaps in the heavy curtains hanging over the windows, but there was no sign of T'ang Jian-Shan. From the throbbing in her hand, she suspected she'd slept through the effects of the morphine. It hurt so much now that she had to sit up and do something, or scream.

Moving made her groan. She might have been stabbed through the hand, but her entire body felt bruised. "*Ma vie*, what have they been doing to me?"

"*Anou Okusan*, I help you."

Val turned to see a middle-aged woman in a gray cotton kimono place a tray on a table and approach the bed. "Hello."

"*Hajime mashite.*" She bowed, then gave Val a shy smile as she helped her sit up. "*Daijobu?* Ah, you feel bad, *Okusan*?"

"I've felt better."

"This help." The woman brought her a cup of amber tea from the tray. "For stomach."

"Do I look that green?" Val took a sip and tasted mint and honey. "*Arigato gozaimasu.*" When the woman immediately broke into rapid Japanese, she added, "*Nihon-go ga dekimasen*—I'm sorry, I don't speak much Japanese."

"*Gomen nasai, Okusan,* I speak not good English." The woman made a sympathetic face. "My name Onaba Shikoro, T'ang-san housekeeper, Onaba-san wife."

"Is Onaba-san Mr. T'ang's driver?" Shikoro nodded, and Val drank a little more tea. "This is working. I don't feel like throwing up anymore. Thank you."

"You need, *Okusan,* you tell Shikoro. I get for you."

Val smiled. "You can help me learn more Japanese and tell me what '*Okusan*' means."

"Mean 'madam, lady, wife.'"

Wife? She nearly choked on her tea. "What exactly did I do after they gave me that morphine?"

"You sleep." The woman looked perplexed, and made an elegant gesture over the bed. "Just sleep."

"Thank goodness." Val produced a raspy chuckle. "You had me worried there for a minute."

After Val drank her tea, the housekeeper helped her walk a few feet to a door that led into the large bathroom, then politely waited outside.

When she emerged, Shikoro pointed at the opulent black porcelain tub inside. "I make bath for you? Doctor say not get hand wet."

"Maybe a little later." Val felt too shaky to do anything but sit down. She made it to the edge of the bed before she dropped and winced.

The housekeeper brought the tray to the bed and set it beside her. "You eat, feel better."

"What I really need to do is get to a hospital." She saw the housekeeper politely avert her gaze. "I know Mr. T'ang is being a nice guy about this and all, but I can't stay here. Not like this."

"There is no medical reason to transport you to a hospital," Dr. Toyotomi said as he came in, carrying a medical case. "I am quite capable of treating you here, Ms. St. Charles."

Val's stomach clenched again as Shikoro bowed to the doctor and hurried out. "No more drugs, okay? I'd rather deal with the pain."

"You must continue to take antibiotics to prevent infection." He took his stethoscope and something she couldn't see from the case.

"Must I?" She eyed the second man who walked into the room. "What if I'd like to get a second opinion on that?"

Jian-Shan came to stand on the other side of the bed. He was wearing an unadorned black cheongsam that reminded her a little of a priest's cassock. "I will summon another doctor if you like, Ms. St. Charles."

That was what she'd been afraid he would say. "Why can't I go to the hospital?"

"You must stay on bed rest for at least another day." The doctor's sad expression turned reproachful as he handed her two pills and a small glass of water. "You know, I have treated Mr. T'ang's family for several years, my dear."

Val studied the pills, and then glanced up at Jian-Shan.

"Take them," he said, his voice as compelling as his gaze. "You are quite safe here, I assure you."

She remembered her dream, and how he had chased away the knives. A wave of weariness rolled over her, making her feel like curling up and crying herself to sleep. "All right."

Toyotomi removed a blood pressure cuff from his bag. "Now, allow me to examine you, and then I will change the dressing on your hand."

Val wasn't squeamish, but her nausea returned when Toyotomi uncovered the short rows of stitches on the back of her hand and her palm. Her host leaned over to examine the damage.

"She will be able to use it again?" Jian-Shan's calm expression never changed, but the question sounded strange—almost menacing.

"There may be some stiffness at first, but with continued use she should regain full function. I am going to immobilize it for now so it will heal properly." He took two rigid pieces of plastic and foam from his case and used them to create a short splint from Val's wrist to the tips of her fingers. "You must keep this dry when you bathe. I will check in on you later." With that, the doctor picked up his bag, bowed, and departed.

Although she liked the odd, gloomy little man, Val was glad to be alone with Jian-Shan. Maybe now she could get some answers. "Have you contacted the police, Mr. T'ang?"

He reached down and pulled the coverlet up over her. "For what purpose?"

"Whoever that man was, he meant to kill you.

And nearly did." When that didn't provoke a response, she added, "Someone should tell them what's going on, don't you think?"

"I prefer to handle such matters privately. Let me see this." He lifted her injured hand and inspected the splint. "Are you in much pain?"

"No. I mean, yes, a little, but it doesn't matter." The way he was tracing his thumb over the ovals of her fingernails distracted her. "You can't go after this man by yourself. It's too dangerous."

"You worry too much, Ms. St. Charles." He lowered her hand until it lay at her side. "I will let you rest now."

"But, Mr. T'ang—" Before she could think of what to say, he was already out the door. "Damn." The clicking sound after the door closed made her look up. "Oh, no. He wouldn't."

She carefully got to her feet and after balancing for a moment on decidedly wobbly legs, walked across the room to try the doorknob.

T'ang Jian Shan had locked her in.

Kalen Grady switched off the lamp on his desk before grabbing his keys and his coat and heading out to the elevators. He had at least five more hours' worth of reports to review, seven domestic operations to evaluate, and countless other bureaucratic tasks waiting for his attention. He couldn't keep his mind on any of it, not since the call had come in from Paris.

So she's working directly for T'ang now.

It had been more than six years since Sarah had deserted the Central Intelligence Division. As far as the army was concerned, she was AWOL and subject to prosecution for same the moment she came under military jurisdiction. Unfortunately, no one knew where she was—or who she was—except Kalen, and he wouldn't turn her in.

Not yet.

A gust of chilly air slapped him back to awareness. He was standing in the parking garage under his office building, staring blindly at the car keys in his hand. It was rare for him to become so lost in thought that he shifted into automatic. Given his position, it was also incredibly stupid.

Once he was in his car, he made a phone call and roused his secretary out of bed to cancel his remaining appointments for the week. She promised to rearrange his schedule and have the plane tickets waiting for him at JFK. Then he called Sean.

A deep voice rough with sleep answered after the third ring. "This had better be good."

"It's Grady. What have you heard from our friends in the tong lately, Irish?"

Sean Delaney produced a convincing sigh. "I'm on medical leave."

"That didn't stop you the last time. Where's T'ang Po?"

"Hang on." There was a rustling sound, then the clink of glass, and liquid pouring. "I'm too old to be doing this in the middle of the night, General."

Next to Kalen, Sean Delaney knew the most about the Shandian tong, which had spread Chinese organized crime from Asia throughout the U.S. He had been directly involved in two important cases in Colorado and Montana, playing the role of an assassin for hire for some major players in the tong syndicate.

Kalen also knew that Sean enjoyed the game too much to give it up entirely, and his network of sources remained a legend in the intelligence community. Sean Delaney might retire from fieldwork, but he would always keep his connections alive. "I can haul your ass back in front of an inquiry board again, if you like."

"Ah, no, once was plenty, thank you. According to my sources, T'ang Po left the country just after we recovered the microdisk in Montana." Sean drank something. "He hasn't entered China, and he hasn't come back. My guess is he's back to looking for his son."

Which confirmed Kalen's suspicions. "You're staying on medical leave this time, Irish."

"I'm a short-timer now, General." Sean chuckled. "Soon as the base doc clears me, I outprocess for a well-earned retirement."

Kalen wasn't convinced. "Because if I found out differently, Colonel, I would nail you to the nearest cross. Starting with your balls."

Sean made a pained sound. "Not necessary, boyo. The girls are keeping me busy, what with baby-sitting for my two great-nephews. Laney's Matthew brings me rocks he digs up with his da, and Neal's boy, Liam, is already wanting his own horse."

"Good." Kalen knew how fond Sean was of his nieces and their families, who would also keep the retiring colonel out of his hair. "I'm leaving the country, but I'll be in touch. Call my service if you hear anything about T'ang."

"I will, General." Sean yawned. "Have a safe trip."

Chapter 4

"She thinks I am a nice guy, Han," Jian-Shan said as he stood by the window in the library.

His bodyguard, who was cleaning one of his practice blades with a chamois cloth, paused. "I am sure she meant no deliberate offense, *kei*."

His mouth quirked as he turned around. "Indeed. And on what do you base that observation?"

Han ran the cloth over the steel one last time. "'Nice' is a well-used American honorific, is it not? They say, 'Have a nice day' to virtually everyone they address."

"True enough." Jian-Shan inspected the Nagatoki, then nodded. "Good. Place it with the others to be packed."

The big man hovered near the door for a moment. "You should try to eat, *kei*. And perhaps rest for a few hours."

"I will, later," Jian-Shan lied.

Valence St. Charles had complicated everything, and still he found himself thinking about her constantly. She wasn't aware of the security camera in his bedroom, which permitted him to watch her, as he had last week when she had shown up at his office. He had watched her closely, telling himself he was only waiting for her to reveal herself as an operative.

Instead, she had been a model guest, only occasionally showing hints of impatience and a little indignation.

He turned away from the monitor and spent the next hour sorting through communiqués from the different sources he used to gather information throughout Europe. As he read, Raven called to warn him that General Grady was on his way to Paris.

Jian-Shan knew the personal and professional history that Raven shared with Kalen Grady. "Perhaps you had better relocate to London for the interim."

"I'm not worried about the general," she said. "Now, how many passports do you want, and what names should I put on them?"

He instructed her to make four, then added a fifth for the American woman.

Raven made a tsking sound. "You sure you want to haul this civilian around with you all over creation, Jay?"

"No." Another lie. "Make it up anyway. Keep me updated on Grady as well."

Bitterness tinged her laughter. "My pleasure."

After ending the call, he rubbed his tired eyes. Asking Raven to monitor Grady's movements may not have been the wisest decision. He knew she had an old score to settle with the general, and it was one that could very well get her killed.

Another call came in from his business manager.

"Monsieur, I have been in contact with Drake Scribner, the head curator at the New Orleans Museum. The St. Charles woman is employed by him, though apparently on very shaky terms."

"But she has actually worked there for two years?"

"*Oui, monsieur*," Madelaine said. "I have also had a number of calls from members of the society. Evidently this woman has paid a visit to nearly every import dealer in the *zaibatsu*, inquiring about you. She has made herself quite a nuisance."

Movement on one of the monitors made him turn, and he saw Valence standing in front of the window, looking out into the garden. Though he could see only her back, something in the way she stood made him frown.

She turned, tightened the belt of her robe, and went to the door. He panned the camera over to see her inserting a small, thin square between the door and the frame, just above the lock. A moment later, she smiled, pulled the door open, and walked out of the room.

Chikusho, he swore silently. What was his fallen angel doing now? "I must call you back, Madelaine. Adieu."

He found her walking down the hallway near his training room. He waited until he was right behind her, then spoke. "Are you lost?"

Val yelped and spun around, then sighed her relief. "Are you trying to scare me half to death?"

"No." He held out his hand. "Give me the credit card, please."

"How did you—" She stopped, scowled, and removed a slim leather case from the pocket of her robe. "Here."

He took it and opened it. "Does Dr. Toyotomi know you have his wallet?"

"He will now." She looked around the corridor. "I didn't see any security cameras. Where are they?"

"Why would I tell you that?"

She nodded. "Good point."

Had he not been so distracted by the hunt for his father, Jian Shan might have anticipated her getting out of the locked room—she had, after all, found a way to get to him. Now he had to think of another method to keep her safe, secure, and under control.

Which meant making her *want* to stay.

"Come with me." He gestured for her to walk ahead of him. "I want to show you something."

He led her into his training room, where Han was packing the last of the crates. "Han, would you excuse us for a moment?"

The bodyguard looked puzzled, but obediently left them alone.

Valence was already moving toward the open crate. "Is that what I think it is?"

Jian-Shan saw the pleasure lighting up her face and felt suddenly annoyed with her. "Is that what you're trying to steal from me?"

"No." She chuckled as she crouched down by the crate. "But I'm awfully tempted to try." She didn't touch the sword, but bent so close that the tip of her nose nearly brushed the blade. "Middle Edo Period, Shinto-smithed, close-forged. God in heaven, the *hada* looks almost grainless." She glanced up at him. "Kunisuke, isn't it?"

"A thief generally doesn't know how to identify a seventeenth-century Japanese blade on sight." His tension inexplicably eased. "I am impressed."

"I'm not a thief." She openly admired the sword for another moment, then rose to her feet. "No, that's not true. I *was* a thief, when I was a kid, but I'm reformed. It's been a good fifteen years since I've had to steal anything."

That he would verify through her juvenile records, but her words had the ring of truth to them. "And Dr. Toyotomi's wallet?"

She shrugged. "I don't like being ignored and locked up like a crazy person, any more than you would." She walked around the other crates. "This is it, isn't it? Your collection?"

"Part of it."

She came to him, and the longing on her face was almost painful to see. "Would you let me have a look at the other blades? Please?"

"The Nagatoki are no longer here."

She blinked. "Where are they?"

"I have moved them to a safer location." He took her arm and guided her to the door. "You can see them after we arrive in Provence."

"What do you mean, 'we'?" She tugged him to a stop. "I'm not going there."

He gathered his patience. "We will be leaving in a few hours. For your own protection, you must accompany us."

"Mr. T'ang, I can't go with you," she said, shaking her head. "I'm here on business, and my time's almost up."

"Do you truly wish to see the Nagatoki?" Her eyes strayed to the cases, and she bit her bottom lip. He didn't wait for an answer. "Then you will come with me."

"It's not that simple." When he didn't comment, she blew out an exasperated breath. "Look, I'm sorry about what happened, and I'm very grateful you're so concerned about my safety. But you don't understand. I have a job I need to get back to. I can't go chasing around France. If I am in danger, as you say, then this is an excellent time for me to leave the country."

"You are injured, and you have no protection." He opened the door for her. "Is your job more important than your life?"

"The police will protect me." She turned toward the front of the house. "Thanks again for your hospitality, but I must go. Now."

"Stop." He took her by the shoulders and pulled her back to face him. "This is not a fantasy. The danger is quite real. The moment you leave, that assassin will track you. He won't care what you have, or what you want. He's a professional; the police can't stop him. He will kill you, Valence."

Touching her was a mistake—the tension between them immediately tripled. Her face had paled, and he could feel the shudder that ran through her at his words.

"Why would a professional killer be after you?"

"The swords," he reminded her.

"Oh, right. Well, I'll go to the American embassy, then." She looked down at the floor. "They have the marines stationed there."

"You can't even provide them with a description of the man," he reminded her, then lifted her chin to look into the black crystal of her eyes. "You saved my life. Let me protect yours."

"What if you went with me?" Hope brightened her eyes. "You know a lot more about this hit man than I do, *cher.* That could help them catch him."

She was so naive that he wanted to shake her. In spite of a knife through her hand and everything he had told her, she still believed it was something the authorities could handle.

Jian-Shan shook his head and handed her the wallet. "I trust you will return this to the doctor when he calls tonight. In the meantime, you should rest. We will be leaving before dawn."

Val did return the wallet to Dr. Toyotomi's jacket that evening—minus one credit card—and relieved him of his car keys at the same time.

She didn't understand what was happening with T'ang Jian-Shan, but his insistence on her avoiding the authorities and traveling to Provence decided everything for her. As much as she was tempted to go along for the ride just to study the swords, this bizarre situation had gotten completely out of control.

I'll find another source for the Nagatoki research, she told herself as she made her plans. *He's not the only collector in the world. If Scribner fires me, I'll just find another job until I can finish the book.*

She had to get out of the house tonight, which meant getting rid of the doctor for a few minutes. Her blouse had been ruined, so she settled for wearing a robe over her leather pants and borrowing Shikoro's zori.

Before Toyotomi removed her sling, she got up

from the bed. "Would you excuse me, Doctor?" She pressed her hand against her belly and looked in the direction of the bathroom. "All this excitement has got my stomach upset." She sighed. "I sure could use some of that special tea Shikoro makes."

"I would not mind having a cup myself," the doctor told her. "Go ahead. I will get the tea."

As soon as the sound of his footsteps faded down the hall, she pulled on her pants and tucked the zori under her arm. Her odd appearance, reflected in the standing mirror, made her wince. *I'll be able to change as soon as I get back to the hotel.*

She used the credit card to let herself out of the room. She had been unable to locate the security cameras, so she figured she had only a few seconds to get out of the house, at the most.

The moment she stepped out into the hallway, she ran.

Conversations with Shikoro had supplied her with enough information about the general layout of the house for her to swiftly locate the nearest door to the garden. Once outside, she raced into and through the garage, where a small sedan sat parked behind the big limousine.

Grand theft auto is probably a felony in this country, her conscience reminded her as she spotted the gate release switch and flipped it, then hurried to the car. She glanced over her shoulder at the sound of a door being slammed toward the back of the house. Quickly she jerked the driver's side door open. *But then, kidnapping should be, too.*

As she fumbled to get the key in the ignition, Han barreled into the garage. "Come on, come on," she begged the car.

At last the engine started. She threw the car into reverse, and slammed her foot down on the accelerator at the same time Han hit the gate switch. The tires shrieked as she hurtled backward down the drive and through the gate, just before it closed.

She drove frantically, taking several turns through the narrow streets, passing houses with architecture dating back to the fifteenth century. As soon as she felt confident that she had eluded Han, she slowed down to get her bearings.

The next time I get stabbed and held hostage, I am definitely bringing my guidebook and map.

The sun had just begun to set, but there was enough light for Val to navigate through the exclusive residential quarter. Maseratis and Ferraris were parked openly on the streets, while banks of colorful tulips seemed to border every house she passed.

As she had suspected from the glimpses she'd gotten from the trunk of the limousine, T'ang lived among the wealthiest Parisians. A sign she passed read RUE VIEILLE-DU-TEMPLE, and she recalled writing to a museum named the Hotel de Rogan with the same address. That meant she was in Le Marais, one of the oldest sections of Paris, and not far from the White Tiger society's office building, where she had left her motorcycle.

I'll leave the car there, and his people or Han will find it.

Guilt sank into her as she thought of how worried Jian-Shan might be now. After all, he *had* been prepared to whisk her away to Provence, simply to keep her safe. And it really wasn't his fault that someone wanted his swords so badly that they were willing to hire a professional killer to get to them.

Or was there more to it than that? Was Jian-Shan still in danger? What if something happened to Lily?

I can't feel sorry for him; I can't get involved. This is none of my business.

Val wondered how many times she would have to repeat that to herself before she started believing it.

Working with members of the White Tiger *zaibatsu* had taught Madelaine Pierport the value of reserve paired with elegant courtesy. Tonight's reception would initiate the fall season of showings, so everything had to be discreet, perfect, and utterly unforgettable. T'ang Jian-Shan demanded nothing less.

She had arranged for the string quartet playing Debussy, the formally dressed waiters offering hors d'oeuvres and flutes of pale champagne, the carefully orchestrated display of Ming vases. As the patrons and guests arrived, she greeted them and apologized for her employer's usual absence, pretending dismay when she was rather happy to be running the entire event by herself.

Madelaine would never admit that she secretly enjoyed the fact that her job allowed her to constantly take the spotlight.

"Madam Pierport?"

She turned to reply, saw her guest's mildly shocked expression, then saw the American woman.

Not her. Not tonight.

Valence St. Charles walked boldly through the front entrance and stalked directly through the crowd toward Madelaine. Unlike the last time she had intruded, her blond hair hung in complete disarray. Her face was bare of makeup. Her business suit had been replaced by far less formal attire.

What is she doing in leather pants and a bathrobe?

"You." The American stopped in front of her. As Madelaine glanced down, she saw that the blonde was wearing zori on her bare feet. "I want to talk to you."

Her long nails curled into her palms. *Was there no peace to be had from this annoying female?* "How may I be of assistance to you, mademoiselle?"

"First, you can tell me what you did with my motorcycle, and then you can call the police."

"A motorcycle?" Madelaine took a wary step back. "I have no idea what you're talking about, mademoiselle."

"I left it out in the alley across the street when I—oh, never mind." Val looked around. "Where's the phone?"

Guests began to drift over and form a circle around the two women. Most of the men took the opportunity to surreptitiously inspect the American's scandalous garments. That was when Madelaine realized that Valence was wearing nothing under the robe but the leather pants.

"You may wait for me in my office"—Madelaine gestured in that direction—"while I summon the police. You saw someone steal this motorcycle you refer to?"

"No, I wasn't here." The American nodded toward the door. "Your boss has been keeping me locked in his house for the last couple of days."

"Are you referring to Mr. T'ang?" Madelaine smiled for the benefit of the many eyes watching them. "You must be mistaken. He does not entertain at his home."

"He wasn't entertaining me." The American held out her left arm, which was splinted and bandaged. "I got this when I saved his life."

It was becoming more impossible by the moment for Madelaine to make sense of what the woman was telling her. Evidently Valence St. Charles was under the influence of some mind-altering substance. "I'm sorry to hear that you hurt your arm, mademoiselle. Now, if you would be so good as to wait in my office, I will—"

"I stepped between him and a man who was throwing a knife at his chest. The knife went through my hand."

Madelaine blinked. "What?"

"I was in his garden. That's how I saved his life."

"Let me understand this correctly: your motorcycle was stolen while you were preventing a knife thrower from killing Mr. T'ang in his garden. For that, he then imprisoned you in his home." A few titters erupted behind her. "Is this what you wish to tell the police, mademoiselle?"

"That's the short version."

Madelaine could think of only one way to handle this debacle. She looked around the circle of mesmerized faces, then laughed. "Americans. They watch so many spy movies."

Valence's eyes narrowed. "I am not making this up. I can prove everything."

"Of course you can, my dear." She placed one of her hands on the woman's robe sleeve and lowered her voice—but not enough that what she said escaped the ears of her guests. "I know you're determined to meet Mr. T'ang, and while I admire such a creative approach, I cannot allow you to go about relating such ridiculous stories. Mr. T'ang is a very important man, and he will not take kindly to being slandered."

"He didn't take kindly to having a knife thrown at him, either." Rather than slink away in defeat, the American went around Madelaine and headed for the reception desk. "I need to use the phone now. What's the number for the local police?"

"I beg your pardon, young lady." Li Shen, one of Madelaine's most important guests, stopped the blonde before she got to the desk. "You should think before you speak to the police. They may not take you seriously. Not dressed—or rather, as undressed as you are."

Madelaine stalked over to the pair. "Monsieur Li, please don't concern yourself with this matter. This young woman is obviously under the influence of some drug. Perhaps she wandered from some type of hospital. In any case, I believe it *is* a matter for the police. I will call them myself."

"I wasn't in any hospital." Dark eyes narrowed as the American turned on her. "And I am *not* on *drugs*."

Madelaine signaled two of the security guards. "Ms. St. Charles, you may wait with these gentlemen in my office while I contact the authorities."

"Ms. Pierport, you may go jump in the Seine while *I* contact the authorities." The blonde turned to Li Shen. "They'll listen to me if I have decent clothes on? That's what you're saying?"

"I think they would be less willing to think you irrational or on drugs. Also, you should have your arm looked at by a physician." He thought for a moment. "There's a hospital just a few kilometers down the road. I would be honored if you would allow me to escort you there."

She cradled her injured hand. "I don't need a doctor as much as I need a cop, and I've got my own car, thank you."

The dealer lowered his voice. "It would be for the best if you returned to your hotel and got some sleep. The police will be unable to take your report until the morning."

"You don't believe me either. You're just being polite." The American sounded incredulous. "What is it with you people?"

"This has gone far enough." Madelaine nodded to the guards. "Remove her from the premises at once."

"Keep your hands off me." Before the guards could touch her, the American stalked back out of the building, with Li Shen in her wake.

While the small, slim Chinese woman waited by the baggage gate, the customs official inspected her forged passport without much interest. "You are Yusogi Kuei-fei, a citizen of the United States?"

She was T'ang Kuei-fei, a citizen of China, who had been declared dead two days ago. "Yes. That is correct."

"What is your occupation, madam?"

She had been many things—a concubine, a wife, an agent for the Shandian corporation and the tong using it as a smoke screen to hide their criminal activities. Now she would be what had been denied her since the birth of her son: a mother.

"I am not employed, sir. I am a tourist, here to

see the many beauties of Paris. Maxim's. The Arc de Triomphe. The Eiffel Tower." She touched the camera she had hanging from a strap around her neck. "And take many pictures, I hope."

"Buy plenty of film." The official's sour-looking mouth curled. "How long do you intend to stay in France, Madam Yusogi?"

"Two weeks." *Or two months, or two years. Now that she was free, she would not leave France until she found her son.*

He nodded and stamped her passport, then handed it back to her. "Enjoy your stay, madam."

The trip from the airport to the hotel provided time for further contemplation of her task. A task she had decided to take on shortly before her husband, T'ang Yin, had been arrested and indicted on multiple counts of conspiracy and industrial espionage. Charges she would have faced herself, if not for a timely phone call from a man she had never considered a potential ally.

"I'll arrange everything," Colonel Sean Delaney had told her. "All you have to do is contact Jian-Shan and convince him to work with us."

Kuei-fei had learned long ago never to trust the motives of someone offering so much for so little. "Why does your government not contact my son directly?"

He cleared his throat. "The government's not exactly had a great deal of success in that area."

"Is that so?" She refused to give in to new hope. Not until she knew more. "I would be quite interested in learning how you remain active on this case, given your recent absence from duty, Colonel Delaney."

"Call me Irish." He laughed. "There's no dust on you, is there, lady?"

His laughter would have been infectious, but Kuei-fei had stopped allowing herself to feel thirty-eight years ago. "You have not answered my question."

"All right, I'll level with you." The colonel's voice grew serious. "I've been involved in this operation since before Jian-Shan and Karen left China, and I want to see it through to the end. The men assigned to the case now don't have a leper's chance in a cathouse of getting your son to come in. I don't know your son, but I knew Karen, and this is what she wanted for him."

A man did not offer protection unless he had good reason to do so. "How did you know Karen, Irish?"

"She smuggled a microdisk out of China for Jian-Shan and sent it to me for safekeeping. There was a bit of scandal at the time—she killed her first husband, Senator Colfax, in self-defense—but one of my nieces helped her." He sighed. "It's a tangled story, but in the end I did what I could for her."

"Indeed." Kuei-fei knew all about Karen Colfax, and the Montana operation Sean had been involved with, but she refrained from commenting. "How will you profit from this?"

"Like you said, I'm retired. I just feel like I owe it to Karen to close this case once and for all." He hesitated, and added in a kind way, "I interviewed your husband, Yin, and I know you haven't seen the boy since he was born."

She thought of her husband, to whom T'ang Po had sold her after Jian-Shan's birth, and sniffed. "What does that matter?"

"Family matters. You can trust me with yours."

Kuei-fei reserved her opinion on the subject of trust. Nor did she hand over her agreement to work for the Americans immediately. She bargained with Delaney until she obtained the concessions she wanted: full immunity from prosecution for herself and her son, the promise of new identities, and enough money for both of them to make a new start.

Once they had worked out the deal, Sean Delaney was cautiously pleased. "You drive a hard bargain, lady."

"Nonsense. When Jian-Shan decrypts the microdisk for you, it means the end of Shandian."

"You know about what's on the disk?" He sounded surprised by the revelation. "Yin never said a word."

"He does not know." Yin was a weakling, incapable of making decisions of his own. T'ang Po, on the other hand, was no fool. Neither was the United States government. She would have to go very carefully. "Very well, Irish. I will go to Jian-Shan as soon as I make some final arrangements."

Colonel Delaney had not been involved in the latter. It would be several more days before an anonymous phone call would be made, and the badly burned body of an Asian woman would be discovered in Kuei-fei's Mercedes at the bottom of a cliff. By then, she hoped to be reunited with her son, and they would make their plans.

The hotel concierge escorted her to the reception desk, where she was greeted and given her room keys. The hotel was finer than any she had ever frequented, but she hardly noticed the luxurious appointments of her four-room suite.

Soon, my son. Soon I will find you, and we will never be parted again.

Val couldn't believe how angry she was. Bad enough she'd been stabbed, drugged, and locked up in T'ang's house. But the way those people had been looking at her—as if she'd walked into their snotty society party naked.

A chilly breeze made her shiver, and she looked down at the thin robe she wore.

She took a deep breath. *All right. I'm not wearing a very coordinated outfit, and maybe that looks a little strange. I'll go back to the hotel, get dressed, then go to the police.* She glanced at where she had parked Toyotomi's sedan. *Maybe I'd better ditch the car first.* Her jaw sagged.

The car was gone.

"Someone *stole* my stolen car?" she said out loud, walking toward the empty space. "I don't believe it. This can't be happening."

"Ms. St. Charles?" Li Shen, the nice dealer from the reception, called out to her.

Val had liked him, and would have taken him up on his offer of a ride, but the glare of approaching headlights temporarily blinded her.

She put up her hand, trying to see where the dazzling light was coming from, when someone grabbed her and yanked her to one side. An instant later a car whooshed past on the sidewalk, only a few inches away from her. It quickly jumped the curb and hit the street with squealing tires as the driver gunned the engine.

"*Va chier!* You crazy idiot! What are you trying to do, kill me?" She turned to the person who had grabbed her, and saw Li Shen staring after the car. "I can't believe that. Did you see that car? It was like he was trying to run me down!"

"The French are very poor drivers, mademoiselle." Li Shen glanced down. "Are you injured?"

"No, just angry. What a moron." Val shook her head, then belatedly realized the dealer had been the one to pull her back, which might have saved her life. "I can't thank you enough for what you did, Mr. Li. If you hadn't grabbed me, I'd be squashed all over the road right now."

"You are very welcome." The art dealer managed a more natural smile. "Perhaps now you will allow me to escort you back to your hotel?"

She glanced at the empty space, then at the street where the hit-and-run car had disappeared. "You couldn't get rid of me if you tried."

The older man offered her his arm and led her to the adjacent parking lot, where his Porsche was parked. He drove to the hotel at a sedate pace and commented on life in the city until Val shook herself out of her self-induced trance.

"I appreciate the small talk, Mr. Li, but quite frankly, I'm not up to it."

"I thought it might distract you from dwelling on your unpleasant experiences." As he turned to join the heavier traffic streaming through the Champs Elysee, he glanced at her. "Are you part Asian, Ms. St. Charles? Forgive my curiosity, but your eyes and skin color are unique."

"I'm not sure. I never knew my real parents, though it's obvious one of them wasn't white." She ran a tired hand over her messy hair. "Do you know Mr. T'ang well?"

"Only by reputation," he said. "He has united the entire Eurasian community in Paris over the last two years. I myself arrived in France only recently and have not had the pleasure of meeting him in person. You probably know him better than I do."

"I'm not making this up, you know." She held up her injured hand. "Someone really wants him dead."

"By publicizing the existence of the Nagatoki blades, T'ang has made himself an instant legend among weapons collectors around the world." He looked at her and smiled. "I would love to see those swords."

"So would I." Val rubbed the side of her head. "It's the reason I came to France."

"You mean, you did not see the swords when you were with T'ang?"

"No. He moved them out of the house before I had the chance."

"Where did he take them?" When she glanced at him, he shrugged. "If they are on exhibit, I would schedule a visit to see them."

"I don't know, but I'm pretty sure they're not on exhibit anywhere. To tell you the truth, I'm beginning to doubt that the Nagatoki blades even exist."

"To the Chinese, swords are more than weapons—they are symbols of power and familial piety, especially among the tongs." Li Shen gave her a sideways smile. "It is not something about which our people boast."

"Tongs?" She frowned. "You mean the Chinese mafia?"

"They are similar to the Italian criminal organizations, but much more complex in structure. For example, in one region, the head of the tong gives his son his sword only when he is prepared to relinquish his position and power to him." He pulled up to the service entrance of the hotel and parked. "You will be less noticeable if you go in through this entrance. Let one of the stewards know you have been locked out of your room, and he will provide you with a replacement key."

"Thanks." She grimaced and held out her right hand. "I'd invite you to have a drink with me, Mr. Li, but I'm leaving France as soon as possible."

"Have a safe trip home." He clasped her hand briefly between his, then removed a business card from his wallet and pressed it in her palm. "Take this. Should you need help before you go, leave a message for me at that number."

She smiled, nodded, and stepped out of the car. The outside temperature was dropping, so she didn't linger but hurried into the service entrance. As Li Shen had predicted, she found a helpful steward, who not only got her a replacement key for her room but brought one of the courtesy toweling robes provided by the hotel for her to wear over her thin robe.

She took the service elevator up to her floor, thinking about what she would do in the morning. *Call the police first, of course. Then contact the American embassy. It never hurts to cover all the bases.*

Val pushed the coded key card in the slot above the door handle, then let herself into her room. It was dark, so as soon as she shut the door and turned the dead bolt, she flicked on the light switch.

And saw who was standing by the window.

"Don't scream," Jian-Shan told her, without turning around.

Chapter 5

How had he gotten into her room?

Everything Li Shen had said to her came rushing back into her mind at once. *Swords are more than weapons . . . symbols of power and familial piety . . . among the tongs.*

Val backed against the door, then whirled and clawed at dead bolt. And froze when she felt his hand on the back of her neck.

"You will do as I say, Ms. St. Charles." He turned her around, then pointed to the closet. "Open the wardrobe."

She moved a foot to the left, then opened the small closet where she'd hung her clothes. "Why are you here? Why are you doing this to me?"

"Take the clothes and put them in your suitcase." His voice remained flat. "Leave out the blue trousers and the gray blouse."

"Why? Don't you like them?"

"You will be wearing them."

She eyed him over her shoulder. "Do you want your robe back that badly?"

"I am in no mood to banter with you." His expression darkened. "Get dressed."

"I see you've already packed everything else. What an efficient valet you'd make." She grabbed her clothes from the closet and stomped over to the bed. "I'm not dressing in front of you."

"I will wait outside in the hall for you. If you do not come out in two minutes, I will dress you myself."

She nodded. Two minutes was more than enough time.

"In the event you are thinking of leaving through the window"—he nodded in that direction—"there is no fire escape, and it is twelve stories down to the street."

She *had* been thinking of going out the window, damn him. Without another word she folded the clothes in her arms in half and stuffed them into her suitcase.

Two minutes later, Jian-Shan returned, and gave her half-dressed state a stern look. "I did warn you."

"*You* try doing up buttons with one hand," she said, ready to thump him, "and see how fast you can get dressed."

He came to her and began buttoning the front of her blouse. "I should have chosen one easier for you to put on. I apologize."

"Why? You're not sorry about any of this."

He grabbed her suitcase, closed it, and nodded toward the door. "We will go now."

Val wasn't surprised to see Dr. Toyotomi's car parked outside the hotel entrance, or to see Han behind the wheel. She was briefly tempted to make a

scene, especially when a group of young Parisians
came up the sidewalk to enter the hotel, but a look
from Jian-Shan made her quickly discard that idea.

No, he means business.

The air seemed much chillier now, and she shivered as she stood beside the car. He indicated she
should sit in the front seat, and clipped the seat belt
over her personally. Then he traded places with
Han and started the engine.

She frowned as the bodyguard walked away
down the street. "Isn't he coming with us?"

"No, he will take another car." Jian-Shan
frowned. "One that is not stolen."

"I wouldn't have stolen the car if there had been
any other way to leave." She stared through the
front windshield, hating herself for feeling guilty. "I
just want you to know that."

"Desperation does not justify criminal behavior."
He pulled away from the curb.

She folded her arms, then grimaced as the movement jarred her injured hand. "You've obviously
never been homeless or hungry."

"You would be surprised what I have been, Valence."

What had Li Shen said? *The head of the tong gives
his son his sword only when he is prepared to relinquish
his position and power to him.*

"Do you belong to a tong?"

"No."

If he did, would he tell me? She rested her head
back against the seat. "I don't know what to believe." She could be in the middle of some Chinese
mafia war. With the head warrior dragging her off
to the countryside. Not knowing made her resent-

ment inch up another notch. "I never wanted any of this, you know. I'm just a museum curator, not a James Bond girl."

Jian-Shan didn't respond to that, and remained silent for most of the trip back to Le Marais. She tried to see where they were, but it was too dark, and her eyes felt odd. Heavy, and hot, as if she'd been reading for hours.

Finally she broke the silence. "What happens now?"

He glanced at her. "To whom?"

The growing aches and pains in her limbs made her snap back at him, "Me. You know, the victim here."

"I have not decided what to do with you yet."

"You haven't *decided*?" Disbelief only sharpened her temper. "*Cher,* you don't own me, you certainly don't get to decide what happens to me. This is your mess, not mine."

Jian-Shan pulled off the road, put the car in PARK, and shut off the engine. For a time he simply sat and stared out through the windshield.

When he spoke, his voice crackled with ice. "The only reason the assassin who attacked us found my home was because you led him there."

She snorted. "That's impossible."

"He planted a transmitter on your clothing and followed the signal." He turned his face toward her, and his eyes glittered in the dim light. "You wanted to know more about tongs, didn't you? Do you know how their assassins prove they have made a kill? *Do you?*"

Horrified, Val shook her head.

"They cut off the ear, the nose, and a finger, and

deliver it to the tong leader in a box. If the target was important enough, they will skin off the entire face, so it can be dried and hung in the private rooms of their leaders, for all to see what happens to those who cross them."

He made a sound of utter disgust. "I have been in such a room. There were three hundred and forty-one faces hanging from small hooks on its walls."

She wanted to clap her hands over her ears and beg him not to say anymore. "I didn't know."

"Now you do." He turned back to the wheel. "Perhaps the next time you think to place my household in danger, you will remember this."

She would have assured him that she would, but the pain from her hand and the heat in her head grew too much to bear, and all she could do was let it pull her down into the numbing darkness.

"Why did she run from me, Han?" Jian-Shan watched as Toyotomi checked his reluctant, unconscious guest.

"She does not recognize the danger of her situation," Han murmured. "It is also difficult to make Western females understand the need for protection. They are excessively . . . liberated."

"I was too harsh with her." He clamped down on the inexplicable wave of anger he still felt from the night before, when he had carried her in from the car. "Doctor?"

Toyotomi, who was heavy-eyed from being summoned in the middle of the night, removed the digital thermometer from Valence's ear and sighed as he read the display. "Her fever has returned. I should begin an IV to prevent dehydration, and begin antibiotic treatment for the infection."

"Give her the drugs, but no IV. I will see to the rest myself."

Toyotomi looked puzzled. "There is no need for that, Mr. T'ang. I can start the intravenous and return in the morning."

"We will not be here." Jian-Shan nodded to Shikoro, who went to retrieve his sleeping daughter from her bed.

Once Toyotomi departed, they left the villa. Han kept the car on the back roads from Paris as they traveled into the heart of the French countryside. Shikoro sat in the front of the big car, holding the sleeping Lily in her arms, leaving Jian-Shan to watch over the feverish American.

His loss of temper had been unfortunate, and convincing Valence to stay with him voluntarily seemed unlikely now. Yet he would have to come to some sort of agreement with her, or keep her prisoner. Transporting her out of the country under the current conditions—with Shandian operatives monitoring every international flight, train, or boat—would prove challenging, if not impossible.

I cannot leave her behind. I cannot leave her to die.

He looked down at her face. In sleep she looked younger, more vulnerable. The mask of self-confidence gone, her stirring sensuality became even more evident. The fullness of her lips, naked of cosmetic concealment, curved into a slight smile.

Headlights from a passing truck revealed a faint sheen on her skin, and he pressed his hand to her brow. She still felt hot to the touch, but her fever was breaking.

The long, straight lashes swept up, and she looked at him, confused. He took his hand away. The open expression became quickly guarded as she eased her head up and took in their surroundings. "New car."

He nodded. "We're moving to a safer location."

"A safer location where, exactly?"

"In Provence, as I told you." He pulled up the chenille throw Shikoro had covered her with, being careful not to jar her arm. "You have been running a fever. Are you in any pain?"

She shook her head, but he could feel her shivering under the throw. He reached for the case of medical supplies Toyotomi had given him and extracted a flask of water and a bottle of pills. "This will help."

"No. I don't want any more drugs." She reached out to him with her good hand and slipped her hot, damp fingers between his. "I can't stand them, *cher.* Please don't."

He stared down at her hand in his and put the pills aside. "Then drink some of this. It's just cold water."

She took the flask and sipped from it, then grimaced. "How long was I out this time?"

"A few hours." He kept his expression impassive, but seeing her so weak made him angry. "The pills will help you sleep, Ms. St. Charles."

"Val. And I want to stay awake."

So you can find out where we're going. "As you wish."

She tried out a smile on him. "I'm too old to be

taking naps." She studied his face. "You haven't been sleeping much, have you?"

He shrugged. He rarely slept.

"Don't do the guy thing and pretend you're invincible," she said. "No one is, except Superman, and even he has to deal with kryptonite."

He frowned. "Kryptonite?"

"Pieces of his home planet." She drank from the flask again, then handed it to him. "Didn't you ever read comic books when you were a kid?"

"No."

"That's a shame." Val shifted her weight, then winced. "You can't intimidate me, you know. I've been stabbed. Everything else seems kind of piddly in comparison to that."

"Piddly?" He drew out the word into three separate sounds.

"Trivial. Insignificant. No problem." She grinned. "Besides, I work for a man who makes snakes look friendly."

"I think," he said, assuming a bored tone, "that you should rest now."

"You aren't ever going to tell the police about this, are you?" She shifted, moving closer. "You're hiding me in the country for my protection, okay, but who's going to look out for you and your little girl?"

"We are safe," he assured her.

"Like you were in Paris?" She lifted her bandaged hand in emphasis. "Forgive me, *cher*, but I have the proof right here."

"That was an exceptional situation that will not be repeated."

"I took a knife for you, and you've dragged me

right into the middle of it." She looked up at Han, then leaned back on the seat. "That Frenchwoman who works for you thinks I watch too many spy movies. I wonder what she'd make of this." Val abruptly huddled down under the throw. "I'm cold."

He reached over to close the air-conditioning vents nearest to her, then felt how violently she was trembling and moved closer. "Come here." He pulled her against his side, draping his arm around her shoulders.

"Hmmm." She closed her eyes and rested her cheek against his chest. "Better." A few moments later she was asleep.

Jian-Shan meant to set her aside, away from him, as soon as she quieted. But it had been too long since he had held a woman in his arms. He looked down at her bright hair, and began smoothing back the damp tangles from her face. It would become tousled like this when she made love, he thought, admiring the silky strands wrapped around his fingers.

He wanted to see her like that. He wanted to see her fallen angel's face flushed with desire and pleasure.

Val stirred in her sleep and shifted her injured hand until it rested close by the wound in his chest.

Desire ebbed, replaced by something deeper and more complex. *What brought you to me? What am I to do with you? How can I keep you safe from the nightmares we both fear?*

There was no answer. His only solace was holding her in his arms for the rest of the journey and imagining what it would be like, in a world that could never be possible, where he would never have to let her go.

Val woke up in another strange bed to find Shikoro coaxing her to drink from a cup of her warm mint tea.

"Good morning," she said, strangely glad to see the Japanese woman.

"*Ohayou-gozaimasu*, good morning to you, *Oku-san*." Shikoro stepped back to bow, then made a polite gesture. "You wish bath before you eat? I have ready."

Val felt sticky and sweaty as well as achy with fever. "Yes, please."

"Take pills first." She handed her two of the antibiotics she'd taken before. "Doctor say take bandage off, no wet hand," the housekeeper warned after Val swallowed them.

Shikoro helped Val out of bed and guided her to the bathroom. This one didn't adjoin the bedroom, but lay just across the hall. She retrieved towels and soap from a lovely white cabinet that looked about a hundred years old. "I help you, clothes, wash hair?"

Val felt dazed, but then, she had absolutely no idea where she was. For the second time in as many weeks. *Provence? Is that where he said he was taking me?*

"*Okusan?*"

"Um—yes, if you don't mind." Val took off the bandage and splints, then examined her hand. The wound was healing, but it still hurt too much to do anything more than wiggle her fingers. She felt a little self-conscious as she slipped out of her robe and sat down in the warm bath, but Shikoro went right to work.

"Give proper bath soon," the housekeeper told her as she tilted her head back to wet her hair, then began applying shampoo.

"This sure feels like a proper bath." Val closed her eyes for the rinse.

"My country, no sit in water and wash. Wash, then sit in water." Shikoro applied something to her hair that felt silky and smelled like spices and fruit. "*Okusan* hair like gold on fire."

Her head felt like it was on fire, but that was from the fever. "Americans call it strawberry blond."

Shikoro giggled. "You no look like strawberry."

"That's exactly what I've always said."

After her bath, the housekeeper showed her where her clothes had been stored and helped comb and dry her hair.

"You look better," Shikoro told her, sounding very satisfied. "Master come see you later, he say."

So Han's wife called Jian-Shan master, too. "Probably to yell at me."

"Master never yell."

"I think this time he'll make an exception." Val contemplated her reflection.

Shikoro fussed with her hair, brushing most of it back from her face to spill around her shoulders. "You make him not want yell at you. Man like woman please him."

"It's safe to say I don't please him."

"How you know?" She wagged a finger at Val. "You not try yet."

Her lips curved. "So what should I do?"

"You be pretty for him. Talk soft voice. Drink tea together. I bring you." The housekeeper stepped back from the vanity table. "No ask question. No make mad. Give him smile. Make master smile."

Val knew Asian women had a totally different perspective on relationships, but all that sounded positively *medieval*. "And if I do all this, he'll be happier?"

"You still . . ." Shikoro thought for a moment, as if trying to find the right words. "You not know man in bed?"

Val couldn't help but laugh. "Oh, no, *cher*, I've known a few in that department."

"Then you know." The housekeeper smiled. "That please him most. Feel better, take him in bed."

She sighed. "Americans don't settle arguments with sex."

The other woman shook her head. "Master sad. Very lonely. Need woman please him."

Something in Val's heart twisted. She'd already sensed some deep, abiding sorrow in Jian-Shan, as if some tragedy had set him apart from everyone around him. Yet that wasn't her concern—not after what he'd done to her. "Shikoro, a woman doesn't go to bed with a man just because he's depressed. Especially if the man is involved in criminal activities."

"Master no criminal." The housekeeper looked offended. "T'ang-san honorable man. Keep you safe."

Feeling hot and weak, Val went over and sat down on the bed. "I appreciate the advice, but that's not how we do things in my country." Or how she would handle Jian-Shan.

"Then you stay sad, lonely, like master." With that, the housekeeper bowed, and left her to brood.

Val drifted off to sleep, and although she woke up several times, she felt too exhausted to do more than roll over and try to find a cooler spot on the pillow.

After an indeterminate amount of time, it felt as if her fever had ebbed, but it had left in its wake a migraine of epic proportions. She sat up and squinted at the old-fashioned bell pull beside the bed. Shikoro had said to use it if she needed anything, but she felt a little reluctant to do so.

"You're awake."

His voice was so near that Val jerked around, inadvertently propping herself on her injured hand. Pain flashed up her arm as she hissed in a breath. "Yes. Hi." She grimaced as she took in the tray he carried. "Have you got an extra hacksaw around here? I'm getting tired of this hand."

"A hacksaw is certainly no remedy for pain." He set the tray aside and came to the bed. "Does your head hurt, too?"

"I think there's someone in there, redecorating with a sledgehammer." She flinched a little as he placed his fingertips at her temples. "What are you doing?"

"Tui-Na—Chinese massage." He began rolling his fingertips in small, intricate patterns against her temples. "It promotes relaxation and restores the internal balance of energy."

"As opposed to, say, abducting someone."

"Close your eyes and relax." He moved one

hand over, coaxing her eyelids shut. "Small wonder you have a headache; you're still dwelling on what happened last night."

"Aren't you?" Val had expected him to be angry, not to perform some kind of ancient holistic therapy to give her relief.

"I was angry. I didn't think you would run away from me." His fingertips strayed from her temples and glided in circles over her brow. "I should not have taken my temper out on you, but you put yourself at great risk."

She thought of the car that had nearly run her down in the street. "I think you were right. Someone tried to make me a hit-and-run last night, outside your office building."

"Tell me about it."

As he continued the exquisitely gentle massage, Val related everything that had happened, adding, "Was it a tong who sent that man after you?"

His fingers stilled for a moment. "It is possible."

"Why would they do that?"

"My collection is very valuable, but to the tongs, the swords have special meaning. Some of our emperors refused to carry anything but Nagatoki swords. They are symbolic of supremacy and power, and there are men who would kill to have them." His voice went low. "You understand now why I was so angry with you?"

"Yes." The pounding pressure inside her head had gradually decreased, and Val discovered that she could open her eyes to the light without squinting in pain. "Hey, it's working."

Jian-Shan was sitting on the bed beside her, his hands buried in her hair as he rolled his fingertips against her scalp. So close she could see a pulse ticking at the base of his throat. His brows were drawn, but there was something different about his eyes, and the way he was looking all over her face, as if searching for some flaw.

Immediately her feminine side kicked in, and she felt color scorch her skin as she shifted back against the pillows. "I must look terrible."

"You are flushed"—he skimmed three fingers down her cheek and followed the line of her jaw—"and your skin is damp, but the fever is nearly gone." He slipped a hand under her neck and worked on the tense muscles there. "You still look a little lost, Valence."

"I don't know where I am."

"You are here, with me." He bent closer, shifting one hand to support the back of her head. With the other, he traced a delicate, swirling line around her lips. "And you are more beautiful than the first moment I saw you."

"Any girl looks better without a knife sticking in her," she murmured, unable to look away from his eyes.

His mouth hitched, then without warning he closed the gap between them and kissed her.

The hands that had chased away her migraine moved differently now, holding her still for his mouth, which had already coaxed her lips apart and was slowly demolishing every rational thought she had left. He kissed her with finesse, as if she were something fragile, but passionately, as if they were already lovers.

"Jian." She managed to turn her head, and inhaled sharply as his mouth traveled over her cheek and up to her temple.

"I know," he murmured against her ear, and the touch of his breath sent quick, darting tremors of delight down her spine. "Yet I see your lips move"—he brushed his over her brow—"and I find that I want them on mine." He lifted her, pressing her against his chest for a moment as he nuzzled her hair. "You feel it, too."

Of course she did. No woman alive could resist this strange, burning attraction he summoned inside her. Then Shikoro's pretty, practical voice echoed through the heat.

Master sad. Very lonely. Need woman please him.

She went stiff against him and brought up her good hand between them. "Mr. T'ang, I'm not here to entertain you. I came to borrow your swords for my museum. Under the circumstances, I have to be . . . professional about this."

"Yes, of course." Jian-Shan released her and withdrew behind his calm, expressionless mask again. "Forgive me for disturbing you." He rose and indicated the tray as he walked to the door. "Try to eat something if you can."

Before she could blink, he was gone.

Raven was waiting for General Grady when he walked out of customs at the airport, but she didn't allow him to see her. She told herself that gave her the opportunity to assess him, to see where he went, whom he spoke with, and if he'd brought any of his CID puppets along for the ride.

You don't want to face him, fear whispered.

No, she didn't. Not yet.

It had been seven years since the last time she saw Kalen, plenty of time for some changes. She'd certainly been through enough of her own. Secretly she'd hoped to see him balding or getting paunchy around the waist. Yet when he walked out of the gate, the only alterations time had made were some scattered streaks of silver in his short, dark red hair, and a few more lines around his eyes and mouth.

My, my, General, don't you look all tough and world-weary? The old desire flared up for a moment, before she stomped it out with ruthless determination. *Maybe I'll put a little more gray in your hair before you go home.*

It amused her to keep him under surveillance, although she knew her chances of continuing it for very long without getting caught were slim to none. Kalen had been one of the best field operatives in army intelligence, before he'd made too much rank to escape the desk work. And if he was as sharp as he had been in the old days, he'd know it was her.

He should—he trained me to do it.

She lost sight of him out by the long line of taxis waiting by the loading zone curb, then felt something like a touch on the back of her neck. Only one man in the world made her feel that way.

Without turning around, she smiled. "Hello, General."

He walked around to stand in front of her. "Raven."

They could have been two statues carved out of ice, stuck in the middle of some extravagant banquet table, the way they stood there, facing each other, not moving, not speaking, just staring and waiting.

I've been waiting for you.

Yes. And now I'm here.

Finally a taxi driver broke the stalemate by demanding to know if they were going to stand there until Paris crumbled into ruins and rolled into the Seine, or help him feed his starving children by giving him gainful employment.

"Will you share a cab with me?" Kalen asked with precise, wintry courtesy.

Raven wouldn't share the same planet with him, if it were left up to her. However, she owed Jay. And maybe in settling that debt, she could get Kalen out of her system.

She definitely wanted the general *out*.

"I brought my own wheels." She pushed a bill at the cabbie to shut him up and pointed to her Lotus, parked at the head of the line. "Come on, I'll give you a lift."

He plucked a parking ticket from under her windshield wiper and handed it to her. "Did Jian-Shan send you to tail me?"

"If you're going to interrogate me, you can go get a cab." She crumpled up the ticket, tossed it over her shoulder, then unlocked the car. "If you want a ride, shut up and get in."

For a moment, she thought he might just stand there and watch her drive off. But when she started the Lotus's engine, he climbed in.

Raven smiled a little. *Oh, Kalen, you still like to take chances.*

"Put your seat belt on, General." She rammed the car into gear before he closed the door. "This could be a rough ride."

* * *

Jian-Shan spent hours in meditation, and then worked through nineteen of the most complex *iaido* forms before he exhausted himself enough to sleep. The rest of the night he spent dreaming of a fallen angel with a flaming golden sword, who guarded the gates to paradise.

He woke before dawn with the answer to his problem—namely, what would persuade Valence to willingly remain under his protection until the game was finished and the danger was over.

He found her wandering around the bedroom, examining the art and books there. "Good morning." The small jump she gave at the sound of his voice gratified him, on a basic male level. "How are you feeling?"

"Better, thank you." She turned to him, her professional facade firmly back in place. "I'd like to make a few phone calls, if I may?"

"You haven't seen the rest of the villa yet. Come." He gestured toward the corridor. "Let me show it to you."

Again, he startled her. "You mean you're not going to lock me in this room, too?"

"Since the locks are old, and you were obviously an accomplished thief, that would probably be an exercise in futility." He didn't wait for an answer, but held out his hand. "Come. You really should see the rest of the house. It's magnificent."

He gave her a complete tour that ended in Raven's library. The large room was more like a treasure vault than a study—heavily gilded and ornate Baroque wall and ceiling panels stretched out for yards, showcasing a few seventeenth- and eighteenth-century paintings.

"They're genuine," he said as Val wandered a little closer to examine them. "The owner has an extensive collection, but keeps most of it in Paris."

"Wow," she murmured, running a fingertip over a complicated whirl in one corner of a Delacroix. "I feel like I'm in the Louvre, minus the tourists."

"Please, sit down. I will have Shikoro bring tea." Jian-Shan indicated a wing chair upholstered with ivory and gold tapestry to match the walls, then called the kitchen extension and requested the tray. "Your color is better this morning. Has the fever returned?"

"No." Val sat down and assumed a serious expression. "Mr. T'ang—"

He took the chair across from hers. "I believe we dispensed with any need for formality last night, Valence. Jian-Shan, or Jian, will do."

She nodded. "Jian, then. I do appreciate everything you've done to safeguard me, but I must return to America."

"Of course." She was so determined to be a professional. Which was exactly what he wanted. "However, you came to Paris to speak with me, did you not?" He made a casual gesture. "Before you go, why not tell me about your proposal?"

Her jaw dropped open for a moment. "I didn't think you were interested."

"Everything about you interests me, Valence." Jian-Shan enjoyed the brief flash of pleasure in her eyes before her business demeanor took over.

"As I've told you, I'm a curator for the New Orleans Museum of Art and Antiquities. You must have known how much interest the news about your swords would generate, or you wouldn't have gone public with the information."

He smiled a little. "I did."

She traced one fingertip over the intricate needlework covering the chair's armrest. "You must have also guessed how many museums would become immediately interested in your collection."

The way Val was leading up to making her offer was interesting—so serious and yet so carefully diplomatic. He could see how easily she would have charmed the taciturn Scots into lending her their claymores. "I did not make the knowledge available in order to sell my swords, or loan them to museums."

A small line appeared between her fair eyebrows. "Then why do it?"

Because it would bring my father to me. "Let us say, it was the proper time to let the world know."

"All right." Val linked her hands. "Let's say it was. You've just told the world you own more Nagatoki blades than we ever knew existed. Do you have certified provenance for them?"

"Yes. Why?"

"If you had obtained them through the black market, they could not be publicly exhibited. Interpol monitors all the museums in the world, and they would confiscate them as soon as they were shown. Also, I can't allow my museum's name to be associated with anyone trafficking in stolen goods."

He admired her for attacking first what others would have avoided altogether. "These swords have been in my family for over three hundred years, and I have the legal, certified provenance to prove that."

"Terrific." She released a small sigh, and grinned. "Stolen antiquities are such a problem these days.

Now, how would you like to change what the world knows about the Nagatoki?"

"I believe you said that by revealing their existence, I have already done so."

"Not quite." The side of her mouth curled for a moment. "Do you know the history of the sword maker himself?"

"Nagatoki Kan is considered one of the finest Japanese sword makers who ever lived. His work rivaled Masamune in strength, beauty, and serviceability." He inclined his head. "Everyone knows the swords are priceless, of course."

"Few people know that Master Nagatoki went blind in 1641," she said, startling him. "Yet I'll bet every dollar I have that carbon and tang etch dating will prove that half of your blades were forged in the decades *after* he lost his sight."

He hadn't anticipated this, and thought quickly. "You wish to disprove their authenticity?"

"No, I believe your swords were made by Nagatoki." She paused. "In order to prove my theory, I must examine the blades. If I can do that, I can not only date them, but I can verify exactly who made them."

Again, the guarded look. *What was she hiding from him?* "But that is not all you want."

"I would also like you to consider showing your collection for the first time at our museum in New Orleans. Before you say no"—she held up a hand—"let me tell you what we're prepared to offer. If you agree, I will give you all the research data I have on the swords and the sword maker. I am a trained expert in identifying these weapons, and I will also provide my services to photograph, catalogue, and publicize the collection, not only for the exhibition but in the book I'm writing about Japanese swords. It will cement your position as the premier collector of Nagatoki in the world, and no one will ever be able to take that away from you. Not even if you sell part of the collection, or decide to donate them to a museum."

Jian-Shan admired her presentation, and the sincerity invested in every word. She might come from an impoverished and unfortunate background, but she had polished herself to diamond-like brilliance. He felt an almost perverse sense of pride in her, as if she had done it to please him.

And it did please him, for her proposal worked perfectly with what he had planned—to offer her the collection for study, as long as she remained in Provence.

He had no intention of lending the swords to her museum, naturally, but he made a pretense of thinking it over.

"I am intrigued by your offer. Very well, Valence. I will allow you to study the blades, and I will consider lending them to your museum."

She hadn't expected the answer, and her smile became blinding. "You won't regret it, Jian, I promise you. I—"

"On one condition."

She leaned forward, intent. "Name it."

"You will stay here, in Provence, and catalogue the entire collection for me." He watched her *kurozuishou* eyes grow wary. "And you will help me identify the man who attacked us in the garden."

Chapter 6

So he found a way to make me stay here after all.

Val sat back in her chair and groped for an excuse. Time—she had none left. "I've only been given a week's vacation from my work, and that's up tomorrow. I would stay, but I can't. I'll lose my position."

Jian-Shan picked up the telephone. "Your employer is as eager as you are to obtain the collection, is he not?"

"He'd kill for it." What she said hit her, and she cleared her throat. "I mean, yes. He's very eager to get the loan."

He spoke in rapid French to the operator, then glanced up at her. "His name?"

"Drake Scribner."

He repeated that to the operator, then waited. After several minutes, he said, "Drake Scribner, please. This is T'ang Jian-Shan calling."

Val imagined her boss's reaction when he heard that. Then got another shock when Jian pressed the speaker button and returned the receiver to its cradle.

Scribner's voice over the speaker sounded more than eager. He was practically panting. "Mr. T'ang, what a coincidence! We were just discussing your incredible blade collection during our morning staff meeting here, and—"

"Thank you, Mr. Scribner. I have one of your curators here with me, a Ms. St. Charles. She has been of great assistance to me, and I find I require her services for some weeks further." Jian's dark eyes never left Val's face. "Do you have any objection to her remaining in France to help classify some of my swords?"

"No, no objection at all." Scribner chuckled, but it was a forced sound. "Ah, is Ms. St. Charles there?"

"Yes, as it happens, she is. Would you care to speak with her yourself?"

"Please."

Jian picked up the phone and held it over the desk to her.

"Hello, Mr. Scribner," Val said politely after she took the receiver from Jian.

"I can't believe you nailed him."

Val eyed the phone base. Jian still had it on speaker, which meant he could plainly hear every word they said. "Mr. Scribner, I didn't—"

"How'd you do it?" Her boss sounded out of breath, as if he'd run a marathon around his desk. Probably after the redheaded grad student. "Hell, girl, do you know what this means?" He hooted out loud. "The board's gonna have a field day."

Jian said nothing.

Val could feel her face getting hot. Yet as much as it pained her, she had to be honest. "Mr. T'ang has given me permission to examine his collection, Mr. Scribner, and catalogue it for him. However, he hasn't agreed to the loan of the swords as of yet—he does want to think it over a little more."

"Well, then, Val, you help the man make up his mind. Do whatever it takes to persuade him." There was no mistaking the innuendo, or the threat behind it.

She was tempted to reach across the desk and flick off the speaker switch, but that would only make things look worse. "Mr. Scribner, there are circumstances involved here, and I'm not sure—"

All the "good-ol' boy" humor fled from Scribner's voice. "Now you listen up, little girl. This man's real interested in what you've said you'd do for him. I don't care what that is, or how long it takes, you do it and you get those swords."

Jian raised one brow at that, and Val could have happily crawled under her chair and stayed there for a hundred years. "Yes, sir."

"I want updates, too. You call me and let me know what's happening over there." He chuckled again. "You can even tell me if he likes it on top. I won't mind."

That did it. "Good-bye, Mr. Scribner." She handed the phone back to Jian, who said a few more polite words, then hung up the receiver.

"An interesting man," Jian said, watching her.

"I think I compared him to snakes, didn't I? That was really insulting. To the snakes." She rubbed the back of her neck. "I don't know what to say about his—about what he said. I'm so embarrassed."

"Why should you apologize for him? His mind remains in the gutter, not yours. Forget him." Jian rose to his feet. "You look pale, you must be tired. Let me take you back to your room."

"Here we are. Le Bristol." Raven threw the Lotus in PARK in front of the grand hotel's entrance. "Real roses in the rooms, five-star restaurant downstairs, and everyone speaks English with a pretty accent. You should talk to Washington about a permanent transfer."

"It doesn't have to be this way, Sarah." Kalen sounded uncharacteristically tired.

"Raven." She eyed him. "No one calls me Sarah. Especially not you."

"Whatever you want. Raven. We need to talk."

"You can buy an hour of my time, General, just like everyone else does." She tilted her head to one side. "But somehow, I don't see the army reimbursement officer being very happy about paying you five grand for renting a clotheshorse."

"You make five grand an hour?"

"Half an hour. I was giving you the old boyfriend's discount." She smiled at the doorman hovering outside Kalen's window. "Better go now, General, before I get another ticket that I'm not going to pay."

He didn't twitch a muscle. "If you want money, you can have it. I'd rather take you to dinner."

She stared through the windshield, suddenly aware she didn't want to play the game anymore, even for Jay. "Why?"

"Because it's been seven years," he said, his voice going dangerously soft, "and we have a lot to talk about."

Was he going to apologize for sacrificing her for

their country? Try to justify killing her entire unit? *This could be interesting.* "I'll pick you up in an hour."

"Meet me in the bar." He got out and walked into the hotel.

She drove to the heart of the fashion district, and came to a screeching halt outside Couture du Etienne's main business offices. She didn't bother to sign in with the receptionist, who recognized her famous saunter before she even saw Raven's face.

Honore Etienne was sitting behind an impossibly large desk, sorting through glossy photos and arguing with voracious pleasure with a manufacturer on the phone. When she saw Raven walk in, she told him to go to hell and hung up. "*Cherie,* what is it?"

They had been employer and employee for years, and in that time had made each other filthy rich. Raven went out onto the balcony, which overlooked the Seine. "He's here. I'm having dinner with him."

Honore didn't have to ask who she was talking about, and gave her the once-over. "Dressed like that? Over my deceased body." She hit the button on her intercom. "Amie, Desiree, I need everyone to the preparation room at once." She went to Raven. "How much time do we have?"

She glanced at her watch. "Fifty-two minutes."

"You always cut it too near." The designer sighed. "Let us go to work."

Less than an hour later, Raven left her car at the curb, charmed the doorman into watching it, and went into Le Bristol to collect Kalen. Along the way, every man, woman, and child who saw her stopped whatever they were doing and stared.

She didn't have to glance in the long mirrors edging the lobby to know how she looked. It was her business to stop men in their tracks and make other women want to stab her in the chest.

She found Kalen sitting in the bar, nursing a glass of scotch. *Glenlivet tastes like paint remover*, she'd told him once, teasing him for his wretched taste in drinks. *And it'll make your insides look like the siding on a refugee shack.*

"Hello, General."

He looked up, then down, then up again. "You look different."

"I changed." She glanced down at the clinging sheath of gold, slashed with insets of onyx lace. The strategic arrangement of the lace made her look almost, but not quite, exposed. "Shall we?"

He'd somehow gotten reservations at one of the new gourmet hot spots that catered to the wealthy and discriminating. As they were ushered to their table, she noted the discreet positioning—off in a corner, where they could talk without being overheard.

And where Kalen can sit with his back to the wall.

"How much did it cost you?" she asked as she sat down in the chair the waiter had pulled out for her.

"About as much as half an hour of your time, standard rate." He ordered a bottle of excellent Chablis. "Does that satisfy you?"

"I'm not looking for satisfaction, Kalen." She gave him a slow, lazy smile. "That I have plenty of already."

The steward served the pale wine he'd selected, and she nodded her approval after the first sip. He began to order for both of them and then glanced across the table. "I suppose you want yogurt and lettuce."

"I'll have the lobster Marseilles, the marinated artichoke peels, and crème brûlée," she told the waiter. To Kalen, she added, "You forget, I never had to diet. My metabolism still scorches everything."

"My error." He waited until the waiter left them alone. "We can make this a fistfight, Raven, or we can talk. It's up to you."

"We'll talk first." She drank a little more of the superb wine. "You're here to get to Jian-Shan, obviously. What's the matter, can't the boys in cryptography crack a little Asian code?"

"Jian-Shan made sure they couldn't." He steepled his fingers. "I'm more concerned about this American he's holding hostage.

"You mean his houseguest, the museum lady." She placed her wineglass on the snowy linen tablecloth, and watched the drops of condensation form a damp ring around the base. "She's agreed to stay with him, so you can throw that baby out the window."

"Raven."

She met his gaze.

"T'ang Po wants his swords and his son back, and he'll kill anyone who gets in his way. Including innocent bystanders who have no business being near Jian-Shan." He reached across the table and took her hand in his. "This has gone beyond critical. Beyond what even your friend Jian-Shan can handle."

She let her hand rest in his. "Is Daddy T'ang in France?"

"We don't know where he is. We're trying to find out. If he is here, I'll give the information to your friend. I'll give him transport, protection, whatever it takes."

Kalen didn't make carte blanche offers without meaning it, so Raven's tension relaxed a few degrees. "I'll relay that to him."

His fingers tightened. "You know where he is?"

"Not at the moment, but we stay in touch." She withdrew her hand as the waiter brought their meals. The chunks of lobster on her plate gleamed pink and white under the lacing of wine sauce. "So, why the three-sixty, General? You were never known for your generosity toward the Asian section of humanity."

"I'm no bigot, Raven." He picked up his fork. "Eat. You're too goddamn skinny as it is."

The food was probably incredible, but she couldn't taste it. All she could do was listen to his voice, watch his eyes, and feel the old excitement at being so close to him. She even let herself wallow in her own self-disgust and daydreamed a little.

He talked about the job, leaving in enough details for her to get a sense of what he'd been fighting over in the States. Between Shandian and the other major tongs, he'd been busy. It reminded her of how they'd started out their relationship—working the same cases, partnering up on field assignments, depending on each other to stay alive. Somehow the line had blurred between professional and personal, and they'd grown closer. One night, hiding out in an abandoned old barn in Russian Georgia, huddling together to stay warm, they'd acted on it.

A year later, he had been promoted out of the field, and became her boss. She'd teased him about it, comfortable in the knowledge that however they served their country, they'd end up together off duty. Toward the end, she'd even dreamed of what they'd do when they got out of special ops. She wanted to live with him openly. Maybe even do the marriage bit. And she had dreamed of a child, a little boy or girl with Kalen's red hair.

And then the man she'd loved and trusted and had wanted to have babies with had sent her to die in a foreign country.

Raven knew she'd never gotten over her one and only love. Despite the disaster that had nearly killed her. The time and distance hadn't helped. She'd never asked him why he had let her walk into a trap. Why he'd sent a cleanup crew to kill everyone in her unit.

Maybe it was time she did. "Kalen, if I'm going to help you, I need something in return."

"I'll arrange to clear your records with the army," he said, nodding to the wine steward, who topped off their glasses. When he left them alone, he added, "You'll have to be officially discharged, but I can swing the details for this op. I expect you to give my people total cooperation in apprehending him. Do this right, and you can come back to working for your own country again."

Clear your records. Officially discharged. Total cooperation. What was left of her heart slowly withered into a tight ball. "You want me to help you apprehend Jian-Shan."

"And T'ang Po, if he happens to stray across the international borders. We'll see what we come up with. Any questions?"

"Only one." She rose to her feet and held out her hand. "Come here."

When he got up from his chair, she pulled him back out of view behind the pillar and pressed herself up against him, letting her long, narrow torso slide over his.

His arm came up around her waist, and she felt his hand through the lace. "What are you doing?"

"Asking about this." She breathed the words against his jaw as she imagined slipping the wire from her purse and looping it around his neck. "What are we going to do about it, babe?"

He stroked her back. "It's been a long time, Sarah. For both of us."

"It feels like it was yesterday, though, doesn't it?" She let her hot cheek slide against his cooler skin for a moment, then stepped away. "You're right. I'm not thinking straight, am I? But then, I never could when you touched me."

For the first time since he'd stepped out of customs, he looked uncertain. "Sarah, I—"

"Shhh." She pressed a long, manicured nail against his mouth. "We can do that later. I have to go visit the ladies', okay? Be right back."

After slipping away from him, she sauntered through the restaurant, smiling at the dazed expressions and avid gazes that followed her. But she didn't stop at the ladies'. She kept going, past the rest rooms, through the kitchen, and spoke to the chef for a moment. Then he pointed to a door, and she sauntered out of the restaurant. Once outside, she took Kalen's wallet, hotel room key, and spare-cash clip from the stiff bodice of her dress.

Nice to know her old job skills hadn't gotten too rusty. "Now let's see how you get out of paying for our expensive dinner, General."

She found her car in the valet lot and used her spare key to access it. Then she drove to a lot across the street, and waited.

The gendarme arrived thirty minutes later and led an unresisting Kalen Grady out to the patrol car in handcuffs. With a single phone call he would be released, probably within the next hour, but it was still worth watching him endure a little humiliation.

It's been a long time, Sarah.

"Not long enough, lover," she whispered as she watched them take him away. "Not nearly long enough."

"I have some messages for you, Madam Yusogi." The hotel desk clerk offered a neat pile of slips.

"Thank you." Kuei-fei took them and went to the elevator, where a tall, silver-haired man joined her.

"Beautiful weather we're having," he said as soon as the doors closed.

Another chatty American—Paris seemed to be filled with them. She focused on the panel of floor numbers and kept her tone neutral. "Yes."

"You sound taller on the phone."

She curled her hand around the messages before she looked at him. The slight smile on his charmingly rugged face didn't meet his dark eyes.

"Colonel Delaney, what a surprise. I had not expected to run into you here."

He nodded. "We should talk."

Conversation wasn't all he wanted, she could tell. "Come to my suite. We can have a drink together."

A few minutes later she tucked her messages behind the bar before bringing him a glass of straight whiskey and taking a seat opposite his. "Is there some problem that brings you to Paris?"

"T'ang Po. He left America and is rumored to have arrived here a week ago."

The glass of ice water in her own hand shook, so she placed it on the table between them. "What has that to do with me?"

"Plenty." He cradled the whiskey between his hands. "You were his mistress, and Jian-Shan is your son, and he leaves the U.S. the same time you do."

"I was Po's concubine, not his mistress, but that was a very long time ago. He often travels—the tong operates in many different countries—and the fact that we left at the same time is simply coincidence." She kept her expression bland. "I have kept to the terms of our agreement, Colonel."

"You've added to it, too." Sean sipped his drink and released a sigh. "Why didn't you tell me you were going to fake your own death?"

"You didn't ask."

He nodded. "Convenient, that woman stealing your car and dying in it like that."

"She was already dead. I bought the body from a willing morgue attendant. And she had no family."

She didn't appreciate his insinuation. "Would you care to see receipts?"

"I'll take your word for it. For now." He scrubbed a hand over his face. "With Po here, you'll have to leave the country. Where do you want to go?"

"I am not leaving."

"Once Po learns you're still alive, he'll know you've turned on him. It's over." He made a curt gesture.

"Let me be plain, Colonel." She rose to her feet. "I am not afraid of Po, or your government. There is nothing he or you could do to me that has not already been done. I am not leaving Paris without my son."

He swore in a strange language. "You know what he does to people who betray him."

"I know better than anyone." She regarded him with a faint smile. "Is there anything else?"

He rose to his feet. "I should have you detained and deported," he said, his voice harsh.

"You won't." She gestured to the door. "Have a good evening, Colonel."

"I'll be in touch." He drank the rest of his whiskey, then left.

Kuei-fei retrieved her messages and went through them, discarding most. Four of the women she sought had returned her calls, however, and they were all in positions to help her contact Jian-Shan.

As she picked up the phone, she thought of what Sean had said. Doubtless he worried that Po would kill her on sight, and thus ruin his operation. He didn't know her former owner had more finesse than the average Chinese crime boss. Nor did he realize how ruthless she could be.

For if it became necessary to save her son, Kuei-fei had every intention of contacting Po herself.

Something poked her cheek, and Val woke up to find a small person sitting on the pillow beside her head, and a pair of solemn blue eyes staring at her.

"Hi, there." She'd wondered where they were hiding the little *chaton*. The child didn't say anything, but stared down at Val's bandaged hand. "Doesn't look too good, does it, *cher*?"

The little rosebud lips pursed. "Hur?"

"A little," she told her, easing up into a sitting position. "But that's what boo-boos are supposed to do."

"Boo-boo." She gently touched the edge of the gauze. "Owie?"

Val grinned. "Yes, *cher*, a great big owie."

The little girl hesitated for a moment, then bent over and kissed the bandage with a noisy smacking sound. "Beh?"

She'd have to assume that meant "better." "Yes, much better." Her throat was dry, so she looked around. A tall glass of orange juice and some toast sat waiting for her on a side table by the bed. When she moved to reach for the glass, the child whirled and scooted backward until she slid off the mattress. "No, it's okay, honey. I just want a drink."

"Dink." She hooted and grabbed the glass, sloshing juice over her hands as she offered it to Val. "Dink, dink."

Val pointed to the tray. "Napkin?"

The little girl happily snatched that up and

handed it over. Val wiped up as much as she could before taking a long sip. "Thank you, *chaton*."

A tiny hand pointed to the front of her romper. "Lee-lee."

"Your name isn't Kitten?" she teased.

The blond head shook. "Lee-lee."

"Lily?" The little girl nodded. "That's a beautiful name. I'm Val." She held out her hand. "Nice to meet you."

Without warning, the child clambered back up on the bed and flung herself at Val. A wave of juice went up in the air as they fell back. A moment later, she and Jian-Shan's daughter were sitting in a small orange pool.

"Uh-oh," Lily said, looking down at herself. She was soaked.

"Uh-oh is right." Val ignored the surge of pain as she gave the child in her arms a reassuring squeeze. "We'd better get you cleaned up before Daddy sees."

Jian-Shan looked up from his book as Han entered the study door. "Has Madelaine arrived?" He'd called her the night before and told her to come directly to the villa so they could arrange the transfer of the swords.

"No, *kei*." His bodyguard looked almost agitated. "It is the gaijin." He paused. "She makes use of the bathroom."

Val's fever had not returned—he'd checked on her himself, during the night. He already knew she was quite capable of caring for herself, even with the splint. "Why would that be a concern, Han?"

Han folded his hands. "I believe she intends to bathe the little one."

Jian-Shan found Valence kneeling beside the old-fashioned tub, stirring the water filling it with her hand. She still wore one of Raven's borrowed nightgowns, but had removed her splint. Next to her, Lily stood wearing only a diaper and clutching a small rubber duck.

"Okay, *chaton*, off with the padding." Val removed the diaper, then held the child's hand as she stepped into the tub. "Do you want some bubbles?"

"Bu-buh," Lily agreed as she sat down with a plop.

"What are you doing?"

Val jumped, then turned around and gave him a direct glare. "*Dieu*, how about letting someone know before you sneak up behind them?" She rose long enough to hand him the discarded diaper, then checked the cabinet beneath the sink. "We need some bubbles. Are there any in your bathroom?"

"This is unnecessary." Jian-Shan gingerly folded up the damp diaper. "Shikoro bathes my daughter every night."

"Oh, I don't mind. It's my fault anyway." Val nodded toward a bundle of Lily's clothing, which was sodden and stained. "I sort of spilled my orange juice all over her."

"Duice," Lily told her father, waving her hand in a wide arc. "Duice, duice."

"Duice went everywhere, didn't it, *bebe*?" Val patted the child's cheek. "And what a smart girl you are! You can say 'juice' and 'bubbles.'"

"Duice." The blond head nodded. "Buh-buh."

Before he could say anything more, Val gave him an appealing look. "Would you mind getting something I can use to make bubbles for her? Please?"

"Where is the splint for your hand?"

"I took it off. It was itchy."

Jian-Shan resisted the urge to haul her up on her feet and drag her back to the bed. "Valence, Shikoro is more than capable of looking after Lily's needs—"

"Her name isn't Lily today. It's Little Miss Fishy, isn't it, *bebe*?"

"Fiss." Lily crowed with delight, and started churning the water with her small feet.

Val chuckled as a few drops landed on her face, then glanced up at him. "Girl fishies need bubbles in the bathtub. Would you mind letting me do this for her? She's having such a great time."

He could see that she was. "Very well. I'll see if I can find some . . . bubbles."

"Terrific."

He discarded the diaper, then found a vial of pear-scented bath liquid in the hall closet and brought it back to Valence.

"Here." He thrust it into her hands, feeling slightly ridiculous. "This should suffice."

Val pulled the crystal stopper and sniffed. "Mmmmm. *Bebe*, you're going to smell gorgeous. Just like a little fruit pie." She tipped the vial under the gushing tap, and foam immediately appeared. "I wouldn't mind using some of this stuff myself."

He watched her awkwardly replace the stopper. "I'll call Shikoro to assist you."

"That's not necessary," Val said quickly. "Really. I

feel much better. I can even use"—she wriggled her fingers, then winced—"my hand some."

"So I see." He leaned against the tile wall. "I do not expect you to be my daughter's caretaker while you're a guest in my home."

"I don't mind." She turned to the tub, and after a suitable amount of bubbles surrounded Lily, turned off the taps. "There now, Little Miss Fishy. Lots of bubbles for you and Ducky to play in."

"Duh, duh," his daughter agreed as she lathered the toy with a handful of foam.

"*Senpai?*" Shikoro appeared in the doorway, looking confused, then added in rapid Japanese, "Forgive me. I was receiving an order from the market. Is something wrong with the little one?"

"Nothing at all, Shikoro." As Val got to her feet, she staggered a little, and Jian-Shan caught her arm. "If you would stay here with Lily, I will see to Ms. St. Charles."

"I'm fine, just a little stiff from staying in bed so long—speaking of which, I should really change the linens." Val gave Shikoro a penitent look. "We spilled some juice."

"I change," Shikoro said as she crouched next to the tub, then told Jian-Shan in Japanese that Madelaine was waiting for him.

"My business manager has arrived," he told Val. "If you'll excuse me?"

"How long has Ms. Pierport worked for Mr. T'ang?" Val asked Shikoro as they both watched Lily splash.

"Two year." The housekeeper sniffed. "She stay for dinner, not like anything."

"Strange." She caught Lily's rubber duck as it popped out of the tub and handed it back to the little girl. At Shikoro's glance, she explained, "I didn't think anyone was supposed to know we're here."

"Master trust her."

Something knotted in her chest. "She must be a very dedicated employee."

"Frenchwoman smart." Shikoro tapped the side of her head. "Know how please men. *Use* what she know."

I'm not here to please him. I'm here for the swords. "I think I'll go get dressed." When she saw the other woman move to lift Lily from the tub, she held out a hand. "No, stay with her and let her play. I can manage by myself this time."

After her bath, Shikoro whisked a decidedly drowsy and content Lily off to the nursery for a nap. In the interim, Val got dressed and ate, but she was too restless to go back to bed.

I'll go have another look around the villa, she decided as she walked out of the bedroom and looked down the hall. No one was in sight. *And if I run into Madam Obnoxious, I'll just say hello and ask how the reception went.*

She unerringly found her way to the library without encountering Shikoro or Han, but the closed doors made her pause. She really couldn't think of a good excuse to barge in. Then she recalled the open windows she'd seen the day before.

A walk in the garden would be nice. And innocent.

She exited the house through one of the side doors and made her way through the meticulously landscaped garden until she heard voices coming through one of the open windows—Jian's and a woman's.

Bingo.

Carefully she edged along the wall of the house until she was near enough to hear what was being said.

"—begin transferring the cases tomorrow. Send them in three shipments by truck," Jian was saying. Paper rustled. "Find out which shops she visited, and fax a list to me."

"Jian, I wish you would reconsider." Madelaine's voice sounded completely different—soft and beseeching. "No one we know in the *zaibatsu* would be capable of doing such a thing."

Val ducked down and moved to crouch beneath the window. When she glanced up, she had a clear view of Jian-Shan and Madelaine, standing together beside his desk. The Frenchwoman looked as immaculate and gorgeous as ever, with her head tilted back and an expression of sweet yet sexy appeal on her narrow face.

The whole tableau made her teeth grind. *Is that what pleases the master? Looking like a vacuum-brained nymphomaniac?* When she saw Jian-Shan move from the desk, Val ducked and stepped to the side. *Time to go smell the roses before I get caught.*

Carefully she crept back along the wall, trying to remain as silent as possible, then turned the corner and headed for the garden.

And nearly walked into Han's chassis-sized chest.

Chapter 7

Val gulped. "Oh." Looking up didn't help. "Hello."

"You should not leave the house without telling someone," he said, his broad face completely impassive.

"Okay." She went to go around him.

Han pivoted and paced her. "Do you wish to see the gardens? I will be happy to escort you."

She needed to check out the entire property, and the last thing she needed was a chaperon. "That's not necessary, I can have a look around by myself."

"I must respectfully insist." He gestured for her to precede him on the path.

They toured the beautiful gardens around the villa, which gave Val time to gauge her location. There were no other houses in sight, and the only road was unpaved and nearly a quarter mile from the house.

"This is a really gorgeous place." Val glanced back at the house as a car started and pulled away from the villa. So Madelaine wasn't staying for dinner after all. Why had he asked her to come out here? "Who's the owner?"

"One of *kei*'s friends."

"You mean, Jian-Shan?" He nodded. "What does '*kei*' mean?"

"'Older brother'—my master prefers less formal address."

"Your master." She shook her head. "I'm sorry, I just can't believe such a feudal concept still exists."

"It is not an obligation of birth, or rank," Han told her. "I choose to serve T'ang Jian-Shan."

"Why?"

"He found me in an alley in Hong Kong, after my owner had me beaten for failing to win the *Hon-basho*." At her blank look he tagged on, "The most prestigious of sumo competitions. Most *rikishi* who disappoint their masters do not live long."

Suddenly his size made sense. "How awful for you."

"I was bleeding from my eyes and ears." He rubbed the side of his head, and for the first time Val noticed a long, jagged scar showing through his short-cropped hair. "Had he not taken me to the hospital, I would have surely died."

What could she say? "I'm sorry. I didn't know." Afraid he would think she was prying, she turned toward the house. "Maybe I should go back in now."

"Miss St. Charles—Valence-san." He held out a massive hand to stop her. "The reason I told you about this was so you would understand how *kei* feels. You saved his life."

"I think it's just the opposite." She thought of the car that had nearly run her down outside Jian-Shan's offices, and what she had just heard from the window. Had someone from the shops she'd visited sent the killer? "The man with the knife apparently followed me to the house. It was my fault Jian was attacked."

He nodded. "Then you have a debt you must repay."

"It appears that I do." Her hand was aching, and absently she cradled it with her other arm. "I'm going back inside now. I have a lot to think about."

"You will remember to tell Shikoro or me before you leave the house?" he asked, and when she nodded, he gave her a singularly charming smile that lit up his blunt, grim face. "Good."

Sean had shadowed Kuei-fei from the hotel for two hours as she walked the streets of Paris. His patience began to run out just as she entered the Parc Floral, the sprawling public gardens situated in the center of the Bois de Vincennes.

"Oh, no," he muttered under his breath as she stopped to admire the monumental Stahly granite fountain that supplied water to all the ponds in the park. "I'm not hiding behind rosebushes for three hours."

She didn't seem surprised to see him when he joined her on the path. "Hello, Colonel Delaney."

"You were going to call me Irish, remember?" Sean eyed the manicured lawns around the aquatic gardens. "I don't suppose we could skip the tour of the water lilies and go directly to your son's place?"

"I would, gladly, if I knew where he was." She gestured toward the path. "Will you walk with me, or do you wish to continue your lurking at a distance?"

Sean wasn't accustomed to being caught by pros, much less a civilian. "You made me at that perfume shop, didn't you?"

"Colonel—Irish," she corrected herself. "I made you from the moment I left the hotel."

"Damn." He frowned down at her. "And here I thought you were a delicate, helpless little woman."

"Some of the most dangerous creatures on the earth are small." She nodded toward a nearby tree. "And female."

Sean followed her gaze and saw a tiny spider sitting in the center of a large, intricate web. "So they are."

She led him to a small valley carpeted with flowers. "I kept a little garden in China," she told him as she paused to admire a wide bed filled with tulips and snapdragrons. "Nothing like this, of course, but I enjoyed growing poppies and fresh herbs. My son has left the city."

"How do you know that?" When she didn't answer, he thrust a hand through his silver hair. "All right, then, where is he?"

"I don't know." She bent down to caress the curly dark purple petals crowning a gently waving stalk. The jewel tones of the flamboyant flower seemed even richer against her pale skin. "He left shortly after I arrived in the city. Fate, it seems, is ever determined to keep us apart."

He heard the subtle underlying thread of pain in her voice and touched her arm. "We'll find him."

She straightened and moved so that his hand fell away. "I do not require your assistance, Colonel."

"I got you out of the country, didn't I?" At her

glance, he grinned. "And I have local contacts, too. We'll find him faster if we work together." And he would feel better, knowing he was between her and T'ang Po.

Something flickered in her calm black eyes. "You do not trust me to keep my word."

"About as much as you trust me to keep mine." He spread his hands, palm up. "Should make us good partners."

For the first time, her lips curved at the corners. "I think you will say whatever you must to get what you want, Irish."

He nodded. "We've more in common than you think."

"Very well." She took his arm. "We will have lunch together, and you can tell me about your contacts in the Asian community."

"As long as you tell me about yours, darlin'."

"Jian." Val beckoned to him without looking away from the thousand-year-old *chokuto* blade she was examining. "Can you tell me what you know about this one?"

He had brought some of the swords to the library that morning to allow her to begin her study. Since opening the first case, she had not moved from the worktable for two hours, nor spoken except to ask him what he knew about a particular sword.

He joined her at the table. "That sword was once the centerpiece of a Tashima shrine. The priests who prayed before it considered it a resident deity."

"This would have been forged about the same time Lady Murasaki wrote *The Tale of Genji*. Incredible." She turned to write a few lines in her note-book, then sat back and absently rubbed her bandaged hand. "I wonder what it was like, to be alive then."

"Japan underwent many changes." He watched the sunlight from the window highlight the strands that had escaped the loose knot in her hair. "Poetry replaced religious doctrines. Calligraphy became alphabet and art. Warriors became samurai."

"While their women blackened their teeth to look pretty." Humor lit her dark eyes. "I've never understood that part."

"Neither have I."

"There's something else I've been meaning to ask you. You're Chinese, right?" He nodded. "But you speak perfect Japanese, and you have Han and Shikoro here."

Now it was his turn to be amused. "The last Sino-Japanese war ended in 1945, Valence."

"I know. I just thought with the cultural differences . . ." She shrugged.

"Fortunately I have had the best of both worlds. I was born in China but fostered in Japan, where I studied kendo and *iaido* with my Japanese *sensei*." He inspected the remaining cases. There were enough blades to keep her busy cataloguing for several days. He hoped. "I also went to Oxford for my postgraduate studies."

"Ah, so that's where you got the Brit accent." She thought for a moment. "You know, Japan broke off cultural exchanges with China during the Heian Period, when this blade was made. The two countries haven't been very good friends ever since."

She closed the case. "So how did your family obtain it?"

No one had ever asked him such blunt questions—no one would have dared—and yet he found her straightforward curiosity oddly refreshing.

"According to legend, a mercenary saved the life of Tokugawa Ieyasu during the siege of Osaka Castle. The shogun removed the *chokuto* from the shrine and presented it, along with the name T'ang, to my ancestor." He moved the case to one side and lifted another up to the worktable. "You may find this pair of equal interest."

He watched her face as she opened the case and saw the matching swords. She took in a soft breath as she saw the copper inlay and *shakudo* patinate.

"Are these Masatoshi?"

"You have an excellent eye."

"So did Masatoshi. May I?" When he nodded, she reverently lifted the katana from the case, and removed the blade from its scabbard. "*Mon Dieu*, Jian, why aren't these in a museum? Do you know how rare it is to find a katana and its matching *wakizashi* together from this period, in such superior condition?"

"Tourists would hardly know the difference, Valence." He enjoyed her frankness, but her philanthropic attitude only emphasized her naiveté. "They would probably think a katana was simply a large *ginsu* knife."

"That's why they need to be shown." She gently replaced the blade. "I would have never known the difference if not for an Asian import shop in the French Quarter. The first time I ever saw a real katana was in the display window. I'd never seen a sword up close before, and it was so strange and exotic. I went inside, and there was incense burning, and bamboo growing in pots, and so many things I'd just never seen before. The importer must have sensed how fascinated I was, because he didn't chase me out. He even let me hold the sword."

"And then your career was born."

She chuckled and shook her head. "I got a job there after school, running errands and dusting the shelves. I fell in love with the beautiful things he imported from the East, especially the swords." She paused. "When can I see the Nagatoki?"

"They will arrive soon, with the third shipment." He heard footsteps and closed the case. "You look pale. I'll have Shikoro bring your tea to your room."

"No, please. I've spent enough time staring at the walls. I'd much rather watch Lily play outside." She rose as the housekeeper appeared with the little girl. "You don't mind, do you?"

"Do what pleases you." He frowned as the toddler ran over and threw her arms around Val's legs, wrinkling her trousers. "No, Lily."

"It's all right. Come on, *chaton*." She held out her hand. "Let's go and see the flowers."

Indulging Val's whim to play baby-sitter, Jian-Shan escorted them to the garden, then practiced his daily exercises while observing their play. She seemed to genuinely like children, judging by the easy way she handled his daughter's growing affection.

Lily's response was one of absolute adoration, so

much so that when Shikoro brought their tea and attempted to take the little girl in for her nap, the result was a noisy tantrum.

"Lily." He crouched down in front of the shrieking child and spoke in a firm voice. "That is enough."

She instantly quieted, but two fat tears rolled down her cheeks, and she held her arms out—not for him, but for Val.

"Don't cry, *bebe*." Val picked her up with one arm and held her close for a moment before handing her over to the housekeeper. "I'll see you later, okay?"

Shikoro carried his still-sobbing daughter into the house, while Val sighed and sat down at the wrought-iron table.

"You do not have to cater to my daughter, you know." He noticed the way she rubbed her shoulder. "Your arm is bothering you again."

"I don't cater to her at all, and my arm is just a little stiff." She wriggled her fingers. "I'll be happy to get rid of this splint."

"You will not heal properly unless you rest." He poured a cup of tea, then deliberately filled a plate with sandwiches and fruit for her. "Do not wrinkle your nose at me. Shikoro tells me you hardly touch your breakfast most mornings."

"That's your fault." Unabashed, she took a slice of apple and bit it in half. "You're ruining my appetite."

He sat back. "And how am I doing that?"

"With all the amazing swords you've shown me. How can food compete with a Tashima *chokuto*, or a

Masatoshi katana?" She shook her head. "It's a joke, Jian. You're supposed to laugh."

"I do not understand American humor."

Her eyes rolled. "Maybe it would help if you'd lighten up. Here." She tossed an orange to him, and grinned when he caught it reflexively. "If you peel that for me, I'll stop teasing you."

He applied his knife to the rind. "I would like you to look through some records this afternoon."

As the sun emerged from behind a cloud, she let her head fall back and closed her eyes. "Records on the blades?"

"No." He sectioned the orange into petals, like a blooming flower, and placed it back on her plate. "I will show you after we eat."

She studied it. "That's pretty. Everything you do is so elegant."

He thought of things he had done that would make her run screaming from the garden. "Aesthetics are second nature for a collector."

"Which is why it's so important to share what you have with others who are not as fortunate. It's like this villa." She gestured at the house. "Look at how much beauty and history is contained in this one place, and yet no one ever sees it. It's wrong to hide that away."

Despite her grim childhood, she obviously knew little about the world. "History must be preserved. Beauty, protected."

"You don't have to tell me that," she said, her expression turning stubborn. "It's my job."

"I know what your job entails. You stock a building with antiquities selected to thrill an already apathetic and jaded public. Do you think any of your visitors would look at my swords and think of art?" He stole a section of the orange from her plate, and broke it in half. "No, Valence, they would look upon them and wonder how many men, women, and children were slaughtered by them. If someone important had been executed with them. Whether traces of blood or tissue could still be found on the blades."

Obstinacy became outrage. "That's not true!"

"That"—he placed a piece of the fruit into her half-open mouth and nudged her chin up with his thumb—"is human nature."

She looked angry enough to spit the orange in his face, but subsided and watched him as he ate the other half. He liked feeding her, he decided. The intimacy of it made him want to find some sun-warmed strawberries and a bed with silk sheets.

Her fallen angel's mouth red from the juice, from the touch of his mouth—

"Did I miss something?" Self-conscious, Val ran her fingertips over her lips.

"Wait." He leaned over to brush an imaginary speck from her bottom lip, then spanned her jaw with his hand and lifted her face to see the sun on her skin and hair. "You belong in the light, Valence. It brings out all the colors of your fire."

"Thank you." She would have sounded like a polite child, except that her voice had fallen to a whisper. "But I don't want to get burned."

He saw it then, saw as the molten gold of her hair paled next to the heat in her eyes. She felt the draw of desire as strongly as he did, wanted to sate it as much as he did. Which was why her next words made no sense.

"You know, I can't figure you out," she said, turning away from his hand. "One minute I think I understand you, the next I'm back to square one. You don't seem like a selfish man, yet you hang on to this collection and guard it as if your life depended on it. While you ignore the one real treasure you do have."

"Indeed." He didn't like her pulling away from him, but he accepted it, and drank the last of his tea. "And what would that be?"

"Your child." She rose from the table and dropped her napkin beside her plate. "Excuse me."

The immediate, furious impulse to follow her into the house and eradicate some of that enchanting but foolish naiveté of hers gave him pause. He was not a man used to acting on a whim or anger. Nor would it be wise to justify himself. Valence had no idea of what she had become involved in, or how many lives depended on his swords.

And if Jian-Shan had his way, she never would.

Han summoned Val from the library and escorted her to another room, one filled with sophisticated computer equipment. Ten different terminals circled the room at a series of workstations that together formed a long, crescent-shaped data center. Another dozen printers, scanners, and modems were linked to them by a web of cable. It was so unexpected that for a moment all Val could do was stand at the threshold and stare.

"Who lives in this place?" she asked the bodyguard. "Bill Gates?"

"The owner is quite fond of the Internet, I believe." Han gestured to one of several chairs in front of an active terminal. "Are you familiar with it yourself?"

"A little, but I'm no Bill Gates." She sat down, and cleared the screen saver. The image of a French document appeared, along with the passport photo of a rather surly-looking man. "What's this?"

"Criminal files," Jian-Shan said from behind her.

When Han bowed and retreated, Val nearly called him back. After that disturbing moment in the garden, she wasn't sure she wanted to be alone with Jian-Shan again so soon. "Why am I looking at criminals when I could be cataloguing swords?"

"Because you agreed to both." He came to the terminal and demonstrated how to sort through the massive database, then opened the first case file. "Look through all of the photos. Stop if you see the man who attacked us."

She tucked a strand of hair behind her ear. "I really meant it when I said I didn't get a good look at his face."

"Going through the images may refresh your memory." He brought a phone to her. "If you need assistance, press Seven and I will return."

She didn't relax until the door closed behind him. Then she regarded the computer screen with a frown. The first file was obviously not the man—he was fair-haired, and too fat. She read the list of charges and translated them into English out loud. "Murder. Arson. Conspiracy to commit murder. What a guy."

She brought up the next, that of a bald man with flat, dead eyes. "Murder, murder, attempted murder, assault with deadly intent." She followed the column of homicide and assault charges until she saw that it carried over to a second page. "And they haven't *caught* this man yet?"

She pressed a key, and the third file appeared. This killer was a black man with powdery white hair and a sweet expression that reminded her of an old blues performer she'd known in the French Quarter. His list of charges was shorter, but no less grim. "Ah, *cher*, you could have learned to play the trumpet instead."

She paged through a few dozen more files before she blew out a breath and got to her feet. "This isn't going to work."

"You still have four hundred left."

Val jumped, startled to see Jian-Shan watching her from the door. *How long has he been standing there?*

"Like I said, I didn't see his face clearly." She glanced at the computer screen. "Are all these people still at large in France?"

"Some are. Whoever attacked us may have been brought in from another country."

"I see." No, she didn't. "Where did you get these files? I can read enough French to know that they're confidential police records."

"A friend sent them."

"The same friend who owns this villa and likes the Internet so much?" When he didn't answer, she got up from the chair and went toward him. "There aren't any Asians in these files. If this tong is after you, why wouldn't they send one of their own?"

"I don't know." He took her bandaged hand in his, and his voice dropped to a low murmur. "Look through the files, Valence. Help me keep it from happening again."

The way he said that, the way he looked at her—the same way he had when he'd popped the orange into her mouth—confused her. He had wealth and power and position, while she had nothing. He could probably curl a finger and Madelaine, along with half the women in Paris, would come running.

But he acts like he needs me. Really needs me. Why? It can't be simply mutual lust, can it? "The police—"

"I don't trust the police. I don't trust anyone but my own people." His thumb made a circle against one of her fingers. "And you."

Why can't I think straight when he touches me? She felt feverish again, but the heat was coming from him. "I'm not one of your people."

"You saved me. You saved Lily." He brought her hand up and brushed his lips across her fingertips. Then he turned it over and did the same to her palm—before adding a small, shocking nuance. "Do this thing for me."

She didn't stop him from leaving, but went back to the computer and sat down slowly. Any faster and her knees would have completely given out.

Why is he doing this to me?

Her fingers tingled where he had kissed them, but the tiny nip he'd given her palm made her shudder. The combination of the archaic gesture and the sensual caress had turned her into a babbling idiot, ready to hunt down killers for him.

Stop acting like a teenager with too many hormones, she told herself even as she opened the next file and tried to focus on the image. *If he knows how you feel, he'll use it to make you dance like a puppet.*

Yet she had the uneasy suspicion that Jian-Shan had already mastered every single one of her strings.

The morning after Kalen was arrested, his identity was finally verified and new documents sent over from the American embassy. The chief of police arrived to personally escort Kalen from his cell and alternated between offering apologies for his arrest and subtle indignation over his presence in Paris.

"*Generale*, my men would have notified the embassy last night had we been made aware of your visit." The chief handed him the unmarked envelope containing his personal effects. "It is regrettable that you were the victim of a pickpocket so soon after your arrival—you are certain you cannot identify the perpetrator?"

He had no intention of handing Raven over to the French police. "Quite certain." He strapped on his watch and checked the package from the embassy, which contained cash, replacement credit cards, and a secure cell phone. "Thank you for your assistance, Chief."

Kalen made one call from his cab on the way back to the hotel. "I want an arrest warrant and extradition order for Sarah Ravenowitz, AWOL army officer, case number two-nine-one-seven-oh. Charges are desertion and conspiracy to commit terrorist acts. The file is in my desk," he told his assistant. "Have the entire package delivered to me within the next twelve hours."

At the hotel, he showered, shaved, and dressed in workout clothes before making the next call, to one of his local operatives. "I want everything you can get on an Etienne model named Raven. Residence, shooting schedule, places she frequents in the city. Locate her, tag her Lotus with a tracer, and keep her under twenty-four-hour surveillance. Call me when you've got her."

He knew Jian-Shan had salvaged Raven when her last operation had gone to pieces, and may have gotten her to Switzerland for the face job. He knew she'd later helped him steal his family's priceless swords and smuggle them out of China. Rumor had it they were still close. Knowing Raven, she would probably do anything for her Chinese boyfriend. As she had once done anything her field superior had asked of her.

I love you, Kalen.

It had been stupid, getting involved with one of his own operatives. Beyond idiocy. But for the fourteen months before Major Sarah Ravenowitz had thrown away her army career, they'd been lovers. More than that, she'd told him all about her dreams for the future, and had nearly convinced him he would be a part of them.

I want to have a kid with red hair, like yours. Naked, she'd jumped on top of him and held him down on the mattress. *Be a good sport and knock me up already, will you?*

He could have thrown her across the bedroom. He could have snapped her spine in two short moves. He'd simply watched her face as he shifted her weight, and taken advantage of her spread thighs—

But Kalen had never answered her. Not then, not ever.

Raven had never pressed the issue, always insisting that she loved him enough to wait. The last time he had seen her, she'd been closing up her apartment to make the trip to China. They'd shared a pizza and made love on the floor. Later, when he left her, she'd laughed and threatened to throw her diaphragm into the South China Sea.

Then you'll have to make an honest woman out of me, you gigolo.

To this day, he still didn't know what had gone wrong overseas. The rest of her team had been killed during the op, and for a time Raven was also presumed dead. It was difficult to remember the details; when the news came in he'd gone a little crazy. Then came the phone call from Geneva.

You missed me, Colonel. Raven had sounded odd, her voice slurred, but he recognized it instantly. *What's that going to do to your monthly DOD reports?*

It took a moment for him to find his voice, the shock was so enormous. *Sarah, my God. We thought you were—*

Dead? Yeah, well, almost. Better luck next time.

He'd put a trace on the call at once. *Where are you? Are you in custody? Who—*

I know what you did. You stay away from me, Kalen, or I'll make sure everyone else does, too.

Le Bristol offered a well-appointed gym for its patrons, and Kalen spent the next two hours punishing the equipment. He didn't feel his muscles burn, didn't notice how quickly he became drenched in sweat. All he could think of was the feel of Raven in his arms, just before she'd picked his pockets and walked out on him.

And who had taught her to do that?

"Monsieur." The gym manager hovered beside him, looking nervous. "I am to give you this message."

He stopped to take the folded note and read it as soon as the other man walked away.

> Dear General,
> Sorry I had to eat and run last night, but you know how it is. Nice try with the surveillance. Your operative and his tracer can be found parked outside Maxim's. He'll be napping for a few hours. Try the lamb at Les Britons while you're in town. It's fabulous.
> Kisses, Raven

He crumpled the note, thrust it in his pocket, then added twenty pounds to the upper body machine and worked his arms until the machine levers began slamming together on each repetition.

You know how it is. He didn't know. He didn't know what she'd become, why she'd chosen to betray her own country, and why he'd let her. She was the only woman he'd ever let get close. She was a traitor to everything he believed in.

Nice try. He should have known she would slip through his fingers. He'd assumed all that prancing up and down runways for the last seven years had made her forget her training. He couldn't make that mistake again.

Kisses, Raven. Sarah was gone, replaced by Raven. Whatever love they might have found together was dead—dead as the past, dead as the people they'd been. Sarah would have taken a bullet for him.

Raven, he suspected, would put one through his head.

"Monsieur."

He stopped and looked up at the manager, who was white-faced.

"The equipment is not, ah, made for such strenuous use." The man made an apologetic gesture. "Perhaps you wish to make use of the indoor pool?"

"I've cleared all the names on the list—none of them have gotten any suspicious infusions of cash in the last ninety days," Raven told Jian-Shan. "How are things at my place? Any problems?"

"No, we're very comfortable here." He closed the file, and frowned as static crackled over the phone line. "Where are you, Sarah?"

"On the move—I pissed off General Grady, and he's sent the cavalry after me. Hang on." Raven shouted something pointed in French, then sighed. "Sorry. Damn truck drivers try to run everyone off the road. Listen, Jay, I've checked all my sources, and no one's heard anything. You know what that means."

"It was one of the dealers who had contact with Valence." As he'd suspected.

"Yeah." Raven hesitated, then added, "Connections I got, but even I can't crack the society—and unless you want to play like your dad, I don't think you're going to get any confessions, either. Maybe we should move you and the kid to London now."

"No." The thought of continuing to run and hide from his father disgusted him; it had gone on too long already. "What caterer do you normally use out here?"

"Oh, great." Raven muttered something filthy, this time in Chinese. "Are you sure?"

He thought of Valence, with the sun in her hair. "Yes."

"Fael's got everything you need, and about ten million aunts, uncles, and cousins working for him." She blew out a breath. "What about the museum lady and the kid?"

"They stay here." He wasn't taking the chance of being separated from them; Han would see to their safety. "What are you going to do about the general?"

"Wear him out and send him whimpering back home." The bitterness left her voice as she added, "Jay, are you sure this is such a good idea? What if the old man himself shows?"

His mouth curled. "Then we end it, Raven. Once and for all."

Chapter 8

"Look better," Shikoro said as she helped Val change the dressing on her hand. "Why you scratch?"

"These stitches are driving me crazy." Val eased her arm into her sleeve. "They've been itching for two days."

The housekeeper buttoned the cuff for her. "Maybe take off splint. I have glove, you wear."

"One glove, like Michael Jackson?" She chuckled. "Not my style, Shikoro. I can't even moon-walk."

"No walk on moon. Wear for master party."

"A party?" Val echoed.

"Tomorrow night." She inspected Val from head to toe. "I help makeup, hair. You have pretty dress?"

She had business suits, but nothing approaching a party dress. And why was Jian-Shan throwing a party when they were supposed to be hiding from a hit man? "I'll find something. Who's been invited?"

"White Tiger people. Other from *zaibatsu*." Shikoro's nose wrinkled. "*Sugoi* Frenchwoman-not-like-anything."

Shikoro's comical description of Madelaine made Val clear her throat. "Um, that sounds nice." She thought of the last party she'd crashed. "Maybe I'll stay in my room that night."

The housekeeper tucked her hands in her kimono's sleeves and gave her a disapproving frown. "You afraid of Frenchwoman-not-like-anything?"

Val couldn't help the laugh. "No, she doesn't scare me."

"You want her please master?"

Her smile faded. "That's really none of my business." No matter how much the idea of Madelaine putting her hands on Jian-Shan made her grit her teeth. "Besides, I'm not competing with her for the *master*."

"All women compete." The housekeeper rolled her narrow eyes as if the whole world except Val knew this. "Shikoro should teach you willow way."

"What's that?"

"Willow way what men like." Her cheeks dimpled. "Han my *danna* before he my husband."

Val knew that word from her research—it meant a certain type of patron. One who paid. Conscious that she was treading on unfamiliar ground, she chose her next words very carefully. "You were a geisha?"

Shikoro nodded.

"Okay. That explains a few things."

"Not mean prostitute, *Okusan*." The older woman wagged her finger. "Prostitute *shougi*, not geisha."

"I know—I mean, I know there's a difference."

"Geisha live by arts. Sing, dance, make man forget troubles." Shikoro moved her hands in small, elegant circles for emphasis. "Be always beautiful."

"It takes years of training, too, doesn't it?" Val tapped a finger against her lips, trying to figure out a polite refusal. "I'd probably make a terrible geisha anyway."

"You too old." The housekeeper giggled at the thought. "But you Western woman, not know what please Eastern man. I show you willow way—how dress, what say, what do Eastern man like."

For a moment, she was tempted—what woman wouldn't want to know the secrets of a genuine geisha?—but Jian-Shan would probably end up laughing at her. And then there was the collection. She could hardly present a professional front if she was trying to seduce him in a kimono and Kabuki makeup.

She didn't want to offend the woman, however. "I'm honored by your kind offer, Shikoro, but I really can't."

"Please man not bad thing, *Okusan*. Master lonely. *Sugoi* Frenchwoman-not-like-anything know this." Shikoro shook her head. "She want master money, name. She not care he lonely."

I'm only going to be here a few weeks. I can't compete with Madelaine Pierport, or any other woman in his life. Val produced a shrug. "Best I stay out of it, then."

The housekeeper bowed, but paused at the door to look back. "Best for whom, *Okusan*?"

Val couldn't tell her.

That night after dinner, Jian-Shan found her working in the library and confirmed Shikoro's revelation.

"I'm having a small reception here tomorrow evening, for a few members of the *zaibatsu*." He glanced at her hand. "If you're feeling well enough, I'd appreciate your acting as my hostess."

So she *was* invited to the ball. Val set aside her notebook and glanced up at him. "Is this wise, under the circumstances?"

"These are members of my society. Each has been thoroughly investigated, so they are people I can trust." He bent over to read some of her notes. "You have beautiful handwriting."

And he was great at changing the subject. "I didn't plan on attending anything formal while I was here, so I hope a suit will be acceptable."

"Shikoro already advised me that your wardrobe is limited. I've ordered some additional garments from Paris for you." Before she could protest, he shook his head. "I owe you at least a new blouse for the one I destroyed. And it will serve as very small compensation for the many hours you will have to spend cataloguing my blades."

"Seeing the Nagatoki will be plenty." She stretched, then looked at her notes and sighed. "I'm making some progress, but I wish I didn't feel so tired all the time."

"You have been working too long. You need some fresh air." He gestured toward one of the doors leading into the garden. "Take a walk with me."

Beautiful as it was, Val *had* been stuck in the villa too long. And perhaps she could get him to tell her more about the White Tiger society. "All right. Maybe that will wake me up."

Instead of taking her the way she had walked before, with Han, Jian-Shan led her around the back garden and to a polished-stone path that appeared to lead into the woods.

"Where does this go?" she asked as she peered at the line of yew and pine trees ahead.

"I won't spoil the surprise." He folded his hand over hers and tugged. "Come. It's not much further."

The stone path entered the forest and curved along a narrow alley through the trees. With darkness creeping up over the horizon, the sky had turned violet, and the looming silhouettes of the trees made the woods seem spooky.

"I should have never watched that movie about the Blair witch," Val muttered. Then she stopped as the path ended and the tree line fell away to form a perfectly square clearing. "A garden? All the way out here?"

"It was called a trysting garden." Jian-Shan led her to the small stone courtyard, the center of which had been filled with a rectangular foot pool. Flowers planted together by color formed terraced boundary hedges of white, red, and gold.

"It's amazing." Val sat down on one of the stone benches and looked at the subtle symmetries of the well-maintained landscape. The bold colors of the flowers flared even brighter as Jian-Shan switched on some discreetly positioned spotlights. Rough with the patina of time, iron arches at either end of the garden gleamed under dense swatches of golden climbing roses. "Why is it so different from the other garden?"

"The gardens surrounding the villa were for family, and visitors. This was created exclusively by the master of the house for his mistress. He planted it with her favorite flowers." Jian-Shan sat down beside her. "They came here to relax, away from the prying eyes of his wife and the servants."

"Which explains the name." Feeling restless, she rose and went to the edge of the foot pool. "Did they keep fish in this? It's too shallow for a swim."

"Likely fish. During the time it was built, people believed it was unnatural or unhealthy to bathe." He knelt down and took off her shoe. "Even the sight of a woman dipping her bare foot into the water was considered shocking." He looked up at her. "And highly erotic."

"Like this?" Val couldn't help testing the water with her toes, then made a face as she snatched her foot back. "I wouldn't have made a very good mistress. That water is too cold."

"Hold still." He removed a handkerchief from his pocket and dried her foot, then held it between his hands as if inspecting her for something.

"What is it?" Val propped a hand on his shoulder and leaned down to see.

"You have such a delicate foot." His fingers stroked her skin as he traced the contours. "Small feet are much admired in my country."

"So much so that Chinese women crippled themselves for centuries, binding their feet." She pulled her foot from his hands and slipped it back into her shoe. "One more way to please the master."

"Is that so offensive to you?" He stood, and rested his hands on her shoulders. "I admit, foot-binding is not the best example, but there are many ways to please a lover. This garden does no harm."

"Unless you were the master's wife." She felt breathless, almost unnerved. "I can't imagine she was too happy, knowing her husband was out here, splashing his feet in the pool with her rival."

"Perhaps tolerating the mistress and the garden was how she pleased her husband." He moved his hands up to encircle her throat. "But you would not do that."

"No." She shook her head slowly, yet never took her eyes from his. "I'd make sure he wouldn't want to ever leave my garden."

In this romantic place, haunted by the ghosts of long-dead lovers, Val almost expected to be kissed. Jian-Shan didn't disappoint her. As he bent his head to hers, she sighed his name into his mouth.

This time she felt no urgency, only a slow, languorous need that bloomed like the flowers around them. The perfume from the garden mixed with Jian-Shan's own unique scent, rising up in her head like some mysterious drug, dissolving her bones. He felt her sway, and his arms came up to support her as she relaxed against him. She made a low sound of protest as he lifted his mouth from hers.

"A man could create a hundred gardens for you," he murmured, stroking his hand down her back. "One with golden orchids, to match your skin, another with alchemist roses, to bring out the fire in your hair . . ."

Val felt his heartbeat under her palm. "There weren't any flowers in your garden in Paris."

"Not until the day I found you there."

Someone politely cleared his throat, and Jian-Shan slowly released her.

Val saw Han standing a discreet distance away on the path and gave him a rueful smile. "All good trysts must come to an end, though."

Jian-Shan put his hand at the back of her waist as they walked away from the foot pool. "For now."

Sean already knew women could drive a man to drink. He'd just never met one who could do it at the speed of light.

"These women will not speak openly in front of you," Kuei-fei assured him as he pulled up to the tearoom. "It is better if you wait in the car for me."

He glanced at the front window, which was wreathed with swaths of ivory lace and pastel-colored ribbons. "The deal was, I take you when I go to see my informants, and you take me when you go to see yours."

"They are not informants. They are former pupils of mine," she told him. "I trained each one of them for the tong, but their loyalty is to me."

"Then pretend I'm a new—what do you call it?"

"Customer." Kuei-fei took out a pair of white gloves and slipped her hands into them. "Or master."

"Exactly. I'm out looking to buy myself a new Chinese girlfriend, and you're auditioning women for me."

"That is not precisely how it is done." She gave him a sideways glance as she slipped into her jacket. "Do you speak Chinese, Irish?"

"Enough to know if you're lying to me when you're translating."

She nodded. "As I expected. Come." She got out of the car, and waited for him to join her on the sidewalk. "Stay in front of me, and when I introduce you to these women, inspect each of them."

"Inspect what?"

She led him to one side of the building, away from the tearoom window. "You are purchasing a woman you wish to bed. Look at her face, her breasts, her hips. Lean in to smell her breath and see if it is sweet. Touch her hair."

Sean gave her a devilish grin. "I should practice this first." Slowly he examined each part of her, as she had instructed, then bent down until his nose nearly bumped hers. "Wintergreen is one of my favorite flavors."

"Then you may borrow my toothpaste." She took his hand and raised it to her hair, which she wore in a sleek, ebony twist. "Rub a strand between your fingers, to test the softness."

"I'm not done with your mouth yet," he said, and caught her face between his hands.

"Colonel."

"Irish," he murmured, brushing his mouth over hers. She had the prettiest lips, and the saddest eyes, of any woman he'd ever met. Then he tasted her, and gathered her up against him as he explored her with his tongue. She didn't respond, but she didn't deny him, either. He ended the kiss, and looked into her eyes. "You didn't like that."

"It doesn't matter." She frowned a little. "Do not kiss the women inside the tearoom, of course."

"I don't care about the bloody women in the tearoom." Sean felt a surge of impatience. "Kuei-fei, did you like it, or not?"

"It is of no consequence."

"Is that something else they hammered into your head? That what you feel means nothing?"

"It is what I taught myself, Sean Delaney." Anger made her cheeks turn pink and her eyes glitter.

"How else was I to cope with being handed from man to man, with watching my only child being taken away from me, with being sold to a weakling as a bribe for his continued loyalty?"

"I'm not T'ang Po."

She made a soft, revolted sound. "No, you are not."

"So stop treating me like I am," he said, and pulled her into his arms once more. "And kiss me the way you want to."

Before he could take her mouth again, she turned her face away. "I don't want to become involved with you, Irish."

He kissed her cheek anyway. "You're neck-deep in me, darlin', and you know it."

"Perhaps, after we find my son, we can discuss this further." She extracted herself from his embrace. "For now, we must be professionals."

He didn't like the way she avoided his gaze. "We're partners, Kuei-fei."

"Very well. Partners." She gestured toward the tearoom. "Shall we go and speak to my girls now?"

Her "girls" turned out to be half a dozen of the most nubile, lovely Asian women Sean had ever laid eyes on. Like Kuei-fei, they were all petite, ebony-haired dolls with deep, dark eyes. Each wore Western clothing, but in colors and fabrics that complemented their exotic coloring and frail-looking limbs.

All six women rose and bowed as he and Kuei-fei approached the table.

The eldest straightened first and flicked a glance at Sean before addressing her former teacher.

"Madam T'ang, we are honored by your kind invitation."

"It is good to see you again, child." Kuei-fei smiled and greeted each of the women, then introduced Sean. "This is my new friend, Mr. Delaney. He is seeking a companion to take back with him to America."

Sean dutifully inspected each woman, smiling and joking with each before sitting down at the table. The women spent the next half hour serving him tea and cakes, while inquiring about his health, home, and business, and otherwise competing for his attention.

Hard to believe this sort of thing still goes on these days. He noticed Kuei-fei watching him with keen interest, and winked at her. *And you're not as indifferent to me as you want me to think, are you, darlin'?*

During a small lull in the conversation, he glanced around the table. "Tell me something, ladies. A friend of mine is supposed to be in town, and I'd enjoy a chance to drop in on him. Have any of you run into T'ang Jian-Shan lately?"

The six women eyed each other.

"Master T'ang does not socialize with our masters," the eldest said. "Some say he is a recluse."

"My master sold an ancient dagger to him over the phone, but he would not allow it to be delivered," another of the girls said. "He sent his bodyguard to retrieve it from his shop."

"I heard the master and his wife speaking of a party he might attend," a third girl admitted. "But they did not say where."

"You live with your master and his wife?" Sean couldn't help asking.

The Chinese girl smiled. "Of course. When I am not serving his needs, I care for hers. We are very happy together."

Kuei-fei nodded. "That is what I have wished for all of you—happiness."

The six women quickly reassured her they were all very content with their positions, then by unspoken agreement politely took their leave.

"Such incredibly attractive women." Watching them leave, Sean slowly shook his head. "They could have any man they want. Why do they settle for this?"

"They cannot have any man that they want. All six were born illegitimately and have either no families to endower them or parents who sell them to the tong. Once they leave China, they are completely at the mercy of their masters." Kuei-fei rose. "They make the best of what fate has done to them."

"Like you have."

"Yes, Irish. As I have." While Sean paid their bill, she checked her watch. "We should visit members of the society and see if we can learn more about this party Jian-Shan is rumored to be attending."

"When you find your son, you're going to have one more thing to do," Sean told her as he left the tearoom with her.

"And what is that?"

He gave her soft mouth a quick, hard kiss. "Share your toothpaste with me."

The "small compensation" for Val's blouse arrived the next day when Han delivered a high stack of boxes to her room. They were all marked with the name COUTURE DE ETIENNE, which Val recognized as one of the most famous fashion houses in Paris.

Shikoro brought Lily to her room to serve as an audience while Val opened boxes and held up one beautiful gown after another. Lily clapped her hands and played happily with the tissue wrappings while the women studied everything with a critical eye.

"I don't want to even *think* about the price tags," Val said as she stroked a silk sleeve.

"Master know colors for you," Shikoro said as she surveyed a rich gold brocade skirt paired with a black velvet top. "But too tight."

Val chuckled. "For that, I might cut off my arm."

"Too hot wear inside. Take off splint. Keep arm." The housekeeper shook out another dress made of ivory lace studded with tiny pearl beads. When Val oohed, she shook her head. "More for day, not night party."

"The lace would cover most of my splint, though." Val was opening the last box, and a pile of slithery, golden-red fabric spilled out onto the bed. It shimmered like a pool of liquid flame. "Oh, my. I wish I could wear this." She held it up and sighed. "It's gorgeous."

"Why not wear red?"

"It clashes with this"—Val tugged at her hair—"and it's not my style."

The Japanese woman made a rude sound. "Hair fine, style dull. Go, try on."

In the bathroom Val took off her splint and clothes, and stepped into the polished silk dress. It was classically tailored, with long, gathered sleeves, a high collar, and no pattern to distract from the astonishing color of the fabric. It also fit her as if it had been made exclusively for her, thanks to the clinging, slippery fabric.

"If only I was a brunette," Val said as she walked out to show the housekeeper. But Lily and Shikoro were gone, and Jian-Shan was inspecting the contents of the boxes. "Oh, hello."

"Good morning." He turned, and slowly gave her the once-over. "I thought red would suit you."

"Usually it doesn't." She glanced around. "Where did my fashion experts go?"

"To the nursery, I believe." He didn't sound very interested. "If you need a consultant, try me."

She started to say something, then bit her tongue and walked over toward the freestanding oval mirror in one corner. The dress shimmered with every movement she made, and instead of clashing with the red highlights in her hair, seemed to feed and intensify them.

"Wow." She'd never worn anything half as lovely. "This is some dress."

"So is the woman wearing it." He came to stand next to her, and handed her a pair of spectacular-looking leather pumps in a matching shade of red. "Put these on."

She checked the size, and nearly fainted. "Gianna Meliani? I can't wear these."

He frowned. "I know they are a half size too large—"

"Jian, they cost more than I make in six months." She caressed the beautifully soft leather, then handed them back to him. "I can't, really."

"So much excitement about a simple pair of

shoes." He took them, then knelt and took her foot by the ankle. Before she knew it, her foot was encased in the beautiful Italian shoe. "There, how does it feel?"

"Like Italian heaven." She wiggled her toes and sighed. "Remind me the next time I go shoe shopping to take you with me. Did you get these from Paris, too?"

"No. I borrowed them from a friend."

She glanced down at them. Jian-Shan's friend was a woman who could afford Meliani. An abrupt surge of dislike made her try to slip out of the shoe. "I don't want to take the chance of scuffing them— I'll wear something of my own."

"Stop." His hand moved up and curled around the back of her calf. "Nothing you have is suitable, and my friend has an entire room full of shoes." He stood, and as he did his palm glided almost up to her thigh before he took his hand from her leg. "Wear your hair down tonight."

Val was beginning to feel like a doll. "Would you like to do my makeup, too?"

"If you need me to, I will." He traced a fingertip over the curve of her cheek. "Although I suspect Shikoro is more accomplished with cosmetics than I."

"Why are you doing this?" she asked, not sure if she meant throwing the party, giving her the dress, or touching her face.

"I ask myself the same question, constantly." He looked at her mouth. "Don't be afraid of me, Valence."

"I'm not." She was more afraid of herself. "Jian, I have to go back to America in a week or two. I can't afford to risk . . . my job . . ." She trailed off as his hand touched her waist, and the warmth of his skin penetrated the thin material. Somehow her hand was on his chest, and she could feel his fingers spreading against the small of her back. "I don't know what you want from me."

"I want to warm myself in you." He brushed his mouth against her brow, then her cheek. "Let me taste it again."

Her eyes closed as he glided a hit-and-run kiss over her lips. She had to think sensibly. Somehow. "We do this, *cher*, we're both going to get burned."

"Yes." He murmured the word against her hair, then tugged at her earlobe with his teeth, sending an erotic burst of sensation along the side of her throat. "I can feel the heat inside you. Waiting for me." He turned his head, his mouth now hovering a whisper away from hers. "Give me your heat, Valence. I've been so cold."

Common sense dissolved as she closed the tiny gap and kissed him, open mouth to his, thrilling to the feel and taste of him as he met her tongue with his. The hand on her back tensed, then pressed her hips in, settling her against his rigid erection, moving her subtly against it.

Breathing was impossible, thinking was unachievable. Her hand slid up his chest and around his neck, where the thick black cable of his braid brushed her skin. She wanted to see his hair loose, feel it streaming through her fingers. It would look like midnight silk, falling around her in a dark curtain—

He broke off the kiss, his breath fast, sweat gleaming on his skin, his black eyes scalding as he stared at her. "*Huo weixian*. You are as dangerous as fire." Then he bent and picked her up in his arms, as if she weighed no more than Lily.

That jolted Val back to reality. "What are you doing?"

"Taking you to bed. It is that, or the floor." He didn't sound too convinced they'd make it to the first.

They'd gone from kissing to this in what seemed like three seconds, and that was too far and too fast for her. "I can't. Jian, put me down."

He stopped in mid-stride. "You want me."

"Yes. No. I mean, yes, I do, but no, I can't. I *can't*." She wriggled, but his strong arms didn't budge. "Please."

Slowly he set her down on her feet. "You want me and yet you refuse me."

"I have to." She steadied herself with her good hand against his chest so she could slip out of the beautiful red shoes, then saw his expression and sighed. "I shouldn't have let you kiss me like that in the garden last night, or now. I don't jump into bed with a man simply because I'm attracted to him."

"You feel more than attraction for me." He reached for her again.

"No." Val stepped back carefully. "I don't. I want you, yes, but I don't know you. You don't know me. I can't have anonymous sex with you. I *work* for you."

"Very well." He made one of his elegant gestures. "You are fired. Now, come to me."

In spite of the unsatisfied desire pulsing inside her, she managed a laugh. "I'm sorry. I really am."

For a long moment, he looked ready to toss her

over his shoulder anyway. In the space of a heartbeat, all the emotion disappeared from his eyes and face. "So am I."

That night Shikoro put Lily to bed early, to help Val get ready for the party. Val insisted on reading her a bedtime story as compensation, and the little girl fell asleep happy.

"She's getting too big for that crib," she told the housekeeper after they left the sleeping child. "Jian should look into getting her a youth bed soon, before she takes a tumble."

"Tell master later. Make pretty now."

Val took a quick shower, but Shikoro insisted on styling her hair and putting on her makeup.

"I can do most of it," she protested as she sat with her back to the vanity table, then tried to turn around to see her face.

"No look yet," the housekeeper said. Once she completed her work on Val's hair and face, she went to get the dress from the armoire. "Be patient, *Okusan*, see all together."

Val thought of the Japanese ideals of beauty—namely, white-faced women made up to resemble porcelain dolls—and dragged in a quick breath. "I'm getting nervous again."

"No nervous."

She brought the red silk sheath and shoes, and after helping Val dress, put on her jewelry. Then she folded her hands, gave her a thorough inspection, and nodded. "Now look."

This time, the woman in the mirror shocked her. Shikoro had darkened her eyes and painted her lips with a startling red gloss, and left her hair down around her shoulders in tousled waves. Paired with the dress, the effect was stunning.

She didn't look conservative or businesslike. She looked *available*.

As a teenager, Val had learned how much trouble her looks could get her into on the streets, and gradually she had learned how to tone them down to present a more reserved appearance. Evidently she'd done it for so long that she'd forgotten what she could look like, because she hardly recognized herself.

No wonder Jian practically threw me on the bed this afternoon. "I'm not so sure about this."

"Sure." The housekeeper gave her a small push toward the door. "Show master, see what he say."

"Stay close to Valence tonight," Jian-Shan told his bodyguard as they left the library. "I want to know who talks to her, and what they say, if possible. Never let her out of your sight, not even for a moment."

Caterers from Paris had arrived earlier to set up in the gallery room, where Raven kept the bulk of her art collection. Now the buffet tables were laden with a variety of Provençal delicacies, and a handful of waiters made the final preparations by loading silver trays with goblets of champagne and wine. Everyone, from the caterers to the van drivers, had been handpicked by Raven and would also be monitoring the guests.

Han made a low sound, and Jian-Shan turned around to see what had startled his bodyguard. "Valence."

"Good evening." She came in and smiled as she

inspected the nearest table. "Everything looks wonderful."

Everything paled and disappeared around her, he thought, remembering how the red silk had felt beneath his hands. She wore Raven's designer creation as though born with it, like a second skin. One he had practically ripped from her body only three hours ago.

She is living, moving fire.

His silence made her glance down and pluck at the glowing dress. "If this isn't . . . suitable, I can change."

"No." He brought her a glass of champagne and lowered his voice to a soft murmur. "If I cannot have you, at least allow me this vision of you."

"You're not the only one suffering, *cher.*" She gave him a rueful smile before taking a sip from the crystal flute. "Will the guests be arriving soon?" As she said that, there was a discreet chime, and Han left the room. "That answers my question."

The way her lips curved gave him an instant, ferocious urge to tell his bodyguard to send everyone away, including the caterers.

Everything you touch dies.

"*Kei.*" Han returned with a small, dark Arab man at his side. "This is Mr. Fael, the caterer."

"Mr. T'ang." Fael sketched a polite bow and, after giving Val a swift, appreciative glance, inspected the room. "If all is as you require, sahib, I would appreciate a word with you in private."

Jian-Shan excused himself and took the Arab to the library, where Fael produced a folded article.

"Our friend Raven asked me to deliver this personally." He handed it over. "It is from the morning papers."

Jian-Shan unfolded the page and sat down slowly behind his desk. The photograph of the older Chinese man being led away by uniformed French police was very clear. Quickly he skimmed the paragraphs beneath the photo. "According to this, he was arrested yesterday."

"Yes." Fael folded his hands in front of him and looked pleased. "Raven says to tell you that his associates and a very bad man wanted for several assassinations are with Interpol now. No bail, and he should be extradited to America by the end of the week."

His father, caught and imprisoned like a common criminal. It seemed impossible. "Why did Raven not tell me this over the phone?"

"She told me to say, 'The general has been busy' and 'Cell phones suck for security.'" Fael produced a pained smile. "Forgive my language, but she did ask me to quote her directly."

"Do not be concerned." He put down the clipping and rubbed his eyes. The Americans would never release T'ang Po; Grady had been very clear about that. "This changes everything."

"For the better, I hope."

Uneasy tension filled Jian-Shan as he thought of a future without T'ang Po's cold shadow stretching over it. He could not believe it was over, not like this. "That remains to be seen."

Chapter 9

Val was disappointed not to see Li Shen among the thirty guests invited to the reception. She had hoped to have an opportunity to thank the man again for helping her in Paris. Jian-Shan returned from his meeting with the caterer, but before she could ask him about it, he was drawn into a discussion about the Euro-common market with a group of importers.

Conscious that she was acting hostess, Val contented herself with circulating around the room and making sure everyone felt at ease. No one seemed to recognize her from the reception in Paris, which made things easier.

Good thing Etienne doesn't offer a line of biker-chick outfits, or I'd be in hot water.

"You're looking less dishabille tonight, mademoiselle." Resplendent in a black satin sheath, Madelaine Pierport stopped beside her and scanned the crowd.

She was hostess, Val reminded herself, so she couldn't push her into the chafing dishes. "Thank you."

"Most women in my country prefer to wear black in the evenings, or"—she nodded to a pair of women in navy and brown—"other subtle colors." Then she squinted at Val. "That is a *very* noticeable dress."

"*Merci.*" Val eyed the chafing dishes. Maybe she could make it look like an accident. "I like to be noticed."

"Yes, I have guessed that about you. It is . . . quite charming." She smirked. "Though I had not thought a junior curator could afford an Etienne original."

She handed a passing waiter her half-filled champagne flute, mainly to keep from pouring it over the other woman's head. "We get paid better over in the States."

"Did you borrow the dress from Raven's wardrobe?" She made "borrow" sound like "steal." "I recognize her shoes, of course. She often lets Lily play with them."

What woman went around memorizing other women's shoes? Was Raven Lily's missing mother? "No, Jian had it brought from Paris for me," she said, then decided to get some payback. "He's a very thoughtful man."

"Asian men can be extremely generous, though they are not enamored of Caucasian women. They consider them loud, uneducated, and annoying— particularly Americans." Madelaine gave her a prim smile. "Probably why the *zaibatsu* prefers Paris to say, New Orleans, wouldn't you agree?"

What a bitch. "Oh, I don't know. There are plenty of annoying Caucasian women right here in France." Val watched the other woman's thin lips disappear and became weary of the verbal fencing. "When will the third shipment arrive? I'd like to get to work on the Nagatoki blades."

"You will have to consult with Mr. T'ang about that, though I am glad to hear you are eager to complete your assignment, mademoiselle. It would be tragic for someone just establishing a professional reputation in the art world to take advantage of one of its most important collectors. I would certainly make everyone I know aware that such a person was not to be trusted." Without waiting for a response, Madelaine gave a little wave to someone across the room. "Excuse me, I see a friend."

She should have fangs and a rattle to go with that mouth, Val thought before she forced herself to begin making the rounds of the room again.

The buyers and dealers were friendly toward her, but Val got the sense that she was being not only watched but gauged. Ignoring it took some effort, but as soon as she joined in a conversation on Edo Period blades, her knowledge seemed to act like a charm. Before long she was politely arguing with one of the older buyers over the superiority of *Kambun-Shinto* versus the earlier *suriage* swords.

"The shallower curve allowed for greater mobility, especially with the circling downward cuts being taught in the kendo schools," she said, pretending not to notice the buyer's surprised expression. "They were far more practical for the warrior classes of the time."

"For one not born to an Eastern culture, you have some interesting views," one of the Chinese importers said. "I would be very glad to purchase your book when it is published."

Before she could form a polite reply, a child's distant scream pierced the air.

Lily.

Without another thought Val ran out and up the stairs, nearly knocking Shikoro over in her haste. They exchanged a frantic look as the little girl's cry turned to louder shrieks of pain. When they got to the child's room, Val flipped on the light and saw Lily sitting on the floor, holding her head.

"She must have fallen out of the crib." She lifted the child into her arms and carried her across the hall into the bathroom, Shikoro in her wake.

Lily kept screaming and at first refused to take her hands away, but Val spoke softly to her and eased her arms down. There was no blood, but a rapidly swelling bruise near her hairline. "She's got a bad bump on her forehead."

"I will get some ice." Shikoro hurried out.

"Shhh, *bebe*, it's all right. You just banged your head a bit." Val held her against her pounding heart and stroked the weeping child's back. "I know it hurts, I know."

Jian Shan appeared in the doorway. "What happened to her?"

"It looks like she fell out of her crib."

"Let me see her." He knelt down beside them and turned Lily's face toward his. He felt the area around the bump, then checked her ears and nose. By then the housekeeper reappeared with an ice pack. "Give her to Shikoro. She will care for her."

"I'll stay with her, thanks." Val got to her feet, still holding the child. "She needs to see a doctor."

"That will not be necessary—"

"Call one anyway." She carried her back to the bedroom.

He followed her. "Valence, you are overreacting."

"I don't care if I am." She would have smacked him in the head with a lamp if Lily hadn't been in her arms. "She might have a concussion. Either get a doctor or take her to a hospital. Or I will."

"I will call Toyotomi. He can be here in thirty minutes." Jian gestured toward his housekeeper. "Give her to Shikoro. She will care for her until he arrives."

He wanted her to dump Lily and go back to the party. She gazed into his eyes, feeling the rage building inside her. "Shikoro, do you mind if I take care of her until the doctor gets here?"

"No, *Okusan*."

"Thanks." Val turned her back on Jian-Shan and carried Lily to the rocking chair.

Most of the guests had left by the time Toyotomi completed his examination of Lily. He found no sign of concussion or complication. Despite his prognosis, Val refused to leave the child until she fell asleep, then cornered the doctor in the hallway outside her room.

"This isn't right," she said without ceremony. "Why can't we take her to the hospital?"

"Mr. T'ang feels it is safer for the child to have her examined here," Toyotomi said, sounding as aggrieved as Val felt.

"The same way it was safer to keep me here, and at the house in Paris." She stared at the ceiling and counted silently until her rage level dropped to low boil. "Have you contacted this Raven lady?"

His round face wrinkled into a puzzled frown. "Why would I do that?"

"I think she'd want to know when her child gets hurt."

"My dear, Raven is not Lily's mother."

"But Madelaine said—" She made a frustrated gesture. "Oh, never mind. Who is Lily's mother, and where is she?"

"Her name was Karen—" He halted as Jian-Shan approached. "Mr. T'ang, I'm happy to report your daughter is fine. I can return tomorrow to check on her, but I'm sure she'll recover with no ill effects."

"Thank you, Doctor." As Toyotomi left them, Jian's dark eyes met Val's. "Are you satisfied now?"

"No, *cher*, I'm not. She scared the hell out of me." She flung a look back at Lily's room, then eyed him. "But not you, apparently. How can you be so casual about this? My God, Jian, she could have cracked her skull open."

"The doctor indicated—"

"I'm not talking about what the doctor said. I'm talking about *you*." She poked him in the chest with her finger a few times. "What kind of father are you? Your little girl takes a bad fall, and what do you do? You leave her with me and go back to your party."

"You insisted on staying with her." He got that same, wintry look of disinterest he had every time they discussed Lily. "My presence was unnecessary. Had you wished to rejoin the reception, you should have allowed Shikoro to take charge of her. I didn't ask you to look after her."

"Look after—" Val's jaw sagged, then she snapped it shut. "I was scared to death when I saw her head, and she's not even my child. Lily's just a baby, Jian. You treat your damned swords better than your own daughter."

"That's enough."

"No, it's not. Maybe everyone else in your life is too afraid of you to say this, but you're going to hear it for once. You've got a precious, loving little girl in there who wants nothing but a little attention and kindness, and what do you do? You ignore her. You're the worst father I've ever seen in my life."

He folded his arms. "What would you know of fathers?"

"Ms. St. Charles." Han appeared behind Jian. "My wife wishes to speak to you."

"I'm not done yelling at him yet," she told the bodyguard. To Jian, she said, "You don't know anything about me or my father."

"I know that you never knew him." His lips were nearly white. "Be grateful for that."

"Please." Han stepped between them and touched her shoulder. "Shikoro is very distraught and blames herself. If you would speak to her, perhaps you could persuade her to see this was only a frightening accident, and not her fault."

"She would blame herself, because she loves Lily. At least the poor baby has *that* much." She brushed past Jian.

With a faintly apologetic look at him, Han followed.

* * *

Jian waited until they had gone downstairs before he went into Lily's room. The child was curled up in her crib, the bump on her forehead plain even in the dim light.

He had never allowed himself to feel anything for her. With his father's sword always hanging over his neck, waiting to fall, he could not.

What will I do with you now?

Jian-Shan bent over and trailed his fingers through the baby-soft blond hair. She had been born with those little curls, and the first time he had held her in his arms had seemed like a miracle. Until the miracle had been stolen from him.

You're the worst father I've ever seen in my life.

Valence didn't know how hard he had worked to remain indifferent to Lily. She couldn't understand the ties of blood, and how they could be twisted and snarled by betrayal. He suspected that even if he attempted to explain it all to her, she would call him more names.

I have been a coward in the worst way.

Carefully he lowered the side of the crib and knelt beside it until his face was level with hers. She still shuddered occasionally, and he placed his hand on her back, feeling each small breath she took.

He would have taken her from me. Killed her to show me his contempt for Karen, for everything I ever loved.

"He cannot harm you anymore, child," he whispered. "From now on, we are free of him."

As he watched Lily sleep, Jian Shan didn't see the shadow that passed by the threshold, and moved down the hall into another room. The call that was placed from the phone there was low and succinct.

"It is done," the man said, his gaze fixed on the door. "You will keep your end of the bargain?"

"You do excellent work, Mr. Fael," T'ang Po told him. "Return to Paris now, and I will release your wife and your children."

"You not eat lunch. You not eat breakfast." A wrathful Shikoro thumped the tray down on the table beside Val. "You eat dinner, or I feed you like Lily."

Val set aside the *no tachi* moor sword she was examining and tried to keep her irritation out of her voice. "I want to get these last few blades catalogued before the Nagatoki shipment arrives." She glanced at the tray, which the housekeeper had piled with food. "Han couldn't eat all that."

"Not for Han. For you. I come back, find food on tray, I make Han put you in high chair." The housekeeper forgot her usual bow and stalked out of the library.

Val tucked a wayward strand of hair back into the clip holding the rest of it away from her face and rested her chin on her hand. Channeling all her energy into getting her research finished was important, but Shikoro was right. She *had* been sulking for the better part of a week.

As Dr. Toyotomi predicted, Lily had recovered from her spill without complications. The morning after the incident he also removed Val's stitches, though he insisted she keep the splint on for another week. Val stayed close to Lily throughout that day, and while they were playing with the little girl's endless collection of toddler toys, Han removed the offending crib. That afternoon, he brought up a youth bed. Shikoro had also produced a thick duvet and placed it next to the lower bed, to cushion Lily if she fell again.

Jian-Shan, on the other hand, didn't even bother to check on the little girl, and he no longer shared meals with Val. The few times she saw him over the following week were only in passing, and even then he remained polite but remote—almost as if he were preoccupied by something.

It was probably for the best, Val thought. Everything had been getting far too personal between them, and what she had to concentrate on now was nailing down a firm commitment on the loan of the collection and unraveling the secrets of the Nagatoki.

If they ever arrived.

To please Shikoro, she ate most of the delicious vegetable stir-fry she'd brought, then decided to brace the tiger in his den. After she showered and changed, she came back down to the library to tidy up, and found Jian-Shan reading her notes.

Well, you wanted to talk to him. Here he is.

"I'm finished with the first two shipments," she said. "All I'm waiting on are the Nagatoki."

"Madelaine will be here shortly. You can begin first thing in the morning." He took one of the Edo Period katanas from its case and studied the sheath as if he'd never seen it before. "You seem anxious to complete the work."

Oh, you can tell? She planted her good hand on her hip. "Yes. I'm ready to go home. We still need to finalize details on the loan of the collection."

"I have not decided to lend it to you yet."

"I've given you all the specifics involved. The collection will remain under tight security from the moment it leaves you until it's returned. The displays will be guarded around the clock." She didn't like the way he was ignoring her. "What other assurances do you need to make your decision?"

"I will think on the matter and let you know." He replaced the sword and started to walk out.

She stepped in his path. "When will you let me know? Give me a time frame here."

"You are very impatient for someone asking a favor."

"I've been here almost a month. I've done what you've asked." She winced inside as she thought of the one thing she hadn't done. "I have yet to even see the Nagatoki swords. Now, either make up your mind, or let me go."

He didn't like that, she could tell. "You will not leave until I have made my decision about the loan. As it is, I doubt I will allow you to take them."

She threw her arms out. "What more do you want?"

"Bonjour, Mr. T'ang." Madelaine Pierport walked into the room carrying a briefcase. "Ms. St. Charles, if you would be good enough to excuse us?"

"Of course." Val stomped from the room, then hesitated outside. She needed the Nagatoki blades more than a temper tantrum. With a sigh she hovered near the door, listening.

"Really, monsieur, you should not let that young woman speak to you in such a disrespectful manner." Madelaine sounded different again—the softer, sweeter version. Or maybe that was the way she normally talked around rich men. "Do you wish me to escort her back to Paris?"

No way am I leaving with her. She'd whack me over the head with a tire iron and bury me in a shallow grave by the roadside.

"That will not be necessary," Jian said. "Where are the Nagatoki?"

"En route from the monastery as we speak. Forgive me, but the highway workers' strike had blocked most of the major roads until this morning." There was a pause. "Let me do that. You know, it would be no trouble for me to stay. Lisette can take over my duties in the city."

Why was Jian-Shan keeping the swords at a monastery?

"I have Ms. St. Charles working on the collection. She'll be here for a few more weeks."

Weeks? Val barely stifled a yelp. She didn't want to stay under his roof for another day. The subsequent silence made her inch closer to the gap in the door. Through it, she saw Madelaine practically plastered all over the front of Jian-Shan, doing something to his collar.

"She does not appear very grateful for what you have done for her." The Frenchwoman rose on tiptoe to straighten his collar at the back, and then rested her hand on his shoulder. "Wouldn't you rather have someone who respects you in her place?" She leaned in until their mouths almost touched. "You won't be disappointed. I can do whatever you want."

He put his hands on her waist. "I know you can."

Did he? Val curled her hands into fists for a moment, then turned away. What was she doing, spying on them? It didn't matter to her who Jian-Shan went to bed with—she'd already told him she wouldn't sleep with him, so if he found comfort in cuddling up to that walking rattlesnake, he was entitled.

Now if only I could forget how he made me feel.

Humiliation over her adolescent behavior drove her up to the nursery, where Shikoro was preparing Lily for her bath. Yet not even watching the toddler splash in the tub made Val feel any better.

"You no happy, *Okusan*," Shikoro said as she deftly scrubbed Lily's face. "Make peace with master?"

"Why should I?" She stared blindly at the tile wall. "He ignores his daughter. I can't accept that."

"He no ignore," she said, looking perplexed. "That Eastern man way. Care for Lily, just not show it. Like Han care for me. You not see that?"

Val had already sensed the bodyguard's deep and abiding love for his wife, although Shikoro was right—he rarely demonstrated it. It was more in the way he looked at her, the softening of his voice when he spoke to her. He invested that love in every glance, every word.

Could she have misjudged Jian-Shan? "I didn't have a real father when I was growing up, so maybe I overreacted."

"Lily look like mother, not master. He look her, he miss wife." Shikoro touched her arm. "Master good man, many bad memory."

She'd never thought of it from that perspective, and she felt ashamed of herself. "I didn't know."

She rubbed her temple and sighed. *"Dieu,* I'm an idiot."

"You lonely. Master lonely."

"Not for long." She sat down beside the tub and trailed her fingers through the fragrant bubbles. "Madelaine's here, and it looks like she'll be staying."

"Sugoi Frenchwoman-not-like-anything no good for master. Greedy woman." Shikoro avoided a splash from Lily's kicking feet and offered the child her toy duck as a distraction. "Master see willow way in you, no see her."

"What's this willow way?"

"Be beautiful, like willow. Willow soft, always bend, sway, like music." The housekeeper made a frustrated gesture. "Hard say English. Better show you."

"I don't think I could do anything . . ." Val groped for the right word. "Explicit."

"I tell you, *Okusan,* geisha not prostitute. Geisha beauty person. You beauty, need little work." Shikoro scooped Lily from the tub and held her while Val dried her little body with a towel. "We read bedtime story, Lily sleep, then I show you."

"I'm not Japanese. I'll probably mess it up."

"What that matter?" Her brows rose. "You want Frenchwoman-not-like-anything please master?"

"No," Val admitted. She didn't want Madelaine anywhere near Jian. And if that meant going to bed with him . . . her lips curled. *It's what I want. It's what I've wanted since the first time he kissed me. Why am I fighting it?*

"Hai. I teach willow way, you try." She cocked

her head. "Better do something, Val-san, than do nothing."

Val should have said no. She shouldn't have cared. But the sight of the Frenchwoman pressing herself against Jian still blazed in her mind. "Okay, Shikoro. We'll try it your way."

Madelaine drove back to Paris at a reckless speed, furious with herself and Jian-Shan. Had she not devoted herself to him and his sacred *zaibatsu*? For two years, mindlessly obeying him like any good little slant-eyed woman? She had repeatedly demonstrated all the qualities Asian men desired in their spouses—dignity, loyalty, and utter subservience. She knew that in time her sacrifice would compel Jian-Shan to grow more and more dependent on her, until it no longer mattered that they shared a professional relationship. Why resist a woman who was willing to do anything for him, in and out of the office?

Wasn't that what all men wanted, anyway?

What had happened was not Jian-Shan's fault—it was all due to that wretched, vulgar American woman. Val St. Charles had forced herself into his life and refused to leave him alone. Madelaine would have never advanced her plans toward her employer so quickly had it not been for her potential rival.

Of course the American had already taken every advantage of her situation. She hosted his reception, coddled his brat—she had even convinced him to buy expensive clothes for her.

Those clothes should be mine. He should be mine. I've

worked too hard to gain his trust and admiration to let some American slut steal him away from me.

The child's fall had led to some kind of argument between them. Yet when she'd seen Val with Jian-Shan earlier, it had sent her into a panic. There was something between them, something almost tangible in the air when they looked at each other. It didn't matter that the American spoke harshly to him—the same disturbing, indefinable tension echoed in her words. Then it struck her as soon as she'd walked into the room. Madelaine had interrupted them the way one stumbles on two lovers quarreling. *She* was the intrusion, not the American.

Are they lovers yet?

Her panic had compelled her to make a rash move. One she realized now had been ill-timed. She'd pressed herself against him, so he wouldn't mistake her meaning, and had savored the feel of his long, hard frame against her softness. *I can do whatever you want.*

I know you can. Then he had ruined everything by gently removing her hands from his jacket. *However, our association must remain strictly professional. Return to Paris now; I will call you tomorrow.*

Thus she had been dismissed, like any other employee, and the American remained in Provence, secure in Jian-Shan's household—and likely his bed. She had to be sleeping with him; why else would he reject Madelaine's overtures?

She worried over the problem like a terrier with a rat. No matter what angle she attacked it, the solution remained the same: she could salvage everything, but the American had to go.

How can I get rid of her once and for all?

She found her answer several hours later, at an exhibition of archaic armor at the Akune Gallery. Akune Ogawa, a prominent member of the *zaibatsu* and one of Madelaine's most ardent admirers, listened sympathetically as she related the situation.

"This young woman is in the country as a representative of her employer," Akune said, and stroked the wispy goatee he affected. "Were she no longer employed by the museum, she would have no reason to remain in France."

She should never have come here in the first place, Madelaine thought, still burning with indignation. "If only I could make her employer aware of her improper behavior toward Mr. T'ang. It is simply too much to watch him tolerate her vulgarism out of mere courtesy."

"What has she done?"

"I'm sure you heard about her appearance at my last reception. She burst in, wearing the most indecent garments, and made a horrible scene. She was either drunk or on drugs, I couldn't tell which." Madelaine shuddered. "Mr. T'ang removed her from Paris, and gave her work, but that was not enough for her. She demanded that he buy her an entire wardrobe. Then this morning I arrived to find her shouting at him for refusing to . . . respond to her overtures."

"Mr. T'ang does not strike me as a man who would tolerate such behavior."

"She injured herself on his property, and I think he feels sorry for her. I know if her employers knew how ungrateful and vicious this woman is, they would have her brought back and send a more appropriate representative." She looked through her lashes at Akune. "Of course, it is not my place to interfere with Mr. T'ang's personal life."

"That is a shame. I know the head curator at the New Orleans Museum. He would not condone this at all." Akune patted her hand. "I will call this young woman's superior in the morning and make him aware of her misconduct."

"Would you do that for Mr. T'ang?" Madelaine produced a hopeful smile. "Oh, Akune-san, that would be such a relief to me—and to Mr. T'ang, of course."

"I would be honored." He lifted her hand to his lips.

A man standing a few feet away from Jian-Shan's business manager casually walked out of the gallery, and lit a cigarette.

Damned women are going to drive me to my grave.

The eavesdropper circled around to the back of the building, where an anonymous-looking van sat next to the telephone cables. He knocked twice on the back door, then climbed in. As the door closed, he removed a tiny receiver from his right ear.

"How's it going in there, Irish?" one of the men at the communications console asked.

"Tough. They're making me drink champagne and eat caviar on little toasts. I might not last another hour." Sean Delaney went over to his laptop and initiated a live link. The face of a beautiful brunette appeared on his screen. "Hello, darlin' girl. You're looking lovely tonight."

"Well, well." Raven tapped a few keys. "I won't ask how you got this number, you sly boy."

"I wouldn't tell you," he said, and chuckled.

"Are you ready to put me in touch with our mutual friend?"

She pretended to be puzzled. "Have you been hitting the whiskey again, Irish? I don't know who you're talking about."

He shook his head. "You need to work on that innocent look, girl. Especially after what you did to the poor general, I'm thinking you need a good friend. You know my price."

Raven turned her head, frowned, and glanced back at the screen. "I'll keep it in mind. Taa." She terminated the link.

"I'm heading back in, boys," Sean said, inserting his earpiece before climbing out of the van. "Keep your ears open, and watch our lady."

As Sean Delaney rejoined the gathering inside the gallery, two Chinese women drifted into one of the private offices, speaking avidly about the Heian armor on display. As soon as the door closed, their voices dropped and the conversation took an abrupt turn.

"Madam T'ang, I have been listening as you asked," the younger woman said. "Akune just spoke to a Frenchwoman regarding your son." She went to the window overlooking the gallery and pointed out Madelaine. "From what she said, I believe she knows where he is."

"You have done well." Kuei-fei clasped the woman's hands in hers. "Akune Ogawa, he treats you fairly?"

"Yes, very much so. Soon I will have enough jewels and money saved to leave him and return to America." The young woman touched the diamond studs in her ears and smiled shyly. "I will never forget your kindness to me when I was brought from China, Madam T'ang. If you are in need of anything while you are here in Paris, I beg you to call on me."

Through the large glass window facing the showroom, Kuei-fei saw Sean approaching. "I will. Thank you, child."

"Pardon me, ladies," Sean said as he stepped in. "I was wondering where my date had gotten to, until I saw the two of you. Now my only problem is, how can I get rid of my date?"

Ogawa's young mistress giggled, while Kuei-fei took his arm. "I am your date," she reminded him.

"Then I am not letting you out of my sight."

She walked through the gallery with him, admiring the displays for the second time until Sean steered her toward a private corner and turned her to face him. "Well? Was she any help?"

"No," Kuei-fei said, gazing directly into his eyes. "She has heard nothing about my son. Were you able to pick up any information?"

"Not a thing." Sean glanced over his shoulder. "We'll try making the rounds again tomorrow."

"Yes." She smiled. "Perhaps tomorrow will be a better day."

Chapter 10

"Don't paint the back of my neck red," Val said as she took off her splint and eyed the collection of makeup Shikoro had produced from her room. "I'll rub it without thinking and end up smearing it all over my face."

"Only geisha paint neck. No touch face," the housekeeper told her in her severest tone. "Wear lace dress. Eastern man like woman look like woman."

"I looked like a woman in that red dress, didn't I?" she asked as she went to the armoire.

"Red dress say, stop and look. Lace dress say, come and touch." Shikoro tried to keep her expression stern, but giggled at Val's glare. "Now you face red."

"It's been that way for a good hour."

Which was true. Val had had no idea what she'd gotten herself into when she'd agreed to Shikoro's tutoring. Instead of conducting lessons on a tea ceremony or some other elegant feminine ritual, the Japanese woman had given her a talk equivalent to the traditional birds and bees discussion. With some particular exceptions.

"Eastern man like quiet woman talk. He like woman listen better." Shikoro motioned for Val to turn around and began buttoning the long row of pearl buttons at the back of her dress. "Like woman serve him, sit close to him, by feet."

"I'm not sitting on the floor."

"I make traditional Japanese meal. You both sit on floor." Shikoro gathered her hair up and pinned it in a loose roll with two white hair picks. "Listen what master say. Look in eyes. Smile, look down. Only place you want be with him. No stare, no make angry face." She turned Val around and pointed to the vanity. "I do face now."

Val eyed the collection of jars, powders, and pencils. "You're not going to use that face cream made out of nightingale droppings on me, are you?"

"Use later, take makeup off," Shikoro said, then smiled in the mirror. "That joke, *Okusan*."

Val sat still as the housekeeper draped a towel to protect the dress. "And when we're done eating? Then?"

Shikoro picked up a cheek brush. "Do other thing I teach."

"What if he doesn't like it?"

The housekeeper looked at the ceiling, then at Val. "He Eastern man. He like it. Now sit still. You worse than Lily."

Once more Shikoro transformed Val, but the reflection in the mirror was quite different this time. She sparingly used softer colors to complement the romantic design of the dress, and pulled a few tendrils of hair loose to fall around Val's face and neck. The dress itself was, like the red dress, conservatively tailored, but instead of clinging it hugged her upper torso and floated around her legs.

The entire effect was almost Victorian, Val thought, not recognizing herself again. She really needed to reevaluate her wardrobe choices in the future. "Very nice." She tried to see the side of her throat. "What did you put on my neck?"

"Something for master."

She went down to dinner feeling slightly ridiculous but determined to give it a chance. Maybe if she could get to Jian-Shan on another level, he would open up to her. All she needed was to make him see her as a woman, the kind of woman he wanted.

Shikoro had set up their traditional dinner in a room off the garden, and Val arranged herself on the cushion by the low table the way the former geisha had told her to, and waited for Jian-Shan.

He came in a few minutes after her, paused at the sight of her kneeling, then slowly came over to join her. "I didn't expect you to join me tonight."

"Shikoro—I wanted to." Val remembered to look at his chest instead of his face, and kept her voice low and demure. "I shouldn't have shouted at you when Lily was hurt."

"You were upset."

"Yes, but I didn't think of the cultural differences or how you felt about Lily's—what I'm trying to say is, I was out of line, and I am sorry."

Jian-Shan sat down beside her. "I see."

Shikoro brought in the first course, and Val rose to take it from her and serve Jian. He watched every move she made in complete silence. "

"This is crab tempura, with jasmine rice," she

murmured as she put a generous portion on his plate. It felt silly, as if she were feeding Lily, but Shikoro had assured her Eastern men enjoyed being served. "Would you like some tea?"

He inclined his head, and she poured for him before returning to her place at the table. She took tiny portions for herself, but waited until he had tasted his food before picking up her own chopsticks.

Now if I can get some of this food in my mouth without dropping it in my lap, there is a God. "Was there any problem with the delivery of the last swords?"

"No. Madelaine took care of everything. You can begin work on them in the morning." He toyed with his rice. "You're not wearing your splint."

"I thought I'd let my hand breathe a little tonight." She smiled at him before returning her gaze to the third button on his shirt. "Were you able to work out in the garden today?"

"Yes, as I do every day."

She felt more and more uncomfortable with her unwilling role, but pressed on. "Did you study tai chi in Japan along with *iaido*?"

"No, I studied it in Great Britain." He frowned at her. "Are you feeling well, Valence?"

Great, I'm trying to be Super Eastern Woman here and he thinks I'm sick.

She almost made a face, then remembered Shikoro's orders to keep her expression serene and untroubled. "I'm interested. Does it take a long time to learn how to do all those moves?"

"It can." He went back to picking at his food.

Val tried hard to keep up the conversation through two more courses, but Jian seemed reluctant to talk about anything. The odd kneeling position was making her legs numb. And she was running out of nerve.

By the time dessert arrived she had run out, and as soon as she finished a slice of the almond cake she rose to her feet. "I think I'll skip coffee, if you don't mind. I want to get up early."

Shikoro, who had come in to clear, gave her an incredulous look.

"Stay." Jian came around the table. "That will be all, thank you, Shikoro."

The Japanese woman smiled, bowed, and managed to send one more exasperated glance at Val before she closed the doors on her way out.

Val sank back down on the cushion and tried to look as if it was the only place in the world she wanted to be, instead of the last. She reached for the small porcelain pot on the table. "Would you like to have more tea?"

"No." He took the pot from her and set it aside, then knelt down beside her.

Since he evidently wasn't interested in having any dessert either, the meal was officially over. Which meant it was time to start phase two of Operation Geisha.

Val lifted her hand to the picks in her hair and tugged them free, one at a time, and placed them on the table. Her hair fell around her shoulders and face, until she tilted her head and used her hand to sweep it back.

"There aren't many strawberry blondes in China or Japan, are there?" She wondered if she looked as stupid as she sounded.

He watched her hand as she sifted her fingers through her hair. "No."

"Your hair is so dark." She produced what she hoped was a small, seductive smile as she reached out and touched his hair. "Very thick." She had to raise herself on her knees as she felt for the tie at the end of his braid to pull it free. "A lot longer than mine, too."

He moved as if to stop her, then dropped his hand and let her release his hair from the heavy cable.

"I've never seen a man with such long hair." She drew it out over one shoulder, allowing her fingers to trail down until they rested on his forearm. "I like it."

He bent down until their brows nearly touched. "Do you?" His breath warmed her lips. "What are you doing, Valence?"

"I just . . . want to show you I'm not a complete harpy." She moved her hand to his collar and unbuttoned it. In the process, her fingertips brushed his throat. "Your skin is almost hot. Is it too warm in here? Or"—she turned her head so that her cheek glanced off his—"is it something else?"

He moved his head to the side, gliding his mouth over her cheek in a deliberate caress. "Something else."

Her hand trembled as she reached for the next button. "Then let me make you more comfortable."

"That will take more than a few buttons," he murmured, his mouth barely avoiding a collision with hers.

She felt his arms come up around her. Shikoro

had been right—this submissive female stuff worked. "Okay."

"Are you offering me anything I want?"

Her eyelids felt heavy. "I think so."

"You said you did not want to go to bed with me."

"I changed my mind."

"Is this your idea of an exchange?"

The words didn't make sense, but then she was losing herself in the warmth of his body and the touch of his hands on her back and neck. "For what?"

His touch changed, tightened. "The collection."

Jian-Shan watched the dreamy look fade from her eyes.

"No." She tried to extract herself from his arms. "You've made a mistake, Jian."

"Have I?" He watched her eyes. "You have repeatedly refused me. Yet when I tell you I am considering turning down the loan of my swords, you offer yourself."

"You're wrong."

"You demanded to know what more I wanted, but you already knew, and you decided to take the direct approach."

Her cheeks turned pink. "No, this was Shikoro's idea—she just wanted to—*Dieu*, let's just forget about it, okay?"

"You obviously want my attention, and my swords, Valence. You have the first." He felt the sudden tension in her body as he moved his hand around her throat, the weight of her hair brushing against his wrist. "Negotiate your terms for the second."

"I'm not negotiating anything, and I'm not having sex with you to get you to loan the collection to my museum," she told him, anger making her voice tight. "If that's what you think, you can take your swords and—"

"Shhhh." He smoothed some lace down, away from her skin. "I'm very willing to consider your offer."

"There's no offer." She turned her head as he bent down. "If you want to discuss the possibility of an exhibit, let go of me and we'll talk."

"Later, perhaps." He breathed in the scent of her hair, and thought of roses and ginger. Then he saw a small calligraphic mark on her neck, just behind her ear. The Chinese symbol for the White Tiger. He touched it with a fingertip. "You wear my mark like a jewel."

"Your what?" She tried to reach up, but he caught her wrist to keep her from smearing it. "Oh, God, what did she paint on me?"

"I like seeing it on your skin." He brought her hand down to his chest, felt her fingers curl against the fine white material of his shirt. "I want to see more."

"There's nothing else to see."

"Let me look anyway." He followed the line of her high collar, back to the row of ivory buttons, and began releasing them one by one. Fine tremors ran down her spine as the air touched her bare skin. He spread his hand over the gap, urging her closer as he bent down.

"Jian?" Her eyes widened a fraction.

"Let me taste," he murmured against her lips.

He let her have her moment of resistance, and simply enjoyed the feel of her fallen angel's mouth on his. She was everything ripe and luscious, and he knew he could spend hours just like this, with her trembling in his arms.

When at last she opened her mouth for him, he found she tasted of almonds and tea. And heat—so much that he forgot to taste and sank into the kiss, wanting more, taking more.

The tension in her body melted away, until she was pressed fully against him, her uninjured hand clutching at his arm. He could feel the edge of her fingernails through his sleeve, and heard the low sound she made, a sound that stirred something inside him he'd thought long dead.

My woman.

And she was, in that moment, everything his— her lips, her slim body, her heat and her passion. He knew that what had been simmering between them for weeks would not be denied any longer. Tonight he would take what was his.

He lifted his head so he could see her mouth, damp and red from his kiss. "Valence." He rose, bringing her with him, keeping her pressed against him. "Come with me."

"I want to." She ducked her head and laughed once. "God, I really want to. But not like this." Her dark eyes met his. "Not with what you think."

"You don't know what I think." He touched her cheek. "You don't know how I feel, being near you, unable to touch. Seeing your smiles, hearing your laughter, feeling your warmth. Denied all of it."

"That's not true." She sounded dazed.

"Isn't it?" He tugged open his shirt, ignoring the buttons that popped as he gently pushed her injured hand inside, until the scar on her palm touched the scar on his shoulder. "Do you remember how it felt, that day in Paris? In the garden?"

She paled, and her eyes shadowed. "I remember."

"Your flesh to my flesh. But this time it will be different. You can feel it, can't you?" He brushed his mouth over hers. "No pain, *xia*, only pleasure."

"I feel it, *cher*." She closed her eyes for a moment. "I simply can't think straight when you do this to me."

"Then don't think. Feel." He buried his face in her hair, enjoying the coolness against his hot skin. "You hide your desires, but there is nothing to fear from me. I know what you are, Valence, and I know what you want. I only want to give you pleasure."

The world went away then, as she curled her hand around his neck and brought his mouth back to hers. She gave him everything he'd felt her holding back before, the heat and need that echoed inside him, the desperate hunger that seemed endless and insatiable.

He forgot to be gentle as he gathered her close, his hands curling into the delicate lace of her dress. Distantly he heard something tear, felt fabric part under his grip. He wouldn't make it to the bed this time.

"Da?"

Val froze, and he lifted his head to see his daughter standing a few feet away. She held a small blanket and had her thumb in her mouth.

It was impossible for Jian-Shan to see the child without seeing her mother. Karen's face, contorted with agony as she endured the hours of labor pain. Screaming as she pushed Lily from her body. The fist she'd struck him with when they'd shown her the tiny infant she'd delivered.

You can't hold her! Then, to the nurse, *Don't let him touch her! Everything he touches dies!*

He took his hands from Val and stepped away, and watched the little girl toddle over to clutch at her legs. "Put her back to bed," he told Val, then stalked out.

Val had scrubbed off the makeup and thrown the torn, expensive dress into the closet, but nothing could induce her to lie down on the bed. She didn't want to think about how humiliated she felt. She wanted to pack her suitcases and leave.

All I have to do is examine the Nagatoki, photograph the etching marks, and then I can go.

She was thirsty, and a glance at the clock told her it was probably safe to go down to the kitchen. It would give her something to do, and if she ran into Jian-Shan, she could just walk the other way.

Yet the moment Val stepped into the hall, she heard the sound of his voice. She would have retreated, but she realized it was coming from Lily's room, of all places, and she walked silently down the hall until she could see him, standing beside the little girl's bed.

"She's growing so fast now, Karen." He sounded odd, as if he were praying. "You should see her. She's the image of you; she even has your hands." He knelt beside the bed, picked up one of Lily's tiny hands and watched her fingers curl around his.

Karen—the name Toyotomi had mentioned. Lily's mother.

"Every time I look at her, I think of the day I lost you." He tucked in the blanket around the sleeping child, then rested his hand on her small head. "I would do anything to go back to that day, to be there at the hospital with you. Maybe I could have kept you alive."

Val closed her eyes. He had no idea she was listening, of course, or he would not be having a conversation with his dead wife. It hurt to hear him; she'd had no idea he felt such despair.

"I will keep my promise to you." Jian-Shan bent over and kissed Lily's brow. "I will never love anyone the way I loved you."

Val turned and slowly walked back to her bedroom.

The Lotus screeched to a stop, blocking in the Mercedes. The woman who climbed out had to run to catch her target, but in ten seconds she had him pinned up against his car, a switchblade at his throat. "Hello, Fael."

The Arab swallowed hard. "Raven, h-h-how good to see you."

"You don't call, you don't write. Makes a girl think you're avoiding her. Then I hear your cousin has gone into the specialty printing business." She leaned in. "I don't want to be in Paris right now, Fael, and it really pisses me off that you've dragged me back. Talk to me."

"You must let me go." His wide eyes bounced

from right to left. "He took my wife, my children—if he sees you—"

"In the car." Raven shoved him toward the Lotus.

She drove to one of the crowded parking lots surrounding the Eiffel Tower, then shut off the engine. Fael was dabbing his damp face with a white linen handkerchief. "All right. Who grabbed Fatima and the kids?"

"T'ang Po." He looked ready to weep. "I did not want to help him, but he said he would send them back to me one piece at a time."

"Great. Just great." She rolled her hand. "Tell me the rest of it. All of it."

Fael made a strangled sound. "You don't understand. He will *kill* them."

"He'll kill them anyway." Raven grabbed him by the front of his shirt and shook him. "You tell me, and we may have a chance to get them back alive."

Fael wept openly as he told her everything—how T'ang Po had given him the faked photos, instructed him to forge the Paris newspaper, then use his people to search the villa in Provence. "The swords were not there."

"Bastard is waiting until Jay moves them down from the monastery. God *damn* it." She grabbed her phone and began to dial Jian-Shan's number, then felt something hard and deadly nudge her side. "Don't mess with me, Fael."

"I am not, Raven, I promise you." He pressed the gun to her ribs and took the phone away from her. "You're going to help me first. Then you can save your friend."

*   *   *

Val refused breakfast the next morning and went immediately to work, examining the first of the Nagatoki swords.

No more playing around. Get the job finished and get out of here.

When she'd arrived in the library, Han had been waiting to help her. And she wouldn't let herself ask where Jian-Shan was.

Not after last night.

The blade she removed from the case was a *koshigatana*, carried by warriors on the field specifically to behead fallen enemies. For a moment, she wondered if any of the samurai had ever considered using it on themselves.

"I need to remove the hilt and examine the tang," she said to Han, lifting her still-useless left hand. "Will you help me?"

She showed him how to carefully remove the ancient pegs and slip the hilt off, revealing the *nakago*, the last six inches of the blade traditionally signed by the sword maker. The name was written vertically, with the characters marching down from the *hamachi* to the end of the tang.

"Good, it's not folded." At his blank look, she explained, "Fighting styles regularly changed, and long swords were often cut down to a more convenient length. Sometimes the tangs would be folded over to preserve the inscription, but more often than not, they were cut off."

"That looks like a dragon," Han murmured as he bent to inspect the carving.

"It is. Nagatoki was obsessed with dragons. He thought they lent mystical strength to his swords. He also named all of his swords." She took out her magnifying glass and slowly examined the row of faint Japanese characters running alongside the pictograph. "This one is called . . . Crest of the Billowing Storm Wave."

"The steel is as bright as the rest of the sword," Han said, touching the shiny surface. "What are these marks?"

"That's the *hamon*, the grain pattern of the blade. Each sword maker had his own methods of forging, and they produced a consistent pattern. It's one way we identify who made the sword." She showed him how the marks continued up the entire length of the blade.

"It looks like mist."

"The best do. The forging process produced distinctive metallurgical structures on the surface— shadows, lines, and clusters. Some are coarse and obvious, others are more subtle. Nagatoki's *hamon* are called *noi*—visible fragrance—and are the finest of grain patterns." She turned the blade over and examined the etchings on the other side. "A Shinto prayer for peace. The warrior he made this sword for was an important samurai and a philosopher."

As she set her magnifying glass aside to make her notes, Han read the prayer. "They understood the value of peace, these warriors."

"Despite what you see in modern movies and on television, most samurai weren't really violent men. They often looked for peaceful solutions so they wouldn't have to use their swords." She finished noting the information and measured the blade with a flexible tape. "But when they had to, they could cut a man in half with a single stroke of a blade like this. And frequently did."

"You have rare understanding." At her glance, he added, "Most Americans cannot fathom that kind of dual nature."

"Maybe if they were exposed to your people's history more often, they'd stop thinking anyone with a katana was a homicidal ninja." She sighed. "That's why these blades should be on permanent display in a museum, so we can educate people."

"Blades are not merely pieces of history," Han said. "In China and Japan they are symbols of power. Power that men will kill and die to possess. As such, they must be guarded."

She frowned. "Maybe three hundred years ago they were, but that's hardly true today. People are more civilized now."

He gave her an unreadable smile. "The lust for power never fades. It is reborn in every generation. More so in times when men no longer use swords to wage wars."

She thought of the cutting rejection she'd gotten last night. "Some of them still do." She took a deep breath. "Where is Jian-Shan? I need to speak with him."

"I have never seen such a fine example of Naga-toki's work," Akune Ogawa told Madelaine over the phone. "I plan to display it in my gallery immediately, unless Mr. T'ang would prefer I show it to him first." He listened to the Frenchwoman, then nodded. "Excellent. I trust Mr. T'ang can return to Paris to examine it this evening? At seven? I will have it ready for him."

The dealer hung up the phone and turned to the assassin. "The bodyguard should accompany him to the city, leaving only the women to deal with. You can kill the housekeeper, but T'ang Po has changed his mind. He wants the American and the child brought to him alive."

Outside his office, Ogawa's young mistress inched back from the door and retreated on silent feet until she left the gallery. She went directly to the first phone booth she could find.

"Madam T'ang, I have news," she said as soon as Kuei-fei answered her call. She rapidly relayed what she had overheard, adding, "What can I do?"

"You must leave Akune Ogawa immediately. Do not bother to pack your things. Go to the airport, I will arrange to have a passport and plane ticket waiting for you."

The young woman gave a little cry and gripped the phone tighter. "I must leave him? So soon?"

"T'ang Po does not leave witnesses behind, child—he will send the assassin back to kill Akune, and you." Kuei-fei's voice hardened. "Do as I tell you. Leave now, right away."

The Chinese girl stepped out of the booth to hail a taxi, then spoke into the phone. "But what of your son, madam?"

"I will go and speak with the Frenchwoman. Go now, and the gods be with you, child."

"She claims she is your mother," Madelaine told Jian-Shan from Paris. "I have her waiting in my office now."

"My mother died when I was a year old," he said, and looked up to see Shikoro enter the computer room with an express envelope in her hands.

"Take her name, address, and phone number, but tell her nothing."

The express envelope contained a series of photos from Akune Ogawa, a dealer in Paris who had recently joined the *zaibatsu*. He went through them slowly, occasionally using a magnifying glass to examine some details. Only when the scent of roses and ginger reached his nose did he look up.

"Good morning." Val came to his desk, then saw the photo in his hands and moved around to stand beside him. "What's this?"

"The dealer thinks it is a late Nagatoki." He handed her the photo and sat back in his chair. "What is your opinion?"

"I'm not sure." She held the photograph up to the sunlight streaming through the window. Then she went still. "I have to see this blade."

"Why this particular blade? You have twenty swords here you haven't examined yet."

"There's a phoenix design on the scabbard and the hilt." She handed the photo back to him. "This is it. This is the one I needed to find."

He placed it back in the envelope. "You've spoken of the phoenix before—what significance does it have to you?"

She avoided his gaze. "You won't believe me."

"You assume I will not." He gestured to the chair beside his desk. "How did you say it? Try me."

Carefully she sat down and took a deep breath. "Okay. This is the sword that will prove that Nagatoki had help forging the blades later on in his lifetime. According to a journal I have, he began to lose his sight, probably to glaucoma, when he was still a young man. At the time, his only child—a son—was still an infant. Before he went blind, he passed along his knowledge to the one person who could continue making swords in his place, and eventually teach his son the skills he himself had learned from his father."

"And you know who this person was?"

"Yes." Her dark eyes met his. "It was his wife, lady Nagatoki Kameko. The journal is hers."

Disbelief held him in silence as he contemplated what would directly contradict more than a thousand years of research and study.

A woman sword maker. It cannot be possible.

He rose from the desk and went to the window as he considered how to respond to her provocative statement. "I don't have to inform you that women of that era were forbidden to make weapons, particularly swords. You would already know this from your studies."

"Jian, I didn't invent this. It really happened." Her voice remained quiet and steady. "Lady Kameko wrote in her journal that she had personally forged over half of the swords her husband made—always to his specifications, with his methods. The only difference was that unbeknownst to her husband, she signed the blade differently."

"The samurai would have never accepted a blade signed by a woman," he said. Val was utterly convinced by her own outrageous theory. "Besides, I have already examined the tangs of all the Nagatoki swords in my collection. The signatures are identical."

"Did you notice the extra notches just below the *hamachi*, above the Nagatoki signature on the tang?"

He felt her just behind him and resisted the need to turn and touch her. "Yes, I saw them. They were random marks made during hilt binding, nothing more."

"No, you're wrong. They weren't random. Lady Kameko also made one sword she never told her husband about—the phoenix sword. When the notches from two other key sword tangs are lined up in a certain way against the phoenix sword, and the swords she made aligned with them, the notches all form the characters of her name." She brought him the photo from his desk. "I can prove everything I've told you. All I need is to see this blade, to make sure it's one of the key swords."

"I will look at it this evening, in Paris."

"It's in the country? That's wonderful." She put her hand on his arm. "Please, can I go with you? You don't know how long I've waited to find this sword."

He would not put himself through the torture of spending several hours alone with her in a car. They would never make it to Paris. "It is best that you stay here."

Hope faded from her expression. "You don't believe me, do you?"

"Valence, Japanese women were prohibited from even entering the sword maker's forge rooms. If, as you say, Nagatoki employed an assistant, he would have chosen a male relative. Not his wife."

"I have been studying these blades for ten years, *cher*, and I'm telling you, she made them." She made a frustrated sound. "Okay, you don't have to believe me. Just let me examine and photograph it."

"If it is a Nagatoki, I will consider purchasing it."

"You'll *consider*?" She threw out her hands. "Jian, I don't care whether you buy it or not. All I have to do is see it, photograph it."

"Akune is an old-fashioned man. He would not allow a woman to touch a sword worth a million francs." Jian-Shan knew he would if he was ordered to, but that was beside the point. "I am not jeopardizing an important acquisition by offending the man."

"Fine. Then you can handle the sword. Let me take two of your Nagatoki and go with you. You can tell the dealer I'm there to photograph it, that I won't touch it—whatever it takes to let me see it personally."

The fact that she cared more about a sword than about him enraged him. "I do not believe it would be wise at this moment to offer me whatever I want."

"If that's what it comes down to, *cher*." She took a deep breath. "But let's make it fair: if I prove I'm right, you agree to lend my museum the collection for the fall exhibition."

Her wager amused him. "And if you discover that your theory is incorrect?"

"Then I'll look like a complete fool and I'll also be out of a job. I can stay here as long as you want me to." She looked at the floor. "You still want me, don't you?"

"Oh, yes," he said as he went to her and buried his hands in her hair. Resisting her nearness was one thing, listening to her offer herself to him was another. "That is what I want."

"Then we have a deal." She stepped out of reach. "You'll take me with you to Paris?"

"No. I will go to Paris and bring the blade back to you."

Chapter 11

The drive to Paris gave Jian-Shan a chance to think about Val's shocking revelation and even more provocative offer.

You still want me, don't you?

There was nothing he wanted more. The constant ache of desire for his unwilling guest had been a nuisance at first, interfering with his practice and his preparations to deal with his father. Now that he no longer had to contend with T'ang Po, it should have been simple.

Sex had always been an uncomplicated business for him in the past—there were any number of willing women within the White Tiger *zaibatsu* eager to share his bed. Since Karen's death, he had chosen the few who had not expected more than sex and enjoyed them.

It would have been a great deal more convenient if Valence St. Charles had been like them.

I'm not having sex with you to get the collection.

What she didn't realize was that she could have had almost anything from him. From the moment he saw his mark on her neck, the need to put his hands on her and strip away the lace and silk covering her sensitive skin had been the only thought in his mind. The way she had looked at him, with her dark eyes wide and questioning, had driven him past all restraint.

He would have her, and there would be no more tension between them. He could sense the strong emotions inside her—she likely thought herself in love with him already. One only had to consider how she'd used their confrontation to offer herself to him. He had no such romantic illusions, but he also had no intention of refusing what she wanted to give him. He would be indulging her, not taking advantage of her.

I feel it.

There was no question of him loving her—not after what had happened with Karen. What she stirred inside him came from physical hunger for her, nothing more. She was beautiful, soft and warm under his hands, and unlike any woman he'd ever known. Rarities had always fascinated him. Why should she be any different?

What if she is right about the Nagatoki?

Her theory was beyond ludicrous, of course. In all the centuries of Japanese sword making, no woman had ever been taught or allowed to practice the craft. Many had been routinely punished for daring to cross the threshold of a forge room. There were tales of some extremely conservative samurai who refused to touch a sword after it had been used to kill a woman, claiming the feminine spirit polluted the soul of the blade.

Yet there was just enough detail to her theory to make him uneasy: The journal, written by Naga-

toki's wife. The phoenix symbol, which he knew
from his own studies that Nagatoki had always
used in reference to the lady Kameko. Nagatoki's
blindness, at a time when his son was still an infant.

If Valence could prove that Kameko had herself
forged the blades, she would turn the world of
Asian antiquities upside down. And then she
would leave him and try to take his swords with
her. He knew he could no more keep his end of the
bargain than he could let go of her, or the swords.

Valence would have to lose her bet.

Akune Ogawa greeted him at the front entrance
to the gallery, which was closed for the evening.
"T'ang-san! I am thrilled to have you enter my
humble establishment. Come, we will have a drink
in my office."

He accepted a small cup of sake and sat down as
Akune extolled the virtues of his latest acquisition.
"From whom did you obtain it?" he asked when
the other man paused for breath.

"An estate sale. The previous owner was a member of the Kyoto aristocracy, a noble with connections to the emperor's family." Akune beamed and
refilled his own cup. "It is a rare blade, with many
unusual characteristics. I think you will be proud to
add it to your collection."

"Perhaps." Jian-Shan knew that revealing his desire to see the blade would only drive up the
dealer's price. "I have many rare and unusual
blades."

"But none so fine as this, nor with such unusual
markings."

He thought of what Valence had told him. "Markings?"

"There are a series of distinctive notches running down the entire length of the blade. Records of kills with a previous sword, I believe." The other man chortled. "Perhaps an accounting by some samurai to the Shinto gods for his deeds on earth."

Jian-Shan nodded, and allowed Akune to continue praising his acquisition until he glanced deliberately at his watch. Immediately the other man rose from behind his desk.

"Come, I will no longer fill your ears with descriptions of its beauty. You shall see it for yourself."

Akune had arranged the components of the blade against black velvet on an open display pedestal, with two track spots directed to shed the most attractive light on the objects. For a moment Jian-Shan circled around the pedestal, taking in the blade and its scabbard from all angles. It burned like a sliver of fire.

Like Valence burns.

"I tested the inlay on the scabbard and the hilt. It is a gold-copper alloy." Akune stood back and watched him. "The relief work is exquisite. Particularly the pearl eyes and the coral in the phoenix's flaming tail."

He bent to look down the back of the blade. The lines and curls running down the length had been added prior to the final firing and polishing. "How many kill notches?"

"Thirty-nine distinctive marks. But they do not detract from the weapon at all. Here, you must hold it yourself, so you may feel the perfect balance." He picked up the sword and presented it to Jian-Shan with a shallow bow.

The weight of the blade was unexpected, perhaps because subconsciously he had expected a sword that had possibly been made by a woman to be inferior. The hilt fit his hand as if Nagatoki had measured his fingers and palm personally.

Or Nagatoki's wife.

Jian-Shan set the blade carefully back on the display. "It is unusual, but I have other decorative blades with much finer inlay work."

Akune's broad smile faltered. "Surely none are Nagatoki, or as unusually detailed as this. You will not find the like anywhere in the world, T'ang-san. It would become the showpiece of your collection."

"I appreciate the opportunity to view it. However, without verification, I am reluctant to make such an investment." He pretended to consider the matter, feeling Akune's tension increase by the moment. "I will take it to my expert, to have her examine the blade. If it is an authentic Nagatoki, I will meet your price." He would remove the sword, store it in his office vault, and ensure that Valence never saw the blade, and that way, she would never leave him.

"Your expert?" Akune echoed. "I don't know, T'ang-san—"

"Ms. St. Charles is an experienced metallurgist as well as an expert on the Nagatoki Period. I have her cataloguing my collection at the moment." He gave the man a cool look. "Of course, if you are unwilling to allow me to remove the blade from your premises—"

"No, not at all. Let me prepare it for you." Akune

glanced at his watch. "I could deliver it in the morning to your office."

"I am leaving early in the morning. It is best if I take it with me tonight to my hotel."

Akune's tension instantly evaporated. "Very good, T'ang-san."

A storm was brewing, but not like any Val had ever known. The sky had turned a hot, brassy blue, as clouds had been swept away toward the horizon. The wind, on the other hand, was getting worse.

When a man from the village stopped by to deliver fresh bread, he noticed her by the kitchen window, and nodded toward the wind whipping through the garden.

"*C'est le mistral, mademoiselle.*" When she looked at him, he touched a weathered, gnarled hand to his equally ancient cap. "*Si le vent se lève le vendredi, il va jusqu'à la messe du dimanche.*"

If the wind starts on Friday, it ends before mass on Sunday. She smiled; his Provençal accent reminded her of bayou Cajuns back home. "*C'est bon, merci, monsieur.*"

For the rest of the day, no matter what she did, Val couldn't stop thinking about the phoenix blade. Not when it promised to validate everything she'd been working for since discovering Lady Kameko's journal five years ago.

It has to be the one.

After dinner she volunteered to read Lily her bedtime story so Shikoro could drive down to the village to pick up some milk and eggs. She sat in the rocking chair holding the little girl for a long time after she fell asleep, then gently placed her in the new youth bed.

"I know I'm right, *bebe*. Your daddy's collection is going back with me to the States." Her heart constricted as she studied the child's face, so innocent and unguarded in her sleep. It was going to be hard to leave her. "Maybe I can even talk him into bringing you and coming to visit me sometime."

She left Lily's room and went down to the library to retrieve the photos and study them again. There she found Han working at Jian-Shan's desk, writing some figures in a ledger book. "Why are you working overtime tonight?"

"A little bookkeeping." He glanced up. "Did you need something?"

"There was an express envelope that came today with some photos of a sword from a dealer named Akune Ogawa. Did Jian leave it here? I'd like to look at them again." Han produced the envelope and handed it to her. "Thanks." She carried it over to one of the chairs and sat down.

There were twelve photos in all, evidently taken for insurance purposes, as they showed the blade being unpacked, measured, tested, tagged with an inventory number, and arranged for display.

"Has to be the one," she muttered to herself.

"I beg your pardon?"

She met Han's gaze and grimaced. "This sword—I wish I could see it. It's the one I need to finish some research for my book."

"You are writing a book?" Han seemed impressed. "On Nagatoki?"

She nodded. "Him and other sword makers. I've been working on it since I was in college."

"I had not thought you a book writer," he said.

Val shrugged. "I never thought of you as a book-keeper." She looked at the photos again, and noticed a Chinese man appeared in several of the photos—Akune Ogawa, she would assume—with two other men who appeared to be assistants of some kind. She was about to put the photos back in the envelope when one slipped out of her hand to the floor.

She bent to pick it up, then stopped in mid-motion. From the angle she was standing, the image of one man carrying the empty packing crate appeared different, as if he were turning away. "Han."

"Yes?"

"This is the man I saw. In the garden." The photo shook in her hand as she stared at it. "The one who threw the knife."

Han came over and took the photo from her. "Which one?"

She swallowed a surge of bile and pointed. "Him. The one with the crate. Same shape head, same bulge in the neck, and his right shoulder droops a little. It's the same man."

"He is not dressed like the other workmen." Han met her gaze. "You are certain of this."

"Yes." Sudden panic flooded her with adrenaline. "Oh, God, Jian's going there to see that blade. If that man is waiting for him—" She looked around, frantic. "Can we warn him somehow? Call the gallery? Maybe he hasn't arrived yet."

"The master always carries a cell phone with him." Han went back to the desk and picked up the phone. He listened, tapped the cradle, then slowly

put the receiver down. "This phone is not working."

"Kitchen." She ran. By the time Han caught up
with her, she was hanging up the phone in the
kitchen. "It's dead, too. Shikoro took the other car
to the village. She said she wouldn't be back for an
hour or two."

"Someone cut the lines." The bodyguard drew
his gun and checked the kitchen door.

That was when all the lights in the villa went out.
Val stifled a cry with her hand.

"You must get Lily. Take her out of the nursery
and hide with her," he told her. "I will follow and
cover you. Go, quickly!"

Finding where T'ang had stashed Fael's wife and
children took three phone calls, several thousand
francs in bribes, and more time than Raven had to
spare. Fortunately, Fael had many connections
among the Parisian Arab community, and once
Raven provided the location of the condemned ten-
ement where they were being held, he sent in his
own men to retrieve them.

"They are safe," Fael told her after receiving the
call from one of his innumerable family members.
He handed back her cell phone. "There were only
two men guarding them."

"T'ang assumed you wouldn't go after them."
Raven didn't bother to ask if the two were still
breathing. "You'll have to get them out of the country as soon as possible. Tell the rest of your rela-
tions to lay low for a while, too."

"Yes, I must." He sighed, then regarded the gun

in his hand before shoving it in his jacket pocket. "Thank you, Raven."

"You're welcome." Her fist clipped him across the jaw, snapping his head to the side. "And next time, ask without the gun. Get out of my car."

Fael rubbed his chin before he climbed out. "Always a pleasure working with you."

She drove at high speed back toward her apartment, where she had stashed the forged passports and tickets that Jian-Shan would need to leave the country. Yet when she tried to call him, he didn't answer his cell. She had to settle for leaving a message with his service, which she did in succinct terms.

"You tell him Daddy never went to jail, and knows where he is." She parked the Lotus in the alley behind her building and hurried up the back stairwell. "Tell him I'm on the way."

Once inside, she quickly retrieved her cache of forgeries and enough money to get Jian-Shan settled in London comfortably. As she was stuffing a duffle bag, one of her hall sensors beeped.

"Oh, sweetheart," Raven murmured as she watched Kalen and two of his operatives on the security camera, approaching her door. "You should call me before you bring friends home for dinner." She ran to the window.

Standing on a fire escape seven stories above the busy streets of Paris wasn't her idea of fun, but she didn't have time to play with Kalen. She leaned over to see that two of his men were standing at the base of the fire escape watching the front entrance to the building, totally oblivious to her.

General, you really need to hire better help.

Carefully she stepped off the iron ladder onto the ledge and used it to walk around to the other side of the building, looking down to see if Kalen had doubled on backup. And got her answer when she spotted the two large men standing directly under the east fire escape, watching the back entrance to the building. The Lotus was also gone.

There was literally no way out—no conventional way.

"Can't a girl get five minutes to powder her nose?" She sighed and stepped back onto the fire escape, but climbed up instead of down. The rattling of the metal alerted the watchers below, and extra weight suddenly jerked the rungs beneath her hands and feet. "Guess not."

She climbed quickly to the rooftop, swinging over the ornate facade and dropping to her feet. Sounds of footsteps pounding up behind her made her sprint for the other side of the building. Kalen and his duo burst out of the building stairwell just as she reached the edge.

"Raven! Hold it!"

"Not this time, darling." She shouldered her bag and blew him a kiss, then picked up a cable coiled neatly under a curve of the facade. One end she clipped to an eye hook she'd driven and cemented into the brick. The other she clipped to her waist.

Then Raven jumped off the building.

She'd had the bungee cord made to her exact length and weight-bearing specifications, of course, and had terrified a few neighbors testing it earlier that summer. It broke her fall with a jerk halfway down, then elongated slowly to allow her to land with ease on the pavement.

Can't leave without a little parting gift.

She took two seconds to clip the end to the handle of an overflowing garbage can, then released it. The can silently rose back up to the top of the building, where it landed with a terrific clatter of sound. As she ran down the street, she heard faint male cursing, and the sound of someone drop-kicking metal.

"Next time you'll call first, won't you?" She grinned as she wove in and out of the stream of tourists packing the sidewalks. When it was safe to emerge onto the street, she hailed a cab and directed the driver to take her along the Seine.

She made sure she wasn't being followed before she took out her cell phone and dialed it.

"T'ang," Jian-Shan answered.

"You've got problems," she said in Japanese. "The clipping Fael showed you was a fake. Your father knows where you are." She filled him in on the rest as quickly as possible.

"He must have been waiting for the right opportunity."

Raven watched the driver give her a curious glance in the rearview mirror, and smiled at him. "Don't leave the villa. I'm en route to you."

"I'm in Paris."

She swore in English, startling the cabbie. "Are the Nagatoki there?"

"Yes."

"Kalen just raided my place, so I need time to get mobile." Raven checked her watch, then her location. "I'll meet you at the villa in two hours. Watch your back." She ended the call, then leaned over the front seat and switched back to French. "You know, I think I'd rather go see Madame Gourdan's. Take me to rue Saint-Sauveur."

"La Gourdan's?" The driver made a comical face. "If you say so, mademoiselle."

La Gourdan had once been the finest brothel in Paris, offering its notorious services to only the wealthiest of courtiers and merchants of the time. The discreet corner house it occupied on Saint-Sauveur had not changed a great deal in three hundred years. Raven paid the cabbie, then slipped into the building. From the first-floor changing room where clients had once masked and cloaked themselves to hide their identities, she entered a passage hidden in a cupboard and emerged in a former antique shop two doors down.

The men working on forging new automobile registrations looked up at her unexpected entrance, then put their guns away. She was no threat to their thriving enterprise—in fact, Raven was one of their best clients.

"Hello, boys," she said as she brushed off some cobwebs. "I need some fast wheels. What have you got in stock?"

On the other side of the city, Jian-Shan replaced his phone in his breast pocket and noted the trickle of sweat that inched down the side of Akune's face.

The dealer discreetly blotted it away with his jacket sleeve while pretending to smooth his hair. "All is well, I hope?"

"No." He placed the phone in his breast pocket and regarded the sword again, seeing it differently. "How much money did my father promise you?"

"I do not understand, T'ang-san." Akune produced a reasonable facsimile of confusion. "I have never had the honor of meeting the man myself."

"You wouldn't be alive if you had." He picked up the phoenix blade and held the tip in front of the dealer's nose. "He wouldn't have you kill me; you'd probably bungle that, too. Were you to lure me here to get me away from the house?"

The terrified man's eyes crossed as he looked down at the razor-sharp blade and swallowed. "T'ang-san, I assure you, I do not know what you are talking about."

"Tell me the truth."

The dealer jumped back and shoved the pedestal forward into Jian-Shan. By the time he righted it, Akune had vanished.

He took the sword and searched through the back of the gallery, only to open an outer door and see the dealer in his sedan, speeding off down the alley outside.

There was no time to pursue him. Jian-Shan dialed the number to the villa, but all it did was ring—as if the lines had been cut.

Valence and Lily.

It seemed to take forever, but Jian-Shan made the trip back to Provence in half the time it had taken him to reach Paris. The lack of light from the windows forced him to abandon the car a few hundred yards from the villa. Before he left it, he armed himself with the phoenix blade he had taken from Ogawa's gallery.

They're still alive. Han will protect them.

He saw the body on the ground beside Raven's estate car first, and hurried over to find Shikoro, unconscious but breathing steadily. He left her and went around to the library windows, which were still open to the night air. With a jump he caught the edge of the windowsill and boosted himself up and into the room.

At the sounds of a struggle just outside the room on the stairs he silently exchanged the antique sword for a short dagger and one of his practice katanas. He kept to the shadows as he drifted around the door and approached the stairwell.

Han and a shorter man were wrestling with something between them. A gun went off, and his bodyguard stiffened, then fell over and tumbled down the stairs. The other figure immediately turned and started up toward the second floor, then paused and looked over his shoulder.

By then Jian-Shan was standing three steps below him. "Were you looking for me?"

The assassin lifted the gun to fire it, then squealed with pain as Jian-Shan's dagger pierced his wrist and pinned it to the wall. *"Fils de pute!"*

"That is for Valence." The gun fell to the stair, and he kicked it away. "Does my father pay you a great deal of money? You're not worth that much."

"Neither is your aim," the killer said as he yanked the dagger out of his arm. "He'll have to take you dead."

The assassin launched himself at him, hacking and slashing with the bloody dagger. Jian-Shan stepped down and under the blade, bringing his katana up in a swift, tight curve that sliced open the killer's other forearm. "Where is my father?"

"Vas te faire enculé." The assassin lunged, then came up short and choked. His eyes bulged as he

looked down at the blade buried in his abdomen. "No . . ."

Jian-Shan stepped up and took the dagger from the killer's nerveless fingers. "He'll pay you in hell." He withdrew the blade and watched the dying man sag and crumple over, then went back down to where Han lay.

His bodyguard stirred and blinked as he checked him. "Master . . . Shikoro . . . Valence . . . in Lily's . . . room . . ."

"Be quiet, brother. Your wife is alive. Let me see this wound. The shot went through your side." Jian-Shan stripped off his jacket and folded it over the injury site. "Can you press this down?"

"*Hai.*"

"Don't move. I'm going to up to get them, and then I'll be back."

He found the nursery empty, as well as Val's room. After a rapid search of the entire second and third floors proved futile, he started back down the stairs. Then he heard something thump over his head, and stopped.

"Valence?"

He ran into the nursery and flung open the window to the roof. A shadow moved above his head, and he leaned out.

She was huddled on the peak of the window gable, ten feet above him, with Lily bundled in a blanket cradled in one arm, and a *wazitashi* blade in her uninjured hand.

As she saw him, Valence extended the short sword and scrambled backward. "No! You stay away from her!"

"Wait." He tossed the sword back inside, then

eased out onto the roof. "It's all right now. You're safe. Give me the child."

She was already trying to climb over to the next roof flat. "I won't let you hurt her, God damn it, get away from us!"

He knew then she couldn't see his face, and spoke in a calm, clear voice. "It's me, Valence. Jian-Shan. I'm not going to hurt you."

"Jian?" Val hesitated, then nearly slipped and grabbed Lily even tighter. "Oh, God, where have you been? There's someone in the house—he has a gun, there were shots—Han—"

"The man is dead, and Han is only wounded." Quickly he hoisted himself up on the peak and held out his hands. "Don't be afraid. I'm here. Come back to me, slowly."

"You're sure there's no one else?"

"Yes." He was lying to her; he had no idea if the assassin had come alone or with accomplices. It didn't matter. He'd killed one, he would kill the others if he had to, but he wasn't going to leave her and Lily out here in the open. "Come to me now."

She moved cautiously back to the peak, then rubbed her cheek against the blanketed bundle. "Take Lily inside first." She waited until he dropped back down and into the nursery, then lowered the child into his arms.

Lily stared at him with drowsy, confused eyes as he placed her on her bed. "Da?"

"Go back to sleep, child," he murmured, and went to the window. Val was already lowering herself over the sill, and he caught her by the waist and lifted her in the rest of the way. "Are you hurt?"

"No," she said, then looked down at the sword in her hand and handed it to him. "I borrowed this."

He propped it against the wall. "You were very brave."

"No, I wasn't. I was so scared." Tears spilled down her face. "I didn't know what else to do, and I thought when I heard the gunshots . . ." She trailed off and covered her face with her hands.

Hearing her weep made him take her into his arms. "You did exactly right. This is the second time you've risked your life to protect what is mine." He stroked her hair. "I think I shall have to let Han go and have you guard me from now on."

She made a low, choked sound and shook her head, rubbing her brow against his chest.

He tipped her face up. "Don't cry, *xia*. It is over." He kissed her brow. "I do not wish to leave you like this, but I must see to Han and Shikoro now."

"Shikoro?" She gave him a stricken look. "Did he hurt her too?"

"I believe she is all right, just knocked unconscious." He held her for a moment longer, then set her at arm's length. "Stay here with Lily and wait for me."

Val sank down into the rocking chair as soon as Jian left them, and tried to regain some control. Her stomach had become a clenched fist that wanted to surge up into her throat, and she couldn't stop crying. As the silence stretched out, she began to shake.

She'd been so convinced they were going to die, the moment she heard the first gunshot ring out on

the stairs. Han had shouted at her to run and returned fire, and she'd sprinted the rest of the way
to the nursery, stopping only to wrench the sword
from one of the wall displays, then snatching Lily
out of bed, blanket and all.

Where do I go? Where can I hide her?

Climbing out the window with the baby hadn't
taken courage. She'd been frightened out of her
mind; that was what had forced her out onto the
roof. Not even the day in the garden had terrified
her as much. As she sat out on the roof, holding the
child and the sword, ready to kill the first thing
that came near her baby, she realized why.

She should have been my child. Our child.

That was when the calm had settled over her,
enough to keep her from screaming every time she
heard a gunshot, enough to keep her hand firmly
on the hilt of the short sword. She loved the child
in her arms. She loved Jian-Shan. She would fight
whoever tried to hurt his baby.

Now the calm mask finished cracking to pieces,
and Val could stifle her sobs only by pressing one
fist against her mouth. She had fallen in love with a
man who could never love her back.

How can I stay? Mon Dieu, how can I leave him?

The muffled sound of her weeping made Lily
stir, and the little girl yawned and sat up. "Da?"

"No." Val quickly wiped her face on her sleeve
and went to the child. "It's me, *cher.* I'm here with
you."

The child blinked up at her. "Owie?"

Val's lips trembled, and all she could do was
nod.

"Tiss?" The little girl climbed out of the blanket

and into Val's arms, and bestowed two noisy kisses, one on each of her wet cheeks. "Beh?"

Nothing would ever be better. Not now, not when she left them to go back to the States. Never again in her life.

"Yes, *bebe*, I feel much better now." She pressed her lips to the blond curls on top of the small head and held her against her heart. "Thank you."

She allowed herself the cruel luxury of sitting down in the chair again holding Lily, rocking her back to sleep. As she hummed an old lullaby, she blinked away the last of her tears.

I've been through worse, and survived. I'll get through this. I'll start over. I'm good at that.

To Lily, she whispered, "I wish I could have been your mama, *chaton*. I think I would have been a good mama to you."

"Mama," Lily muttered, as if in agreement.

She wasn't aware of how much time passed, but Lily sighed and snuggled against her, and she must have dozed. A gentle hand stroked her cheek, making her jerk upright and snap open her eyes to see a decidedly weary Jian-Shan standing over her. The movement disturbed Lily, who grumbled and burrowed closer to Val.

"Han and Shikoro?" she asked him at once.

"Shikoro has a headache but will be fine. So will Han, in time. Dr. Toyotomi is with him now."

She slumped back against the chair and pressed a hand over her eyes. "Thank God."

Lily opened her eyes and yawned, then spotted her father. "Da?"

"Come, Lily." He held out his hand to her. "We will go have your breakfast. Valence needs to get some rest."

His daughter pouted and clung to Val. "Wan mama."

The little girl's demand seemed to hang in the air between them, and Val's heart sank as she saw his gaze grow cold.

"No, *bebe*. I am not your mama. Go with your daddy now." She handed the small, resistant body over to Jian and hurried out of the nursery.

Akune Ogawa had not dared return to his own gallery, for fear of finding T'ang Jian-Shan or members of the White Tiger *zaibatsu* waiting for him. He drove around Paris until dawn, then risked stopping at a phone booth to contact T'ang Po.

"Forgive me for not calling sooner," the dealer said after he related the incident with Jian-Shan. "Your son's rage was all-encompassing, and he is a powerful man. I dare not return to my home or business, in fear for my life."

"There is no need to be concerned, Akune-san," T'ang said in a soothing way. "These things occasionally happen, and I will deal with it. Now you must come to me, before Jian-Shan finds you. Can you come to rue Dussoubs?"

"Yes." Akune scribbled down the address and directions T'ang Po gave him. "Left into rue du Caire, left again into rue des Forges. Place du Hannibal. Thank you, Master T'ang. I will be there within the hour."

It seemed appropriate that T'ang Po's sanctuary had been set up in the Cour des Miracles, a former crime district notorious for offering refuge to every kind of criminal, from pickpockets to cutthroats. The narrow streets were particularly ideal for hasty disappearances into the shadows. The quarter had been restored to its former exotic atmosphere, with its street names commemorating Napoleon's many Egyptian campaigns—rue d'Aboukir, d'Alexandrie, du Caire, du Nil. Imitation Egyptian sculptures even lined the Place du Caire, adjacent the old Cour des Miracles.

Place du Hannibal was identified only by a small brass street plaque, and keeping to T'ang's instructions, Akune parked in the back lot and went to the side door.

A beautiful Japanese woman in a full formal kimono met him with a bow. "Please to come in."

Akune straightened his tie and followed the mincing steps of the woman through a dark corridor, to a large room filled with crates, guns, and a dozen Chinese men dressed in casual tourist clothes. The man standing in the center of the room was polishing a black sword that made the dealer's eyes bulge.

"That is the night dragon," he blurted out, then flushed as the man holding the weapon turned, Swiftly Akune bowed. "Excuse me, Master T'ang. I had thought the dragon blade but a legend."

"You thought the phoenix blade was a legend." T'ang Po tossed the polishing cloth to one of the mercenaries. "And now you have allowed my son to steal that from me as well."

"I would have taken it from him, master, but he meant to kill me with it." Sweat had dampened his goatee, and he wiped his sleeve over his mouth. "Your son is an expert swordsman; there was nothing I could do."

"I know what my son is." T'ang tested the balance of the blade by swinging it a few times back and forth. "Who do you think trained him, Ogawa?"

Akune smiled and bowed. "I should have known."

"Yes, you should have." With a negligent thrust, T'ang Po drove the sword blade into the dealer's upper left arm, jerking it out before the man could scream. "You should have known not to reveal your connection with me," he said over the noise, and thrust again, this time into the right upper arm.

Akune dropped to his knees howling, his arms completely useless. "T'ang-san, I beg you—"

"You should have known what I do to those who fail me," T'ang said as he brought the blade down, cutting off Akune's right ear before he finished the stroke and did the same to his arm. "You should have known much, much more, Ogawa."

It would have taken Akune Ogawa another two minutes to bleed to death, if T'ang Po had skipped the final stroke. Normally he would have toyed more with the dealer, but his rage needed an outlet.

The last cry from the mutilated man echoed around the room, abruptly cut short when Akune's decapitated head rolled off his shoulders onto the floor.

Chapter 12

Val gave up trying to sleep and paced around her room until Shikoro brought her a tray. "Are you all right?"

"Bump on head hurt." The housekeeper made a face as she set down the tray. "You should eat, *Oku-san*."

Val stared at the food before she shook her head. "No. He's not going to give me another time-out."

"What is 'time-out'?" Shikoro called after her as she stalked out of the bedroom.

Jian-Shan met her at the foot of the stairs. "You should be resting."

"I've rested enough. Is Han going to be okay?" At his nod, she let out a breath. "All right. I've calmed down. I'm not going to fall to pieces. Who was that man who broke in last night?"

"A fool." He regarded her with eyes empty of all emotion. "He's dead."

"Shikoro mentioned that." She pressed her fingers against her tired eyes for a moment, then dropped her hand. "I don't have to know where the body is. I don't even have to know *who* he is.

He came here to kill us. All I want to know is why."

"He intended to take the swords."

"That's it? That's the whole reason he cut the phones, and the power, and knocked Shikoro out, and shot Han? For your collection."

He folded his arms. "We have had this conversation before, Valence."

"I'm leaving." She turned to head back up the stairs.

"I've decided to lend your museum my collection."

She nearly fell down the stairs. "What?"

"You heard me."

She'd heard him, but could she believe him? "That's wonderful—I mean, I don't know what to say."

"Under the circumstances, it is best that we relocate the collection immediately. We will be leaving for the United States tonight." He glanced at his watch. "That gives you three hours to pack. Do you need any assistance?"

"No." A sense of wary jubilation settled over her. "Was I right about the sword?" At his blank look, she added, "The phoenix sword."

"I do not know." He didn't sound as if he really cared, either. "I am taking it with us, so you can explore your theory further. After we arrive in New Orleans."

"We're going out to eat first, right?" a woman asked as she walked in the front door. "I'm getting a real craving for some red beans and rice."

Val slowly came down the stairs as the impossibly tall, ridiculously beautiful woman walked in and gave Jian-Shan a casual, one-armed hug.

If she doesn't get her hands off him in ten seconds, I'll tear her moussed hair out by the roots.

Then the vision turned and offered a long-fingered hand to Val. "I'm Raven. Tell me you recognize me or I'll cry."

"Your covers have made me go on at least three diets." Val squelched the vicious urge to wrench the model's other arm away from Jian-Shan's waist. "I'm Valence. You have a lovely home."

"It cost me enough." Raven looked around as if she'd dropped something on the floor. "So where's my favorite blond midget?"

"Ben, ben!" Lily was already trying to fall down the stairs to get to them. Shikoro stooped down, swung her up and carried her the rest of the way, then deposited her in Raven's arms.

"Hey, chickie." The model ignored her immaculate outfit and Lily's damp hands as she whirled the little girl around. "Still can't fly by yourself yet, huh?" Lily giggled and flung her arms around Raven's neck. "Well, we're going on a big airplane all the way across the ocean. How about that?"

"Ben," Lily told Val as she patted the model's face and smeared Raven's glossy lipstick in streaks down her chin in the process.

The beautiful woman only wiped the cosmetic off on the sleeve of her expensive blouse and laughed. "I keep telling you, kid, my name's not Ben." When Lily reached for Val, Raven lifted her brows. "Oh, so I'm not your favorite personal slave anymore, is that how it is?" She handed her over to

Val, then gave Jian-Shan an amused glance. "Usurped in my own villa."

"Mama," the little girl said, resting her head against Val's shoulder.

A funny little silence fell over them. Raven gave Val a wicked smile. Val opened her mouth, then closed it. Shikoro reached for Lily, then dropped her hands. All three women turned to look at Jian-Shan.

"Excuse me. I have business to attend to." He walked off.

"Ho. Kay." Raven's perfectly shaped brows rose. "This is really getting interesting."

"Shikoro, would you mind?" Val handed the little girl to the housekeeper. "I have to get her to stop calling me that."

"Why? She doesn't have one, you know. And much as I love the little rug rat, I'm sure not going to adopt her." Raven tucked a friendly arm through Val's. "Come on, let's go mess up the kitchen and make Shikoro drink tea with us. We can watch the kid smear herself with lunch."

It all seemed like a dream, Val thought twelve hours later as their private jet flew over the Atlantic Ocean toward New Orleans. Yet it wasn't. She had the collection, and Jian Shan, and Lily. Han and Shikoro had even come with them.

Don't forget about the supermodel.

She glanced at the brunette sitting beside Jian-Shan. As if anyone could overlook someone wearing a leopard-patterned jumpsuit that looked as if it was her own natural pelt.

You can't be jealous of someone you like so much.

Oddly enough, she and Raven had hit it off. Maybe it was the model's genuine affection for Lily, or the breezy charm she used on every person who came within a three-foot radius. She was like a long, lean feline, draping herself over the nearest convenient surface, smiling at the world while keeping all of its secrets.

Val noticed the model didn't hang on Jian-Shan, but it was obvious from their conversational shorthand and the looks they exchanged that they were close. Possibly lovers. It made sense—Raven didn't seem like the type to fall in love.

Which means I'm out of the picture.

Val sat back and closed her eyes, willing herself not to feel anything but relief. She had the collection. She had the key blade. The last twenty-four hours might have been the most harrowing of her life, but her job was done. Soon she'd be back in her own territory, and there was no place she worked better or felt more at home.

It'll be easier to let him go there.

Since Lily was napping in the back compartment with Shikoro, Val got up to check on Han. The steward had rearranged three sets of seats to make a comfortable space for the big man, who was still pale and weak from his ordeal.

"Hey." She knelt down beside him. "Can I get you something?"

He shook his head. "Dr. Toyotomi gave me a shot for the pain." He grimaced. "It makes me feel somewhat drunk."

"I remember that shot." She adjusted the blanket over him and tucked it in. "You stay put, or you'll fall on your face."

"Indeed, I think I might." He squinted down the row of seats at Jian-Shan and Raven. "How is he?"

"Quiet and a little grim, though I think he's happy Raven came with us." She tried to sound nonchalant. "Maybe she can get him to relax a little while you're in town."

"We will not stay long, I think." Han shifted his weight and winced. "Dr. Toyotomi assured me this would heal quickly. I hope he is right."

"Why can't you stay?"

"We have never been able to stay very long in any country. Not since we left China, before Lily was born." He blinked a few times. "They would kill us all."

A cold hand seized her heart. "*Dieu*, Han, this has happened before?"

"Are you flirting with my other boyfriend again, Val?" Raven appeared beside her. "How are you doing down there, big guy?"

The sober, serious Han gave her a sleepy smile. "I am drugged."

"So enjoy it." As the bodyguard's eyes closed, Raven touched Val's shoulder. "Would you mind helping me figure out if there's any real food tucked away on this flying yacht? I'm hopeless in the kitchen, and the steward's on his break."

"Sure." She followed the leggy model back to the small section used as a galley, and located an amply stocked little refrigerator near the floor. "What kind of yogurt do you like?"

"The kind that's made out of pure chocolate and butter, if there is such an animal."

Val couldn't help the chuckle. "Best they offer is

this, which is imported, fat free, and has"—she frowned as she read the label—"plums in it."

"Ick." Raven bent down and opened another cabinet, and rummaged alongside her. "You hungry? I noticed you didn't eat much lunch before."

"I'm just excited about going home." And completing her research. And showing Scribner she was worth the slave wages she earned for a little bit longer—just until she found a publisher for her book. And if she worked very, very hard, she might just be able to put the pieces of her heart back together. "Do you think Jian-Shan wants something?"

"No. He's in his stoic samurai warrior mode." The scarlet lips curled on one side. "Listen, Val, while we've got a little privacy going here, I need to talk to you about something."

She's going to tell me that they're lovers, and I should get lost as soon as we touch down. "Okay."

"I'm not going to be able to hang around much while Jay and the midget are in town," Raven said instead, stunning her. "I'm usually busy setting up photo shoots and having some part of my body waxed." She rolled her eyes. "I'd rather Jay and the family not be stuck in a hotel for the duration, so I've rented a house for them in the Garden District."

Val nodded. "Good idea. They'll be more comfortable in a real house anyway." "Exactly. So, I was hoping you could, you know, kind of stick around for the first week or two. At the house, with Jay. Seeing the way Han is, Shikoro's going to have her hands full with him. Jay's going to need help with Lily." She took the yogurt Val was holding, popped it open, and tasted it. "Ack, this tastes like creamed prunes."

Raven doesn't want to baby-sit. Makes sense. "Actually, I think that's what plums become. Prunes, I mean."

"We'll just skip the whole experience, then." The model tossed the container into the disposal bin. "So, will you do it?" When Val nodded, she grinned. "You're a peach. Thanks."

Raven's driver picked them up at the airport and whisked them away to the city, where they arrived at the luxurious home Raven had obtained for Jian-Shan. In the very heart of the Garden District, the Victorian mansion had sizable grounds tucked away behind an eight-foot privacy fence, and was located within blocks of the homes of a famous horror author and a notorious rock star.

"So the vamp writer really lives there?" Raven asked as they drove past the author's home.

"She was born here." Val checked her watch. The museum had already closed, so she would have to call Scribner in the morning. "There's a shop nearby that caters to her fans. They have everything from signed books to coffee mugs."

"I'll have to pick up a T-shirt and some plastic fangs later." Raven directed the driver to pull up through the open gate and got out to meet the waiting real estate agent. She ducked in to toss Jian-Shan the keys. "Everything's ready for you. I had the kitchen stocked. Call me if you need anything. Oh, and if a big redheaded guy in a green uniform with a lot of doodads on it shows up, I'm still in France." She bent over to give Lily a noisy kiss. "'Bye, midget. Val, take care of them for me."

By the time they'd climbed out of the car, Raven was gone.

Jian-Shan had never visited New Orleans before, and found the quiet charm of the Garden District appealing—until he spotted a dozen people standing outside the gates the next morning, taking photos of the house. With them was a tall young woman dressed completely in black, with bleached white hair that bounced around her pale face as she gestured and spoke to the group.

"They're on a walking tour," Val said from behind him, and he closed the blind. "Tourists come through here every day, partly to see the celebrities' houses."

He turned to see her place a file on the desk. "What else is there to see?"

"The cemeteries. The tombs are all elevated. You can't bury the dead in the ground here. The water table makes them pop back up." She picked up the phone. "I need to check in with the museum and let them know we're here. Then we should go over some details."

He thought of his father. "Tell them you are here. Alone."

Slowly she replaced the phone. "Something *is* going on that you're not telling me."

"I prefer to keep my presence here out of the papers." He checked his watch. "Perhaps you should wait to contact your employer. The collection is being transported separately, it will not clear customs until the end of the week."

"Okay." She sat down behind the desk. "It is coming, though, right?"

"I will keep my word."

"I believe you. All right, would you look at these for me?" She waved him over to the desk and spread out some brochures she hadn't had the chance to show him in Provence. "These are some of the brochures we've done for other exhibits. I need to know how you want to publicize the collection, so I can get started on the promotional material. I'd like to have them ready for our publicist to begin finalizing when the swords arrive."

He drew up a chair beside her, and together they worked on the project for the next hour. He kept his name out of the publicity materials, but otherwise let her compose the wording and arrange the design details.

"This is quite good," he said as he read the final draft. "You're an excellent writer."

"I know how to sell an idea." She seemed uncomfortable with his praise, and stuffed the brochures quickly back into the folder. "My apartment isn't far from here. I'm going to head over there now and pick up a few things I'll need."

"I'll send someone to collect what you need tomorrow." Before she could protest, Jian-Shan held up a hand. "Han is still quite weak, and I must meet Raven this afternoon."

She frowned. "You want me to baby-sit."

"If you don't mind helping Shikoro for a few hours, I would appreciate it." He wanted to go upstairs with her, to the opulent room he occupied, and take her on his bed. He settled for leaning closer and brushing a fiery curl back from her cheek. "Then, as it's my first night in New Orleans, I'd like you to have dinner with me."

"All right." Her lips curved into a reluctant smile. "As long as I get to pick the restaurant."

"I was counting on it." He didn't want to stop touching her, so he rested a hand on her shoulder. Knowing what would come in the next week made him wish they had met in another time and place. *Maybe we can pretend, for a few days.* "Do you know what I would really like to do tonight?"

She tore her gaze away from his mouth, and blinked. "I'm sorry, no. What?"

"I would like to start over, as if we had never met until today. Forget the past, and enjoy the present."

She lifted her injured hand. "That's going to be a little difficult, *cher*."

He curled his fingers around hers. "It's important to me. Do you think we could try?"

Val ducked her head. "Why do you want to start over with me?"

"I should have said, as we mean to go on." He cupped her chin and lifted her face. He despised having to lie to her, but he was determined to have this time. He had earned it. "We're safe now, and I want to know you better. This is your city, your home. Show me who you are, Valence."

For a long moment she didn't say anything. "Are you sure you really want to know?"

"More than I can tell you." That much, at least, was true. He caressed her cheek, then forced himself to stop touching her. "I should make some phone calls."

"I'd better go check on how Shikoro is coping with things." Val took the folder with her, then paused at the door and glanced back at him. "Do you like spicy food?"

He nodded.

This time her smile was brilliant. "Great."

When she left, he took out the new cell phone Raven had given him and dialed a number. "Where are you?"

"Checking out this museum," Raven said. "Huge place. About ten thousand things in it you can use to kill someone. It's right up your alley."

"And Paris?"

"Word is the general was none too happy to find out we'd left. He's probably in a room somewhere right now, reviewing customs security tapes." She paused. "Jay, even with the bribes, we've got maybe a week to do this."

"We have to wait for the swords."

"Screw the goddamn swords," Raven said in a lowered voice. "This is a public museum, Jay, with about twenty entrances and exits on the first floor. They've got a couple of overweight retired guys in security uniforms drinking coffee and watching college girls walk by. If your father comes in here with one of his kamikaze ninja squads—"

"He won't. Not for me."

She blew out a frustrated breath. "One day you're going to have to explain this whole honor among Chinese killers thing to me."

"I will." He checked his watch. "Is your man on the way to Miami?"

"Yeah. The swords will be flown in tonight. He'll be driving them here, so it'll take a few more days," she said. "I told him to stick to the speed limit and the back roads."

"Then we wait until they arrive."

A note of unease entered her voice as she said, "I

take it you want to be the one to contact your old man."

"Yes," he said. "I'll call my father and tell him to come and get them."

That afternoon Val showed Lily the delights of the yard and garden while Shikoro tended to Han. The housekeeper brought a tray of iced tea and cookies for them, but the little girl was too entranced by the swaying limbs of an enormous pink azalea to sit still for long.

"She like it here," Shikoro said. "This first time she see her motherland." She giggled. "First time I see, too."

Val insisted she sit down under the wide patio umbrella and poured her a glass of tea. "How is Han doing?"

"Better. Want get up. I tell him I give him pills in food, make him stay." She shook her head. "Shoot man, still not want stay in bed."

Val thought of the man she'd like to shoot, and sighed. "If he is able to get around later in the week, I'd like to show you both some of the city."

"Master need see city. You take him?"

She rose a little as she lost sight of Lily, then spotted her crouched down, examining a butterfly perched on a blade of grass. "We're going to dinner tonight."

"How you say, Val-san?" The housekeeper's round cheeks dimpled. "About time?"

They stayed out for another hour, until Lily was ready for her nap. As Shikoro put her down, Val went to shower and change. She knew exactly where she wanted to take Jian-Shan for his first taste of New Orleans, so she made a quick phone call to an old friend before she went downstairs.

Jian-Shan was waiting for her, dressed more casually than he had been in France, in a tailored gray shirt and black trousers. "Is this acceptable, or should I have a tie and jacket?"

"You're in New Orleans now, *cher*." She grinned. "All you need are shoes and an appetite."

He didn't call for a driver but allowed Val to drive a rental car delivered earlier that day. "I will drive back, so I can become more familiar with the streets."

"Streets aren't the problem," she said as she avoided a convertible filled with college students cruising down Duvalle Street. "The visitors are."

The streets abruptly narrowed as they entered the French Quarter, and Val took advantage of the slower-moving traffic to show him some of the landmarks.

"Jackson Square is the heart of the quarter, where most of the tourists accumulate day and night," she said, speaking louder to be heard over the zydeco spilling out from the open doorway of a half dozen bars. "They eat beignets in the park in the morning and stroll down the sidewalks drinking out of plastic cups at night."

Jian-Shan eyed a cluster of young men gesturing with half-filled cups of beer. "I trust you have other plans for us?"

"Oh, yeah, *cher*." She laughed and patted his arm. "I'm taking to you to my home away from home."

Tailor's Dance was hidden in the center of a street populated by antique shops and luncheon cafés, and only a blue neon sign shaped like a spool of thread marked the entrance. Val parked in a public lot opposite the restaurant, then stopped Jian-Shan.

"Here, wait." She reached up and unbuttoned his collar. "You'll be more comfortable," she said, and took his arm to lead him.

"What sort of restaurant is this?" he asked as he pulled one of the heavy steel doors open. A wave of music rolled out like a lazy caress.

"Not just a restaurant, but a jazz club, too." She tugged him inside.

The black maitre d' had on a beautiful tux and a poker face, which he promptly lost when he saw Val. "Valentine! Where you been, woman? Ain't seen you 'tall for weeks."

"I been back to the motherland, Antoine. Paris, France, and my oh my was it pretty over there." She stretched up on her toes to kiss the man's cheek. "This is my friend, Jian. Jian, this is Mr. Antoine Camille, owner of the Tailor's Dance and one of my best friends."

"Her *oldest* friend," Antoine said with a mock scowl. "Caught my little valentine here filching pralines out the kitchen one night, put her to work washing dishes."

"He knows all about my checkered past," Val said to Jian, and noticed the way he scanned the club. "Is this okay?"

He nodded toward the four-man quartet playing on the small stage. "Is the food as good as the music?"

"Better," Antoine told him. "C'mon, I take you

upstairs, get you a place you can see, hear, *and* talk."

The tables on the second floor were reserved for special guests, and Antoine gave them the best spot, right over the band.

"I'm bringing you champagne, 'less you want something else." The man's teeth flashed, very white against his dark skin. "Special tonight is crawfish tart and jumbled salad."

"Champagne would be lovely." When the man left, she reached out to stop Jian from opening his menu. "Let me order for us, please? I think I know what you'd like."

"Very well." He placed the menu back on the table. "You actually stole from that man's kitchen?"

She nodded, rested her chin on her hand, and gazed down at the quartet. "I was about thirteen back then, and Antoine really did make me stay and wash dishes half the night. Sat in the kitchen watching me do it and lecturing me about the evils of becoming a thief. He would have called child services, but I talked him out of it. Then he gave me a bag of pralines at the end of my shift and told me they'd be my fringe benefits."

"He gave you a job."

"Well, I was one hell of a dishwasher." She chuckled. "He did more than just give me work, though. That night he found me a place to stay for a while, until the social workers caught up with me. Then he tracked me down and came to my foster home to pick me up for work, every evening."

"Had to, or the lazy girl woulda never made nothing of herself." Antoine materialized and poured their champagne. "Running round with all those street kids, way you were back then. You needed an honest occupation, was all. Now, you know what y'all want?"

"The special sounds good—and two sides of Mama Camille's pâté to go with it, please," Val told him. "You got crème brûlée tonight?"

Antoine's white teeth flashed. "Does Mama have the prettiest legs this side of the Mississippi?"

Val laughed. "Two for dessert, then."

Jian-Shan remained quiet through their meal, making brief compliments on the food and otherwise listening to the music. He didn't seem relaxed, though, and it bothered her.

She wanted him to enjoy himself, but perhaps she'd misjudged him. Val knew the noisy, boisterous club would only get louder as the night went on. She was considering asking Antoine for the check with dessert when Jian reached across the table and took her hand.

"I like it very much here," he told her, reading her thoughts. "The food is astonishing, as is the music. Thank you for bringing me."

The band slipped into a slow, sexy blues rhythm that tugged at her, and Val found herself getting to her feet. "Dance with me?"

He led her downstairs, onto the dance floor in front of the stage. There he took her into his arms, and cradled her scarred hand in his hand, against his chest.

"I have not danced for many years," he admitted.

"This isn't really dancing," she said, looking up at him. "It's an excuse to get close to each other."

The quartet's music spun around them like the

other couples, in slow, deliberate circles, and Val found herself closing her eyes so she could pretend they were alone.

She'd danced with other men here, but never felt like this. Never so at ease, so enveloped by her partner. His warmth, the faint herbal scent of his skin, and the feel of his breath stirring her hair were as seductive as the notes spilling like fluid gold from the saxophone on stage.

"Couldn't you just spend the rest of your life here, dancing with me?" She gave him a dreamy smile. "Just you and me and Lily in one of those big old houses? Think of the garden we could make together."

"Valence." He caressed her cheek with his hand, then stopped dancing. "I have enjoyed spending this evening with you."

Her throat tightened at the bleak way he said that. "But?"

"We must talk." He led her off the dance floor and back to their table, where Antoine had their dessert and coffee waiting for them.

She tried to make light of it. "I can ask him to wrap it for us, if you want to go home now."

"Sit." Jian-Shan pulled out her chair, and brought his around to sit beside her. "Eat your crème brûlée."

She picked up her spoon. "I will if you eat yours."

He tasted it, then mainly toyed with it and watched her savor the decadent smoothness. "What are pralines, anyway?"

"Candy." She sipped her coffee and nodded at

his. "Drink some; you won't regret it. New Orleans has the best coffee in the world."

His eyes narrowed. "You're upset with me."

"I'm not, *cher.*" Her eyes strayed to the dance floor. She should have known he wouldn't like this loud, boisterous world of hers. They had come from entirely different cultures on opposite sides of the planet. "I've probably just gone a little too far with showing you who I am tonight."

He signaled a waiter and handed him a credit card. "Valence, I won't be staying in New Orleans for very long. A week at the most."

She pushed the crystal dish away, unable to finish, unable to bear listening to him explain why he couldn't stay, why they couldn't be together. "Would you excuse me for a moment?"

Inside the ladies' room, she washed her hands and stared at her pale reflection in the smoky mirror. She looked afraid, and felt worse. Jian-Shan wouldn't stay, and she couldn't go with him. The silly fantasies she'd been weaving about the two of them were crumbling into dust, just like the old marble tombs around the city.

The dinner had been a bad idea.

Jian-Shan paced the confines of his room, trying to rid himself of the memory of Valence, laughing at the table, moving in his arms, licking cream from her spoon. He had planned to convince her to come with him when he left New Orleans, and discuss the more practical matters of their future, before she became too entangled in her dreams of love and marriage. Then she had looked at him with

those exotic, trusting eyes that promised everything he wanted, and more.

Think of the garden we could make together.

That love, that open, blind trust of hers had driven him back like a whip.

"*Senpai.*" Shikoro opened his door and looked
around it. In rapid Japanese, she added, "Miss Valence just left the house. She walked down and out
of the gate, alone. I thought you should know."

He glanced at his watch—it was after two a.m.,
and she had no reason to leave—then he armed
himself. "Thank you, Shikoro."

"She said before she wanted to go and see a man
friend of hers," the housekeeper added as she followed him downstairs. "She did not look very
happy when you returned tonight."

"I know." Where would Val go? He realized how
little he did know about her, outside of the cold
facts in her dossier. "I made her unhappy."

He saw her at the end of the block outside, and
trailed her. She walked slowly, occasionally stopping to look at the lights of houses or to stare up at
the sky. Suspicion kept him back, in the shadows,
until she entered a gap in a low white wall. When
he followed, he found himself in one of the cemeteries she had described to him, filled with dozens
of white marble tombs.

*Why would she come to a graveyard in the middle of
the night?*

Not knowing made him decide to catch up to
her, and he found her standing in front of a square
tomb with a small angel statue sitting on its high
roof. "Valence?"

She jumped, then pressed a hand to her heart. "Oh, Jian. It's you."

Was she expecting someone else? "What are you doing here?"

"This was one of my favorite playgrounds. When things got bad, sometimes I'd run away and hide in there at night." She pointed to the broken slab at the front of the tomb. "I'm too big to crawl in now, though."

"Why would you sleep in a graveyard?"

"To be alone. To think. To pray, sometimes." She hugged herself with her arms. "I wasn't scared of ghosts, like other kids I knew. I'd already learned it was the live ones who were worse."

"So you came here to escape me tonight?"

"Escaping would mean you were chasing me, and we both know you're not." She turned to him. "You don't know how lucky you are, to have Lily and Shikoro and Han. When you leave, you'll take your family with you. I never had to worry about anyone when I left someplace."

"Family is not always a good thing," he said, thinking of his father. "I wish I had been born alone."

"Don't you ever say that!" Her eyes glittered, and she planted a hand on his chest to give him a shove. "God, you have no idea, do you? Do you know how I got my name?"

He shook his head.

"Come on. I'll show you."

She led him out of the cemetery and down the quiet streets until she reached a corner and stopped. "Here. This is where they found me, wrapped in a filthy blanket in a garbage can. I still had my umbilical cord attached, so apparently my own mother threw me away."

"I don't understand."

"Look at the signs."

He looked. One of the street markers read "Valence" and the other "St. Charles." "I didn't know this."

"So now you do." She sighed. "Jian, you have a daughter. You have friends. You have family. I have my job, and my book. That's all. Don't ever wish to be me. Every time someone says my name, it reminds me of this place. Of how little I was loved."

"You don't know your own good fortune." He seized her arms. "Do you know how many nights I prayed I could be an orphan? That Lily had never been born—"

She slapped him, hard. "How dare you say that! You're crazy. Crazy and blind to the love that's right in front of you, all around you."

"There is no love. No real love—only responsibility." Something tore inside him, and he yanked her close. "I have to keep them safe, keep them alive. That weighs on me every day of my life."

"And they love you for it!" she snapped. "I know why you're afraid to love your daughter. You're afraid of losing her, the way you lost Karen. Let go." She tried to break his grip, but he hauled her up against him and kissed her.

Fury pounded inside him as he controlled her struggles with one arm and gripped her by the hair with his free hand. The gasp of pain she made opened her lips and gave him free access to what he wanted.

And he wanted. Her mouth, her hands on him,

her body naked and trembling under him. For once in his life, he would have what he wanted.

She managed to turn her head away, ending the ferocious kiss. "Stop it," she said, her voice breaking.

"You need this as much as I do." He buried his mouth against her neck, nipping at the fragile skin. "Why not indulge yourself with me? Then you can have a genuine reason to hate me when I leave you."

She stopped struggling, and sagged against him. "I don't hate you, *cher*," she whispered, and shuddered. "Believe me, I wish I could."

He let go of the hair wrapped around his fist, and rested his brow against hers. "I would give you a thousand gardens, if they were in me to give."

Her hand touched his face. "Jian, please. Please don't shut me out. I don't understand what's happened to make you like this, and I want to. I want to know. I want to be a part of your life. Of you. Don't you see, *cher*? We can be strong together."

He could see the love shining in her eyes, and knew she meant every word.

Everything you touch dies.

"I have nothing left to give you." Abruptly he released her. "Go back to the house. Now."

Val left the house early the next morning, taking the rental car over to the museum to report in and escape proximity to Jian-Shan for a few hours. She still felt a sense of failure whenever she thought of how she had behaved, and what he'd said to her.

Who did this to him? Who hurt him so badly that he

couldn't trust himself to love again? Was it losing Karen? Is that why he's running from me?

When she stopped by Drake Scribner's office, his new assistant told her the head curator was in conference with a visiting dignitary.

"Some lady from Europe," the young redheaded graduate student said with a roll of her eyes. "I'll tell him you're back, though. Did you have a good time in Paris?"

"Yes, thank you." Val wrote a quick note and handed it to the girl, then hesitated by the desk. "Is he treating you all right?"

"He treats me like I'm an airhead. So does everyone else since I came here." The girl shrugged. "Could be worse."

Val caught a hint of despair. and made an impulsive decision. "Tell you what—I could really use some help with this new exhibit. If you're interested, come and see me, and we'll work something out."

"You mean that?" The girl sounded shocked. "Do something real for a change? But Mr. Scribner said you were, well . . ." She looked at Val's suit, then down at her own tight knitted top. "I mean . . . I thought you hated me."

"I don't hate you, and Scribner is a jerk." Val produced what she hoped was a convincing smile. "Think about it."

She dropped off the new promotional drafts to the museum's publicist, and then went on to the workrooms to arrange storage space and order what would be needed for the displays. She was at a desk filling out purchase orders when her boss found her.

"Well, now, Ms. St. Charles, it's about time you showed up." Ignoring the NO SMOKING signs, he lit one of his cigars. "You have yourself a good old time catting around Provence with that Chinaman?"

"I don't know what you mean," she said, pushing aside an order for additional display cases and rising to her feet. "I worked on cataloguing the White Tiger swords, and I convinced the owner to lend them to us."

"That's not how I heard it." Scribner cocked his head at the sound of tapping footsteps outside in the hall. "Here comes someone you might want to have a little chat with."

Madelaine Pierport entered the workroom, carrying a briefcase and looking every inch the important visiting dignitary. "Here you are, Drake." She spotted Valence and her expression turned to disgust. "Ah, mademoiselle, you have returned. I would have thought you wiser than that."

Val resisted an urge to throw a three-hundred-year-old bust of Lafayette at her. "This is where I work, Ms. Pierport. Why wouldn't I come back?"

"The Parisian authorities have been in contact with your local police." Jian-Shan's business manager sounded smug. "You are wanted for questioning in the murder of Akune Ogawa."

Val blinked. "What are you talking about?"

"His body was found outside his gallery, shortly after the theft of an important Nagatoki sword. Three witnesses say they saw you leave carrying a case. Your flight from Paris has earned you a temporary reprieve, nothing more." The Frenchwoman sniffed and turned to Scribner. "I cannot allow this woman to have anything to do with the collection, Drake. She is obviously not to be trusted."

"I'm the one who *arranged* for the loan of the swords," Val said, clenching her fists at her sides. "As for this other thing, I have no idea what you're talking about. I never met this Akune Ogawa person, and I certainly didn't kill him or steal any of his swords." She glanced at Scribner. "You're not going to listen to this nonsense, are you?"

"Now, Valence, I know you got mixed up with a bad sort over there, and I'm sure if you turn yourself in the police will take what you say with a bit more respect. However"—he leaned over to crush out the tip of his cigar on the sole of his shoe—"the museum can't have this kind of scandal. I'm afraid I'm going to have to let you go."

"You're firing me?" She gestured toward Madelaine. "All because she tells you some crazy story she probably made up?"

"She's not making it up." Scribner slapped a folded copy of a French newspaper on her desk. "That's your photo, Val. Right next to the one of the dead man." He patted her shoulder. "Best get along now, honey, and find yourself a good attorney. From the looks of this mess, you're sure going to need one."

Chapter 13

Raven missed Val by minutes, according to the receptionist at the museum information desk.

"Something bad must have happened," the girl said, leaning over to add in a low voice, "Mr. Scribner went and fired Val this morning. Nobody could believe it."

A familiar name on the guest register made Raven's eyes narrow. "Where can I find this Scribner guy?"

She followed the receptionist's directions to the administrative wing, where she intercepted Madelain Pierport and a short, cigar-smoking man wearing a cheesy-looking white suit.

"Mademoiselle Raven." The Frenchwoman sounded stunned. "I was not aware you were traveling to the States."

"Yeah, surprise, surprise." She eyed the man, who was practically drooling. "You're Scribner, right?"

"Drake Scribner the third." He gripped the cigar in his teeth as he buttoned his jacket. "It's a real pleasure to meet you, Miss Raven."

"Save it." She took Madelaine by the arm. "Let's have a little chat in private, shall we? Excuse us, Scrubby."

"It's Scribner."

"Whatever." She hauled the Frenchwoman into his office and kicked the door shut, effectively slamming it in his face.

Madelaine jerked out of her grip. "What do you think you are doing?"

"That's my question. You're supposed to be in Paris, watching the store." She put a hand on the opening door and shoved it closed again. "Well?"

"Mr. Scribner invited me to fly over and work with him on the exhibit. As I was unable to reach Mr. T'ang, I felt it was my duty to take over the arrangements." Madelaine lifted her chin. "This is none of your affair."

"You couldn't wait to get over here and make trouble for Val, could you?" Raven sighed. "Okay, Madelaine, run along back to Paris like a good girl."

The other woman sniffed. "I must protect Mr. T'ang's interests."

"Someone protecting his own interests chopped Akune Ogawa into small pieces and sprinkled them in the alley behind his gallery." She saw a flash of unease behind the revulsion on the French-woman's face. "Are you mixed up in that, too?"

Madelaine's face turned an ugly shade of red. "No, of course not! *Mon Dieu*, mademoiselle, how could you accuse me of such a thing?"

Raven kept her gaze locked with Madelaine's, but after a moment stepped away. "Fine. You want to end up like him, keep playing your games. Where is Valence?"

"She left some thirty minutes ago." She made a dismissive gesture. "I have no idea where she went, nor do I care to know."

"I thought I had the whole bitch thing down, but you could give me remedial lessons, Madelaine." Raven stalked out of the office, brushing past the startled head curator on the way to her car.

Madelaine accepted Scribner's apologies, along with an invitation to dinner, and left the museum feeling very pleased with herself. Not only had she rid herself and Jian-Shan of the annoying American girl, but she had bested Raven as well. As she unlocked her car and slid in behind the wheel, she took a moment to preen a little.

Her smug satisfaction turned to a shriek as a man sat up in the back and leaned over the seat.

"Mademoiselle Pierport," Dr. Toyotomi said, holding a scalpel to her throat. "How nice to see you again."

A miserable Lily refused to move from a window in the front room where she sat looking out at the front gate. After she ignored the housekeeper's attempts to coax her away, Jian-Shan picked her up and carried her into the dining room. Yet when he attempted to place her in her high chair, she began to flail and shriek.

"Mama!" For the first time in her life, Lily struck him with her small fists. "Mama!"

"I am sorry, master," Shikoro said in Japanese as she hurried over to take the screaming child. "She has been watching for Miss Valence since she left this morning."

Jian-Shan nodded. "Perhaps a bath will calm her down."

He found he had little appetite for his own meal, and sat contemplating the empty space where Valence should have been sitting. He knew it was dangerous to let her go, but Raven's people would look after her.

And he knew if she had spent another night in the house, he would not have been able to stay away from her.

His cell phone rang.

"Jay." Raven sounded grim. "New problems."

He listened as she related what had happened at the museum, Madelaine's inexplicable presence in New Orleans, and Val's losing the tail Raven had put on her. "There's something else—it appears your dad bought some eyewitnesses to Akune's murder. The French cops want to question Val."

He swore softly in Chinese.

"Yeah, my sentiments exactly. My guys are looking for her now. I'd go myself, but it looks like the general's back in town and he's slightly pissed at me."

"You should have stayed in Europe."

"I don't want to spend the next thirty years in Leavenworth, so I'll be leaving town shortly." Raven paused. "Jay, if there was any other way, I'd stay and see this through with you. Be careful, okay? Kalen is no one to fool with, and the old man'll do whatever's necessary to get you back. You know Val doesn't have a chance on her own."

"I know, and I will. Call me before you leave."

He went up to the bathroom, where Shikoro was washing a sulking Lily. "How is she feeling now?" he asked in Japanese.

"She is sad and a little tired." The housekeeper caressed the blond head with a fond hand. "I will put her down after dinner."

"I have to go and find her," he said, refraining from mentioning Valence's name. "Did she tell you where her friend lives?"

"She said he was a musician. At a shrine—no, a church." Shikoro concentrated for a moment. "Duvall Papist Church, maybe?"

"Baptist."

He drove down to the church, which was closed, but he saw a light on in the back and knocked on the door.

The elderly black man who answered it seemed to recognized him. "She's not here, boy. She's gone on home."

He had the address of her apartment from her file. He turned to go, then hesitated and looked back at the minister. "Is she all right?"

"Lost her job, in some trouble, so now she's moving on." The old man waved him away. "You'd best hightail it 'fore you miss her altogether now."

Val's address, on the fringes of the Garden District, turned out to be an old house converted into a duplex. He checked the numbers on the mailbox before walking up to the left entrance and knocking on the door. She answered it, then saw him and immediately tried to close it again.

"Wait." He stopped the door with one hand. "I must speak with you."

"You said all you had to say last night." She pushed on the door.

"Please." He forced it open, being careful not to hurt her but refusing to be shut out. "It's important."

"Oh, hell, why not." Listlessly she turned away from the door and retreated inside. When he followed, he found himself inside a small but beautifully furnished apartment. Val had two suitcases on the sofa and went over to add a stack of folded lingerie to one of them. "I got fired today."

He closed the door and leaned against it. "I know."

"The police in Paris think I killed someone."

"Raven told me."

She glanced at him with dull eyes. "Why am I not surprised? Anyway, there's no reason for me to stick around. I'm going to Baton Rouge. I know an attorney there who collects daggers. I'm hoping he'll represent me, although I don't know how I'm going to pay him."

"You can't leave, Valence. I need your help."

She closed the lid on one suitcase with more force than was necessary. "You need my help. I've lost my job and I'm facing murder charges, probably because of something you're mixed up in, and you need my help? What do you think my answer is going to be, *cher*?"

"This is important."

"It's always important—to you, Jian-Shan. Never mind that it's cost me my job, my dignity, my research, my book, and nearly my left hand." She stared down at the other suitcase. "You want to tell me why I'm being framed for murdering that man?"

"It is a mistake." He put his hands in his trouser pockets, to keep from reaching for her. "And I am not asking you to help me. It is Lily."

"What?" Her head whipped up. "What's wrong with Lily?"

"She waited for you to return all day. She won't eat. She cries for you." He watched her shoulders slump and knew he only had to press the point a little further. "If you feel you must go, then I will not stop you. But you can't leave without seeing her one more time. She won't understand unless you say good-bye."

"She's a year old, Jian, she'll get over it."

"Please." He walked over to her and put a hand on her arm to stop her from lifting the suitcase. "It will take only a few minutes to do this. Do it for Lily."

"All right." She released the handle. "I'll say good-bye to her." She met his gaze. "Then I'm leaving, and God help you if you get in my way."

Val felt numb as Jian-Shan drove her back to the house. He made a few attempts to talk to her, but she had nothing to say. What was left to say? She had gambled recklessly and had lost—the swords, her future, everything.

· Seeing Lily rush out of the front door and across the lawn nearly broke her heart all over again.

"Mama!"

"Oh, God." She went down on her knees to catch the little girl in her arms. Lily buried her face against her neck and held on fiercely as Val stood

and carried her into the house. "It's all right, *bebe*.
I'm here. It's okay."

An anxious Shikoro stood hovering by the door.
"I try stop her, but she hear car. Miss Valence, you
okay?"

"I'm fine, Shikoro, thanks." She ignored Jian-
Shan and headed for the staircase. "I'll take her upstairs and put her to bed."

There was no rocking chair in this house, so Val
sat on the edge of the youth bed and rocked Lily in
her arms. The little girl was so tired her eyes almost
immediately began to close.

"Don't go to sleep yet, sweetheart." With tender
fingers she stroked back the blond curls. "Lily, I
have to go away for a while. Do you understand?"

The small arms instantly clamped around Val's
neck. "No."

She'd have to lie to her, and the pain of doing
that nearly made her weep. "I'll be back to see you
soon, honey. Real soon. Your daddy needs you to
be a good girl while I'm gone. Can you do that for
me, *chaton*?" Her voice broke. "Can you take care of
your daddy for me?"

The arms only got tighter. "No, Mama."

"I'll be back. I promise." Her voice broke on the
last lie, and she drew in a deep breath. "Now, let's
get you in bed and I'll tell you one more story."

By the time Val reached the part of the book
where Goldilocks tasted the Mama Bear's porridge,
the exhausted child finally drifted off. She allowed
herself to sit with Lily for a few more minutes, to
watch her sleep, to imprint her face in her memory.

Oh, chaton, *will I ever see you again?*

Jian-Shan was waiting for her outside in the hall

when she slipped out of the room. Without a word she started for the staircase, but he stepped in her path.

"I did what you wanted." And it had torn a new place in what was left of her heart. And she hated him for it.

"I have something for you. The sword you were looking for."

"You mean, the one stolen from that dead art dealer's gallery? Keep it." She tried to go past him.

He caught her arm. "I also have a notarized letter stating that I took it from Akune Ogawa's gallery on the night of the murder."

She glanced at him, still suspicious. "Why would you give me that? They're going to think *you* killed him."

His expression remained determined. "It is all I can do for you. Allow me this much as reparations."

If she spent ten more minutes under his roof, she would have a complete nervous breakdown. "Fine. Where is it?"

"On the desk, in your room." He gestured toward the bedroom she had occupied at the other end of the hall.

"Thank you."

He didn't follow her in, she noticed, which was a relief. Being alone with him in a bedroom was never a good idea. And the sword case was sitting on the desk, along with an envelope with her name on it. She opened the case first, and caressed one blazing phoenix symbol, then opened the envelope.

Inside was a plain sheet of note paper, with one

line of handwriting on it. As she read the words, something clicked.

I cannot let you go.

Val threw the letter down and ran for the door, but it was locked. She pounded on it and shouted, "Jian! You let me out of here! Now!"

No one answered, and the fear of waking Lily made her stop. She was so angry she couldn't see straight. She went over to the window and opened it. It was just large enough for her to squeeze through, but the drop to the ground was more than twenty feet.

"I would not recommend jumping," Jian said from behind her. He had let himself in and was locking the door again.

"You are out of your mind if you think I'm going to let you do this to me again." She picked up a lamp. "Let me go."

He pocketed the key. "Put that down, Valence. You are not leaving."

"I'll bash your skull in, I swear to God." When he didn't move from the door, she blew out a frustrated breath. "You did this on purpose—the whole thing with Lily—just to get me here and lock me up again."

"Yes, I did."

His blunt response shocked her so much that she slowly lowered the lamp and stared at him. "I thought you were an honorable man."

"You want to stay, Lily wants you to stay. I want you to stay." His eyes narrowed. "You're better off here, with me."

"I'm not safe around you. I've never been safe around you. People try to *kill* me when I'm around you." She began pacing back and forth, trying to decide if the twenty-foot-plus drop was worth it. "I can't believe I got suckered into this again. How could I be this stupid?"

"You know this is the right thing to do."

"First you want me, then you don't, then you want me, then you don't."

"All I have to do is look at you, and I want you, Valence. That has never been any question of that."

"You're as blind as Nagatoki was, Jian-Shan." She eyed him, then the phoenix blade, and began to move toward the desk. "But you do whatever you want. I am done with you."

"No." What she said must have snapped something inside him, because his voice went low and soft. "If I am truly blind, then you can play Lady Kameko for me."

She came to a dead halt. "This isn't funny."

"I am not laughing." He moved toward her. "You know what to do now, don't you? Or should I have Shikoro give you more lessons?"

Val didn't know how the Nagatoki blade ended up in her hand. One moment it was in the packing case, the next she was brandishing it, with the point three inches away from Jian-Shan's empty heart. "You stay right where you are."

He didn't blink. "Put the blade down, Valence."

"You think I don't know how cold-blooded you are? I do. You think you can use how I feel about you for your convenience? Not in a million years. Not even for Lily, God forgive me." She swallowed hard, then lifted her chin. "You're going to let me go. You're going to get out of my way and let me walk out of here. Now."

He took a step forward, placing the tip of the sword against his chest. "I'm not moving out of your way. You'll have to use it to get past me."

She steadied her grip. "I know how to use a sword."

"You know what you've read in books." He moved to the right, lashed out with his left hand, and popped the hilt out of her grasp. The blade went up in the air between them and ended up in his hand on the way down. "This sword was cold-forged four hundred years ago. It cuts through metal, bone, and flesh." He circled the tip under her nose. "One blow with it can split a body into two pieces."

She looked down the length of the sword at him. "You won't kill me."

"There are other things I can do to you with this blade." He brought it up when she moved so that the flat side of the tip rested against her neck. "Don't move, Valence."

She couldn't move, but she couldn't let him know that. "I'm not going to stand here and let you cut me."

"If you stay exactly where you are, and don't move"—he brought the blade down and sliced off the top button on her blouse—"I won't cut you."

She looked down, then up at him with wide eyes. "You're crazy."

"Perhaps." He moved to her left, sliding the tip down to cut away two more buttons. "You hold a blade on a man, you had better know what you can do with it. You can open his throat"—he brought the blade up to her collar, and cut it away—"or take off one of his arms." With a downward sweep, he sliced open her sleeve.

Val gasped and grabbed her arm, but the skin revealed through the gap was unmarked. "What are you doing?"

"Teaching you something new." He moved to her back, and she felt him remove the button that fastened the waistband of her skirt. Then the material over her buttocks parted, and she felt cool air against the back of her bare thigh. "Your spinal cord can be severed with a single shallow thrust from behind."

She knew he wouldn't hurt her. He couldn't. "That's enough."

He bent down to put his mouth next to her ear, and slid the sword up the back of her blouse, the blunt edge whispering over her skin. "One stroke, and you can lay the spine open, from hips to neck."

She grabbed her blouse as it fell forward in two pieces. "So you can kill someone in a lot of ways. Okay. I understand."

"You do not have to kill." He cut another slit in her skirt, from waist to hem, just above her right thigh. He sliced another on the left, to match it. Her skirt was slowly being reduced to black ribbons. "You can play, Valence. The way a cat plays with a mouse. Extend and slow the torment, and the anticipation of pain becomes worse than the actual cutting." His breath came faster as he circled her. "Until the floor is splattered and slippery from the blood."

Her mouth hurt, and she realized she'd bitten her bottom lip so hard that it was bleeding. "You've never done anything like that. You're just trying to scare me again."

"Oh, but I have." He looked down at the sword in his hand, as if remembering. "My father didn't send me to Japan to get a better education. He sent me to be forged, like a blade. His blade." He put a hand to her throat, making her flinch from the sudden contact. "When I came back to China, I joined the family tong. You already know what that is, clever girl that you are."

She nodded, suddenly more afraid of him than the sword.

"My father liked to use me to impress his allies and deal with his enemies. I didn't have to actually kill anyone; he had other men to do that."

She didn't want to know—and she had to know. "Then what did you do?"

"I taught them fear. The way I'm teaching you now. I became an expert at it. At instilling it in the hearts of men. My father's own bodyguards would begin to sweat the moment I entered a room." He turned and with one smooth motion threw the sword across the room. It buried itself in one of the veneer panels. Then he turned to her. "Now tell me you care for me. Tell me we can create something beautiful together."

She couldn't find her voice, her throat was too dry. All she could do was reach out to him.

That was enough. He yanked her into his arms, and lifted her until her feet left the floor, up to his face, his mouth. She hung suspended between his hands, so close now she could see into the black abyss of his eyes, where there was nothing but blind anger and heat, waiting for her.

He held her for another moment, as if anticipating something, some word, some sign. His control was so utterly ruthless that it hurt her, to know his father had made him like this. By making him inflict pain and suffering on others. A sound came from her throat, something wordless and plaintive, and she rested her scarred hand against his scarred shoulder.

He looked down at her hand, at the scar pressing against his own. "You're mine."

There was no other possible answer. "Yes."

The impact of his mouth on hers was no less of a shock than the knife that had pinned them together, that day in the garden. This time the pain didn't pierce her flesh, but went straight through her heart. The groan she uttered opened her mouth for him, and he took it as if they had embraced a thousand times before. As if they knew every inch of each other, through endless sultry nights of passion and exploration. As if they were longtime lovers, instead of strangers who had barely kissed.

This was what he had been hiding from her, all along. This terrible desire to be loved, concealed under the mask of indifference. How could she have missed it?

One of his hands wrapped around the back of her head, the other clamped around her waist. He went down on his knees, forcing her to hers, pulling her in, welding them together from thigh to heart. He held her head so that she couldn't pull away from his hungry mouth, from his tongue, from the edge of his teeth. He kissed her the way a man did when he climaxed inside a woman, with a deep, primal certainty that shook her even more.

She tasted blood—hers, his, how could she know?—and groaned again.

He lifted his head, and she saw a trace of blood on his mouth. "Tell me I do not see you now. That I am a blind man. That I do not want you."

Want, not love. "Are you playing with me now, Jian?"

His fingers tightened against her scalp. "No. *No.*" He brought her hand back to his chest and pushed it under his open collar until her palm covered the small, ridged scar. "You feel it, here, when you touch me. The same way I do. That blade made our flesh and blood one. It will be the same when you open your thighs for me, and I come inside you."

"I'm scared," she heard herself say.

"Feel me." He took her uninjured hand and guided it down between them, until her fingers slid over the length of his erection. He left her hand there, and moved his fingers to cup her through her panties. "I feel you." One finger ran along the center of the silky fabric, pressing between the folds it covered. The sensation made her curl her fingers over the bulge in his trousers. "Tell me what you feel."

She closed her eyes for a moment, and turned her face toward the hand in her hair, until she could brush her mouth against his palm. "I love you, Jian-Shan."

Raven passed through airport security unnoticed and began walking toward her gate. Out of habit, she strolled by to check out who was in the vicinity. A plainclothes detective stood by the attendant checking passenger boarding passes, studying faces.

Her disguise was good, but not that good. *So much for flying commercial.* She tugged her baseball cap down an inch and made a slow circle to head back out of the terminal. *I'll have to rent a rowboat or something.*

A familiar figure intercepted her a few feet from the metal detectors. "Going somewhere?"

"Bite me." Without warning she dodged around him and took off running.

Shouts and alarms went off all around her, but she wove through the startled passengers, slipped out an automatic door, and sprinted across the road, causing cabs and cars to swerve, until only ten yards of grass stood between her and freedom.

Nice try, General. Maybe some other time.

Some other time arrived when he tackled her from behind, knocking her off her feet and driving her to the ground. She scrambled free and got to her feet, then froze as a brutal hand clamped around her throat and the blunt outline of a gun muzzle pressed against the side of her head. "Don't even think about it."

She dropped and lashed out with her arm and foot, but found herself flat on her back an instant later. "You've kept up with your training. Do you work out with the Joint Chiefs?"

"Shut up." Keeping her pinned between his thighs, he rolled her facedown into the grass and cuffed her hands behind her back. Then he hauled her to her feet. "Let's go."

"What's your hurry?" She eyed the two agents

waiting by an unmarked car at the curb. "Oh, sweetheart. You brought backup. I'm touched."

He leaned close enough for her to see a hint of murder in his green eyes. "Where is T'ang?"

"In a jar at the supermarket." She sent a flirtatious smile toward the younger of the two men by the car. "Hey, can the cute one with the dimples sit in back with me?"

"No." He jerked her toward the car.

"I told him, I didn't date government operatives," she said to the agents while Kalen pushed her into the backseat. "The man simply will not take no for an answer."

He climbed in beside her. "I told you to shut your mouth."

"I don't take orders from you anymore, General. I haven't for seven years." She winked at one of the agents as he glanced at her. "Though I might reconsider, if you assign *him* to work under me."

Raven kept up a steady stream of quips and mild insults as they drove into the city. She was surprised Kalen would take her in to the local P.D. headquarters, but she suspected he wanted plenty of witnesses while he interrogated her.

Which was fine. She liked playing to a big audience.

Kalen handed her off to a uniform, who escorted her in cuffs to an interrogation room where two army officers were waiting. They showed her the arrest warrant, the charges being brought against her in a court-martial scheduled in less than a week, and otherwise did their best to scare the daylights out of her.

"Cooperate, and we'll see what we can do to reduce your sentence." The warrant officer tapped her file. "From my point of view, you've got no choice."

She gave him a gentle smile. "I'd like to see your point of view, but I don't think I can get my head that far up your ass."

As the officers continued to threaten her, Raven yawned, counted the ceiling tiles, and hummed show tunes, keeping time by tapping her sneakers on the linoleum floor.

Finally the army gave up and left her alone for a half hour, which gave her time to collect her thoughts. Unlike the warrant officers, Kalen wouldn't toy with her for long, and when he came in to have a go at her it wouldn't be with threats or intimidation.

No, the general would get exactly what he wanted, even if it meant destroying her in the process.

One of the local cops came in, carrying a cup of coffee. When he set it in front of her, he gave her a sympathetic smile. "Rough night, huh?"

"I've had better, honey. Um, how I am supposed to drink it?" She jiggled her cuffs against the chair back. "By lapping?"

"That general guy out there says not to uncuff you. Here." He lifted the cup to her lips for her to sip, then chuckled at her reaction. "You look like you needed that."

"I'm stuck in a cop shop with the best coffee in the world, and you won't uncuff me. That's cruel and inhuman punishment." She glanced over her shoulder at the door. "So when does the general want to get his jollies?"

The cop looked up as the door opened. "Now, I think."

"Good. I was starting to get bored." She winked at the cop. "Present company excepted."

"Thank you, detective, that'll be all." Kalen waited for the man to leave, and then circled the table. "Enjoying yourself?"

"That's my job description." She noted the shadows under his eyes and the lines of strain around his mouth. The spy business was finally taking its toll on her old lover—or was it maybe a dose of some well-deserved guilt? "Save yourself another ulcer, General. Take off these cuffs and let me walk out of here."

"You knew better than to come back to the U.S., Raven." He took off his jacket and sat down across from her, and turned on the small voice recorder. "Where is T'ang Jian-Shan?"

With a faint pang of regret, Raven bumped the table deliberately with her knee, knocking over the cup of coffee. Kalen slid his chair back to avoid the hot stream that shot across the table and poured off the edge.

"You don't like the coffee?" Raven asked. "Shame, it's really fantastic. Well, maybe not in your lap."

He picked up the recorder, which was soaked, then met her gaze. "Where is he?"

"You keep asking me the same, old, boring question." She tilted her head. "Why not try something else? Like, how was your last show, Raven? Did you like working for Chanel? What's the hottest fashion in Sainte Trophe? Will hemlines go up or down for the fall?"

"T'ang Po won't stay in Paris forever," he told her, in that quiet voice he used to get attention. "He'll find out where Jian-Shan is, and then people are going to die."

She huffed out a laugh. "I seriously doubt that. Though if he shows his face in New Orleans, you can count on sweeping up little pieces of Po off the street."

"I'm not letting your boyfriend start a tong war."

She watched the muscle in his jaw tick. "Ah, gee. Too late."

Kalen never shouted when he was furious. He didn't have to. "If one civilian dies, I make sure you'll get life."

"I'm not going to be around, General. You see, there's a file out there somewhere with the name, location, and activities of every operative you've got in Europe."

"You're not that good."

"Who trained me?" She tilted her head. "This is how it works: I go to jail, that file gets copied and mailed to a number of interested parties." She thought for a moment. "I don't think they're all friends of the United States, though."

"You wouldn't put those men and women in danger. You were one of us, once."

"You can tell their families they were sacrifices on the altar of national security. That's what you called me." She lifted her shoulders. "The fact remains, General, that you backed me into this corner. Can you really afford to find out what it takes to keep me here?"

He stared at her as if gauging every word. "I don't know you anymore."

"Wrong, Kalen." She smiled. "You never knew me at all."

Kalen walked out of the interrogation room and caught one of the detectives watching him—the one who had brought Raven the coffee she'd tried to dump in his lap.

"Any luck with her?" the cop wanted to know.

He hadn't killed her, which he considered to be a minor miracle. "I'm going to have to move her to a secure location. Get me whatever I have to sign."

The cop's expression changed. "Yeah, right." He made a sound of disgust. "We'll be fishing her out of the Mississippi in a week, won't we?"

Suddenly Kalen had the cop by the front of his wrinkled shirt and about two inches from his face. "The United States Army doesn't work that way, officer."

"Sure. No problem." The cop held up his hands until Kalen released him. "I apologize. That was out of line. She's just so . . ."

Beautiful. Brilliant. Bad.

He moved away and rejoined his men, who were waiting silently outside the interrogation room. "I'm going to have to move her tonight. Head back to base and report in."

"Shouldn't we go with you, sir?" One of the warrant officers nodded toward the door. "She's a real handful."

"I know what she is." He checked his watch. "See what intelligence has for us on T'ang Po and if he's made any movement. I'll be in touch in the morning."

*   *   *

Had he had one ounce less control, Jian-Shan might have taken Valence on the floor of her room. But that was not what he needed, or what she deserved. He had to give them both more than a mindless race for release.

He moved her backward, until her legs touched the edge of her bed. As he stripped back the sheets and drew her down with him, he realized how colorless his fantasies had been. Like the black-and-white screens of his security system, projecting the image but not the substance.

Val's hair spilled like liquid gold over the pillows, while her skin glowed against the white sheets. Even the tattered blouse and skirt became ribbons of color, winding around her body, offering glimpses of what she would look like, naked, under him. Her dark eyes, staring up at him from under heavy lids, her slim hands, touching him, clutching at him.

She eclipsed every single thing of beauty he had ever seen.

"I waited too long," he told her, stretching out beside her so that their bodies touched. "My fallen angel. You are like a dream in the night, come to life. Like no other woman I have ever known."

Val went still. "Not even Karen?"

He concentrated on the words. "Who told you about her?"

"You did." She turned her face away. "I heard you talking one night, when you were in Lily's room. I didn't mean to listen, but I'd never heard anything so beautiful, or so sad." She made a small, miserable sound that echoed the hollow sensation in his chest. "I'm so sorry about her. She must have loved you and Lily very much."

The rage came out of nowhere. He grabbed her and forced her over, under him, until he had her pinned to the mattress. "You know nothing about my wife."

"No. I don't."

"Be quiet." Her face paled at his tone, but he would not relent. "The wife you think loved me despised me so much that she killed herself three days after Lily was born."

Val blinked. "What? Why?"

He looked down at her, then rolled off and went to the window. "Karen was the wife of a powerful man in your country. A senator. He traveled with her, and brought her to my father's house. I found her crying one night. She did not want to tell me why, but I threatened to rouse her husband. Her husband, who had raped and beaten her. Not for the first time."

He told her everything. How Karen had turned to him for comfort, then love. How he had tried to protect her, even after learning she was pregnant with his child. But the senator had whisked his wife back to the United States before he could break free of his father's tong.

"After her husband died, she came back to help me leave the country, but we were never safe after that. My father pursued us wherever we went. He sent assassins. We could never stay in one place for more than a few days. Karen lived in terror, waiting for someone to appear to kill both of us. We lived like that for months."

Val felt her heart twist. *How could any woman endure such a life?*

"When my wife began her labor, she begged me to put our child up for adoption. She knew my father would use Lily against us. I refused, and went to make arrangements to move my family to another country. When I returned to the hospital three days later, I found Karen had hung herself in her room." He turned and saw her flinching reaction. "Before she died, she wrote a note, telling me how much she hated me for making her a fugitive, for ruining her life. One sentence I have never been able to forget—she wrote, 'Everything you touch dies.' And she was right, Valence. I killed her."

Val slowly got up from the bed. "Oh, no, Jian. You couldn't have known she was ill."

"I made her ill. I should have known how fragile she was, what her first husband had done to her. Instead, I ignored the signs. When Lily was born and Karen saw her, her mind must have finally snapped."

"Why? Why would seeing Lily drive her to commit suicide?"

"She knew that Lily was not my child." He looked at her. "Blood tests after her birth confirmed that she is the senator's natural child. Probably conceived when he raped Karen, on the night I found her in the garden. My wife must have convinced herself during her pregnancy that Lily was mine, but the illusion ended with her birth."

She came to him, tears running down her face. "You can't blame yourself for any of this, *cher*."

He had known. He had known from the moment he'd taken Karen to his bed that it would end in disaster. "My wife is dead because of me. The child I wanted is not my own blood. All I have left is revenge, and swords. And this night, with you."

Chapter 14

There were no words Val could offer Jian-Shan. His pain was too great, too overwhelming for her. And the love she felt for him swelled until it broke through her, in tears, in the arms she slid around him, in the trembling kiss she pressed on his mouth.

He held her for a long time, then made her look at him. "I cared for Karen. I admired her for finding the courage to leave her husband, and her country. I loved her for choosing to be with me, and to bear her child. But it was not enough, Valence. Not enough to keep her safe. Not enough to keep her alive." He paused. "My love died with my wife."

"No." She stood in the circle of his arms, cradled between his strong thighs, and took his hands in hers. She lifted them to brush her lips over his palms—one, then the other. "You have mine now, *cher*." She stepped back and began taking off the shredded remains of her clothes.

He watched her strip without saying a word, without moving. Only when she was naked did he rise and come to her.

He pressed her against him and ran his hand over her back in a soothing circle. "This is all I can give you."

"I know." She smiled a little. "Come to bed."

Jian-Shan did more than that—he caught her up in his arms and carried her back to the cool, smooth sheets, where he arranged her like an objet d'art, then stood looking down at her for a moment.

Val's face burned. "I know I'm not perfect."

"Perfection is for statues in the Louvre. Something you admire from a distance. Your beauty is warm and alive"—he trailed his fingers across the curve of her stomach, making her muscles tense— "and I can feel it when I touch you."

She watched him reach to unfasten his trousers, then felt shy and looked away.

"Don't you want to see me?" he asked in a soft voice.

Val turned her head and saw him, every inch of him. Undeniably hard and male, from the lean columns of his thighs to the rigid length of his erect penis to the sculpted perfection of his chest. The condom he took from his pocket and opened made her feel both relieved and a little sad. He was protecting her, but she wasn't sure she wanted protecting.

To have a baby of my own . . . like Lily . . .

But that wasn't possible, and she was glad one of them was clearheaded enough to take precautions. She reached up as he bent down, and shivered as his smooth skin slid against hers.

"You're trembling." He stretched out beside her and pushed her hair back from her face. "Are you cold, or afraid of me?"

"I'm burning up for you." She lifted her head so that their lips met, and felt his arms close around her. "I never thought this would happen," she breathed against his mouth.

The way he kissed her then cleared away the last of her doubts—his mouth open and hungry, his tongue searching, his hands splayed over her back, urging her closer, pressing her breasts against his chest. His thigh slid between hers as his palm stroked down the length of her spine.

Feeling his penis pulsing beneath the thin barrier of the condom, pressed now against her belly, made Val slide her hand down to caress him. But before her fingers reached him, he caught her wrist. "Not yet."

"Jian." A low sound of pleasure escaped her as he pushed her onto her back and covered her with his body. The weight and flex of his muscles against her softer, rounder limbs excited her, and she moved under him, adjusting herself to welcome him. "Please, don't tease me."

"Soon." He propped himself on his elbows and looked down at her. "I want to make this last longer than a few seconds."

"I don't care." His taut expression told her he was barely holding on to his control, and she lifted her hips, trying to push him past those last restraints. "I need you."

"I think you are the tease." His hand cupped her breast, and he played his fingers over the peak, watching it pebble even more. "Does it ache here?"

Her "yes" became a moan as his mouth touched her breast and he sucked gently on her nipple. At the same time, he moved his hand down to cup her.

She arched her back and rolled her head against the pillows as sensation and wanting collided inside her.

His beautiful hands controlled her, holding her in place as he moved to her other breast. She went tense as he used the edge of his teeth to scrape over that nipple before soothing it with his tongue. He moved down, stroking and kneading her breasts with his clever fingers as he tasted the indentation of her navel.

Val couldn't catch her breath. She looked down to see him curl his hand around her thigh, felt his hair pool on her stomach as his fingers parted her. Then he was stroking her with his tongue and fingertips, exploring her damp, swollen folds. He lifted his mouth to look at her, and the ache became unbearable.

"Please," she said, and tangled her fists in the sheets as he glanced up at her. "I need you."

"You need me . . . here." Two fingers slowly entered her. "And here." The rough pad of his thumb circled her clitoris.

His eyes never left her as he brought her to the edge, then used his tongue to push her over. One moment Val was helpless, caught up in the rhythmic stroking of his fingers, then his mouth took her and forced her up higher and higher until a wild climax seized and shattered everything inside her.

Jian-Shan caught the last of her cries with his mouth, still damp from her, and she tasted herself on his tongue as he reached down and guided his sheathed penis to press against her. He broke off the kiss and watched her face as he entered her, moving with exquisite restraint to fill her. Her hips jerked as she tried to impale herself on him, but he exerted his strength again, pinning her in place as he continued his slow penetration.

Finally he was deep inside her, his thick shaft filling and stretching her to the point of pain, and yet Val thrilled as she felt the pulse of his heart beating deep within herself.

"Valence." He shifted his weight, gathering her up with one arm so that her breasts teased his chest. Sweat beaded his brow, and he was shaking now. "So many nights I've lain awake, thinking of this moment."

"No more dreaming, for either of us." She curled one leg around him, making subtle movements to bring him even deeper inside her. "Love me now, Jian."

He moved in her gently, testing the narrow confines of her body, still maintaining his control. He was afraid of hurting her, Val realized, and as he slid into her she dug her fingernails into his back.

She began kissing the side of his neck, nipping at him with her teeth.

"Don't," he groaned against her hair.

"We do this right, *cher*," she whispered against his ear. "I give you everything. You give me the same."

It was so exciting to feel his body tense, to watch his control slip away as he thrust hard and deep into her, his hand rough as he took her breast, his chest heaving as he kissed her mouth. To know she drove him to that.

What followed was wild and rough and everything she'd wanted. He held her down, threading his fingers through hers to clench as his hips jerked with each thrust. Her own pleasure peaked again, and the feel of her body convulsing around his hard penis made Jian groan before he buried himself in her over and over.

Through blurry eyes she saw him bend close to her face, saw the savage pleasure in his eyes as his body tensed. He came to her then, murmuring her name as he climaxed, and the joy it gave her made the tears spill down her cheeks.

If this was all he could give her, all she could have, then it would have to be enough.

Setting up a meeting with her former owner took Kuei-fei one phone call and a brief taxi ride. She was amused that he specified the Louvre for their meeting, for in the past T'ang Po had shied from such public places. It would be difficult to kill her inside the museum, but not impossible. And the moment she stepped outside its hallowed confines, she would be a walking target. She knew Jian-Shan would also never be safe.

Unless she could shift Po's focus to a much more profitable target.

She paid the entrance fee, waived the invitation to join a touring group, and went immediately to the second floor. In the decorative arts section she moved from room to room until she spotted a man standing in front of an ancient golden sword.

"It looks crude, doesn't it?" he asked her as she came to stand beside him. "Nothing compared to mine. Charlemagne should have sent to the Orient for a sword maker."

She looked at the precious stones glittering along the length of the sheath. "Men of great power sometimes make such mistakes."

"As you have come to inform me of mine." T'ang Po turned and looked down at her. "When I bought you from your father forty years ago, you wouldn't speak unless I threatened to beat you."

"You never threatened, Po." She met his gaze with a serene expression. "You simply beat me."

He smiled, as if she had recalled a fond memory. "Are you here to demonstrate that you are no longer afraid of me?"

"I am here to beg for our son's life."

The smile faded, and he turned back to the display case. "He is already dead, Kuei-fei."

"He lives, and his child lives." She moved around to the opposite side of the case. "If you will allow them their freedom, it is in my power to give you something you have always wanted, Po."

His silver brows arched. "What could you possibly offer me to compensate for Jian-Shan?"

"The man who has been trying to destroy Shandian for the last ten years. The man who took your son away from you. Kalen Michael Grady."

"I have always underestimated you, my dear."

"Yes, you have." She laced her hands together. "The general's campaign against Shandian obsesses him. An invitation to meet with the former concubine of T'ang Po would lure him to any place in the world. A place where you could be waiting for him. I will bring him to you if you will grant my son and my granddaughter their lives."

"An intriguing offer." He considered that for a moment. "What guarantee would you have that I would keep my word?"

"I have kept mine to you. You demanded my obedience as your concubine, and I gave it to you.

You took my child away from me to be raised by others, and I never protested. You married me to your own nephew, and I was a good wife to him." She bowed her head. "And in all that has happened between us, Po, you have never lied to me."

A small cluster of tourists entered the room, distracting Po for a moment. He reached over the case and took her hand in his. "You know where the general is now?"

"He left Paris yesterday." She hid a spasm of pain when his grip turned crushing.

"Tell me where he went."

"I don't think my boss would appreciate that, boyo." Sean Delaney appeared beside Kuei-fei and allowed Po to see the outline of the handgun in his pocket. "Step up to that wall over there, if you'd be so kind."

"Irish." Po's mouth curled. "I thought you were dead."

Sean nodded to two other men, who moved to flank Po. "Just retiring. The wall, now."

The cluster of tourists came over to crowd around the display case, and T'ang Po snatched a young teenage girl in his arms. The girl and the tourists began to scream as he produced a knife and held it to her throat. "Another time, Delaney. Stay where you are, or she dies."

Holding her as a body shield, he backed out of the room. Sean and his men rushed after him as soon as he disappeared, then Kuei-fei heard a terrified scream. She hurried out to the corridor to see Sean kneeling beside the young girl, pressing his hand against her bleeding neck.

He looked up at her with furious eyes. "You'd

make a deal with that bastard? When he does things like this?"

Kuei-fei removed the silk scarf from her neck and handed it to him. "I would do anything to keep my son and his daughter alive."

"Then you should have trusted me."

Museum security guards surrounded them, and a few minutes later paramedics arrived to transport the wounded girl to the hospital. Sean's men dealt with the authorities while he took Kuei-fei to one of the administrative offices.

"He might have cut that girl's throat on a whim, but I'll not have you doing the same to your own neck."

She sat down and regarded him steadily. "I don't care about myself. Jian-Shan and Lily are all that matter."

"Damn you, woman." Sean dragged her up on her feet and shook her. "I've put my career and my life on the line to help you. I want to save them as much as you do!"

"Then tell me how to do it!" she shouted back at him. "Because Po will kill them now!"

Sean slowly released her, and ran a hand through his hair. "We have to go to New Orleans. Jian-Shan took the swords there."

She nodded, then grabbed his hand in hers. "Promise me you'll save them. No matter what it takes."

"No one else is going to die," he told her, and brought her hand to his lips. "I swear it."

* * *

Raven remained silent on the trip from police headquarters to the expensive, exclusive hotel. There was no need to say anything; she knew what was coming. She didn't even protest when Kalen draped her with his coat to conceal the fact that she was still in handcuffs, and marched her across the lobby.

The elevator took them to the penthouse floor, where he opened the door to an expensive suite.

"Nice place." Raven didn't flinch when he yanked the coat off her and led her over to a straight-backed chair. "Do they leave little Godiva chocolates on the pillows? I'm hungry."

"Sit down." He helped her do that with a push. "Lean forward."

She felt him remove the cuffs, then winced as he pulled her arms around the back of the chair and cuffed them together again. "Would you scratch my right shoulder while you're back there?"

He ignored that and bound her legs to the chair at the knees and ankles, then went over to the bar, where he poured himself a healthy portion of scotch.

"Can I have some too?"

"No." He drank it in one swallow.

She watched him curiously as he paced around the elegant room. It wasn't like Kalen to be hesitant, but maybe he really had bought her bluff about exposing his European network. It was sort of sad, to know the man she'd once loved so dearly had become so jaded—and gullible.

"Are we going to talk, or do you get out the instruments of torture right off the bat, General?" she asked as she tried the handcuffs again. It was no use—he'd adjusted them too tightly for her to wriggle free. "Maybe you could send for some flunkies to do the really messy part."

Kalen went to the window to look down at the city, the empty scotch glass still in his hand. "I do my own dirty work. Unlike your friend."

"I'm not going to tell you anything voluntarily. You know that, I know that. Might as well save yourself some wear and tear on your knuckles and get out the drugs now." She rolled her head, trying to loosen up her neck muscles. "Just remember, I could be taking a counteragent. Something that will either knock me out or kill me before I talk. There's been such an improvement in intelligence-related pharmaceuticals over the past five years, don't you think?"

"I don't need drugs, Sarah. Not with you. There are other ways to get information." He set down the glass and walked over to crouch in front of her.

She let her expression turn to stone. "You don't get to call me Sarah anymore."

"I can call you whatever I like." He rested his hands on her thighs, making her jerk against her bonds. "Let's agree that I already know where all your buttons are. So all I have to do"—he trailed his fingertip across her bottom lip—"is push."

She tried to bite him, but he only dropped his hand down to grip her waist. "That's how it's going to be, huh? You've become a real pig in your old age, General. What a shame. I had such hopes."

"That doesn't say much for your taste, does it?" He gently massaged her hip, and slid his hand a little higher on her thigh. "You never could say no to me. That's why you're sweating now. You remember what I made you feel. What I still make you feel."

She felt something cool trickle down the side of her face. "Sorry, I never got into bondage."

"That's because I never tied you up," he murmured, lowering his head to press his mouth against the inside of her thigh.

Raven nearly yelped when she felt his teeth through the thin material of her jeans, then clamped down on her raging need.

"If you do this to me," she told him, her jaw locked, "I will never forgive you."

"I'm not interested in your forgiveness," he reminded her as he parted the front of her blouse.

"I'll hunt you down and kill you. Very, very slowly. I'll do it, Kalen. I'll"—she hissed in a breath as he buried his face between her breasts "Kalen, for God's sake!"

"Easy. It's so easy, Sarah, just let go." His mouth followed the curve of her breast, caressing the soft skin until he found her nipple. "I missed these. The way they got so tight and hard when I touched them, or sucked on them." He nuzzled her. "You liked me to do that when I was inside you."

"Go to hell."

"If I do, you're coming with me."

He opened his mouth and drew her nipple inside, laving and teasing it with his tongue before he sucked it. His hand began kneading her other breast in time with the hungry rhythm of his mouth.

Raven closed her eyes, feeling the rush and burn sizzling along her nerve endings, taking unwilling pleasure in the tug of his mouth, the stroke of his fingers.

He lifted his head and stopped touching her, and looked up into her face. "More? Or do we end this before it gets ugly?"

"It's already ugly." Some semblance of dignity welled up in her, and she stopped straining against the cuffs and the ropes. "Do what you have to, General. You even might break me down and get me to beg for your cock. I've certainly got enough fond memories of it. But nothing you do will make me willing to betray the one friend I have left. Not to the man who sent me to die for him."

"What are you talking about?"

She stared at the wall beyond him. "I knew we were dispensable, but you know, there was no reason for the cleanup crew. We had them pinned down."

He grabbed her jaw and forced her to look at him. "Explain what you mean by 'cleanup crew.'"

"The backup squad you sent. The one that started firing on us. Jay was on the other side, but when he saw what was happening, he ordered his people to stand down. Your cleaners took off, while the guy you told me was our *enemy* pulled me out of a pile of bodies."

Kalen slowly got to his feet and backed away from her. "There was no backup squad for that mission."

She uttered a harsh laugh. "There's no reason to bullshit me, General. You know I never filed a report. By the time I recovered—to my great surprise—it was all cleaned up, as if it had never happened, and you had me declared MIA and presumed dead. That was when I knew if I came back to the U.S., you'd have to finish the job." She cocked her head to one side and watched him pace.

"That's why you had the plastic surgery, and sent me the photos."

"It wasn't much in the way of revenge, but I imagined you squirming every time you saw my face on the cover of *Vogue*." She smiled. "Did you like that fur miniskirt I wore for the winter fashion issue?"

"Shut up." Kalen stopped in front of her. "I never sent in a backup squad on that op. If I have to haul your ass to Washington and show you the paperwork, I will. I sent the four of you to China. No one else."

"They were Americans, outfitted just like us," she told him. "They knew where we were, what we were doing, and how to take us down. If you didn't send them, who did?"

"Anyone. Maybe someone in the CID. You were recovering missile tech stolen from the army, and it disappeared the same day your unit got wiped out. Someone must have sent in the cleaning crew to create a distraction." He glanced at her. "I always assumed you survived because you sold out to them."

"Oh, really. No, actually, I was recovering from a gunshot wound to the head that should have killed me." Which had been the real reason for her plastic surgery, but she wasn't going to tell him that. She turned her face. "You can feel the biggest scar, just above my right ear. Go ahead."

He came over to her, and touched her scalp. Then

he pushed her hair aside and ran his fingers along the scar. "Christ."

"Part of my skull was vaporized, so they had to install a nice-sized steel plate. I still set off some metal detectors in airports, to this day." She shook back her hair. "Makes it a real bitch to get to the gate on time."

He didn't say anything for a long time. Then he went behind her and removed the handcuffs. He had to kneel in front of her to release her knees and ankles, and she stared at the top of his head, trying to figure this new twist.

"You're free to go." He threw the cuffs and rope on the table. "Go."

She rubbed her sore wrists. "Just like that?"

He swung a hand toward the door. "Just like that."

"If you're playing some kind of new mind game with me"—she curled her fist as he came at her—"you're going to have to get through a quarter inch of surgical steel."

"God damn it!" He shook her. "*I didn't send them!*"

Seeing him lose control shattered her own. "Don't you lie to me, you son of a bitch!"

She drove her fist at his face, he caught her wrist and shoved it away. Then everything exploded, seven years of hate and betrayal and anger, and their mouths collided. His hands bruised her as he dragged them down her back, her fingers snarled in his hair as she yanked him closer.

Kalen wrenched his mouth away even as he reached for her hips and pulled her against him. "If you don't want this, get out now."

"I'm not leaving."

He hauled her into his bedroom then, his hands brutal as he ripped her clothes to get at her skin. She used her long nails on him as payback, and laughed when he swore. Her hair got caught around her neck until he dragged it out of the way to use his tongue and teeth on her throat.

She remembered only too well how it felt to make love with Kalen, but it had never been like this. Not once in all the nights they'd shared, not even after coming off an operation that had nearly killed one or both of them. Their affair had been brief and intensely passionate, but always balanced by affection and respect. Something had put a dark, ferocious edge to both of them, something twisting and simmering inside them for years.

This is what love turns into, Raven thought, *when you starve it long enough.*

He shoved her back on the bed and dropped on top of her, using his weight to spread her legs wide. She dragged his trousers and briefs over his hips, down far enough to free his rigid penis, and arched up to let him rip her panties apart.

"Hurry." She guided the swollen head to the slick, throbbing place between her thighs, and held her breath as he pressed in.

"Look at me," he muttered as he gripped her hip with one hand and braced himself with the other. "Now." When their eyes met, he pushed into her, filling her with one hard, furious stroke.

Sarah gripped his shoulders, gritting her teeth against the staggering shock and pleasure and pain. "Kalen!"

"Hold on to me." His fingers dug into her hip as

he drew back, almost disengaging their bodies. "Are you ready for this?"

"No." She grabbed his hair and pulled his face down to hers, panting as she bit at his mouth. "Do it anyway."

They didn't make love. They mated. Hard and fast and with a violence that stunned her. As if they had been chained away from any pleasure for years and now had no time for anything but immediate, thorough satisfaction. Anything less would have made her scream, anything more might have driven her crazy.

Kalen's hands and mouth raced over her, hard and relentless as the shaft he hammered into her. Their bodies became sweat-slicked and taut, and the elegant headboard of the bed began to slam into the wall. Raven was deaf to everything but the harsh rasp of his voice urging her on.

"Not enough." He yanked her up until he was kneeling and she was straddling him, and she bucked against him, her wet hands slipping as she clutched his shoulders. "Come for me, let me feel it—come for me."

She threw her head back and locked her thighs around his waist as she came with a desperate cry. Kalen laughed and muttered something, then held her motionless as he groaned and shook with the force of his own climax. They collapsed together, panting, shuddering, still holding on to each other.

Raven's eyes burned as she remembered long, sweet nights cradled in the same arms clamped around her now. *No. I'm not going back there.*

She slowly lifted herself until he slipped from her body. His hands slid down her damp back, resisting her movement, then he let her go and watched her edge off the bed and reach for her clothes.

"What are you doing?"

No protests of love or apologies from him—the general was all business. She had the sneaking suspicion that what had just happened would be written off as simply part of that business.

And if he said as much to her face, she'd shoot him in the head with his own pistol.

"I'm leaving." She ignored her abused muscles as she dressed quickly. "Thanks for destroying the memories."

"Sarah." He left the bed and stood before her. The fact that he could do that naked and still look absolutely in charge of the situation pissed her off. "I didn't mean to hurt you."

"I'll survive." She went for the door but was brought up short by his hand catching hers. "You've done more than enough, General."

He tugged to make her look at him. "Leave the country. I'll look into what happened with the op, but I can't guarantee anything."

"You never could." To torture herself a little more, she leaned in and kissed him, hard. "Have fun, babe."

Then she left him, and made it to the elevator before the first sob emerged. But there were no tears. She'd used them all up seven years ago.

"Valence."

A hand caressed her face, and Val rubbed against it like a contented cat. From the press of light against her eyelids she couldn't tell if it was morning or afternoon. It really didn't matter which. She was with Jian, curled up against his warm, naked body, and after the night they'd shared nothing would ever feel as good again.

A polite cough made her eyes snap open.

"I make you cinnamon rose-hip tea, Val-san." Shikoro smiled down at her and lifted the tray in her hands a little. "You sit up, drink now?"

Val felt like diving under the covers and hiding there forever. "Sure, um, thanks."

She had never been served breakfast in bed while there was still someone in bed with her, so the experience was a bit surreal. Jian-Shan was sitting up, reading a newspaper printed in Chinese and drinking coffee from his own tray, and seemed completely oblivious to the housekeeper.

Shikoro, on the other hand, looked as if she were ready to burst into song. "You need anything, call out, I come right away." She gave Val a smile full of meaning. "Beautiful day, yes?"

No matter how embarrassed she was, she couldn't resist returning that grin. "Yes."

The housekeeper departed, and like an old married couple, they had breakfast in bed together. At first Val contented herself with sipping tea and nibbling on toast while she watched Jian-Shan read. When she inched a little closer to him, he absently slipped an arm around her shoulders and stroked her hair.

Val couldn't believe how right it felt, sharing a bed with him. *What would it be like to wake up every morning like this?*

At last she slipped out of bed and pulled on a robe before going to the bathroom to clean her face and teeth. When she returned, the trays were stacked neatly by the door, and Jian-Shan was nearly finished dressing.

Confident after the long hours she'd spent in his arms, she went to him and slipped her arms around his waist. "Thank you for last night. It was incredible."

He nodded. "You should go back to bed and try to get some sleep."

"I feel too good to lie around in bed all day. Besides, I have to call that lawyer and see what my options are." She made a face, and then saw the way his expression became guarded. "What's wrong?"

"It is not necessary to retain an attorney. I will make arrangements to have you cleared from any involvement in Akune Ogawa's murder." He brushed his lips against her brow. "You are mine now."

She frowned. "Your what?"

"My woman." He disengaged himself from her arms and finished buttoning his shirt. "I will see to whatever you need."

She glanced at the bed. "Last night you said that you couldn't love me."

"We have proven we are very compatible, and Lily needs a mother." His dark eyes met hers. "You will go with us when we leave, and we will be together. I will take care of you."

Her heart died a little. "I see."

"It is a sensible arrangement for both of us." He picked up the Chinese newspaper and glanced at his watch. "I have some calls to make."

Dread made her throat tight. "What about my research, and my job?"

His irritation became visible. "There is nothing to stop you from continuing with your research. Since you were fired from your job because of me, I will compensate you, and provide you with a monthly allowance." He went to the door. "We will discuss the financial provisions later."

"Wait a minute." She strode over and shoved the door shut. "I'm not some submissive sixteenth-century concubine you can purchase, like a pretty fan. I'll get a job and support myself."

He regarded her the way he would an annoying pet. "I am more than capable of supporting you."

"I don't want you to. That's not how it works in this country."

"Ah, yes, American feminism. You can redeem your self-respect by devoting yourself to me, and Lily." He stroked the backs of his fingers against her cheek. "Have we not adequately demonstrated that we both need you?"

"You want a wife without the ring."

"I had a wife." His eyes narrowed. "We are together, and we are happy. Why are you making an issue of this?"

"Because it's not enough." Slowly shaking her head, Val backed away from him. "I'm not something you can add to your collection, Jian. I deserve more than that. So do you."

"I will give you whatever you want. All you have to do is tell me what that is."

"Your love." She swallowed. "That's all I've ever wanted. I was willing to wait until you were ready. But you'll never be ready, will you?"

"I can give you pleasure, and a home, and a child."

"For how long? And what if I want to have a child of my own?" She watched his face, then nodded. "That's what I thought. I'm flattered, but I'm going to have to turn you down."

"You don't have a choice." He approached her. "You're staying with me."

"Are we back to kidnapping again?" Her heart jumped into her throat as he settled his hands on her shoulders. "So soon?"

His thumbs caressed the faint indentations around her collarbone. "I can see to it that you never work for another museum again."

She jerked away from his touch and grabbed her clothes. "I'll find something else."

"Very well. If you leave, I'll relinquish custody of Lily and place her with an adoption agency."

Stunned, Val stared at him. "You wouldn't."

"She's not my biological child, Valence." His voice was flat. "No court in the world would expect me to support the daughter of a dead woman and her abusive husband."

"You wouldn't do that to her." Slowly she shook her head. "You know what happened to me. What would happen to her."

"You still do not accept what I am capable of, Valence." He left the room.

Val crumpled down on the bed and pressed her hot face to the sheets. She had known he was ruthless, but not to this extent. Part of her wanted desperately to believe he was incapable of such a callous act, and yet something in his eyes told her he spoke the truth. He was the son of a tong leader.

In China and Japan, blood meant everything. Why would he keep a daughter who shared none of his?

Val knew what Lily's life would be like, once she was turned over to child services. She would go through a series of foster homes, where she would be tolerated for the monthly check she brought in. There would be little love, and plenty of abuse. She would probably end up on the streets, just as Val had, where she would find only drugs and crime and endless despair.

She couldn't let that happen. Not to her beautiful, innocent little girl. That was when the thought she had been avoiding slowly formed in her head.

She's more mine than his now. I should just take Lily and run.

Jian-Shan drove toward the Mississippi, recalling the directions Raven had given him to her rented condominium. Since she hadn't called, he assumed she was still in town—although when he tried to call her, a recorded message told him her phone had been temporarily disconnected.

He felt pleasant muscle aches in several places, small reminders of the night he'd spent with Valence. He would have taken more pleasure in the sensation had he left her a little earlier that morning. Yet waking had not filled him with the usual urgency to rise; instead he had relished the rare delight of holding the warm, resilient body of his lover against him.

I'm not some submissive sixteenth-century concubine you can purchase, like a pretty fan.

For a moment, he envied Nagatoki—the sword maker had undoubtedly purchased his lady

Kameko. Life would be simpler if he could hand over a sum of money and be assured of Valence's presence in his bed for as long as he wanted. He wouldn't have had to resort to threats and blackmail to keep her at his side. He wouldn't be facing the fact that he had stolen her freedom, obliterated her trust, and possibly destroyed whatever love she had felt for him.

Unruly and unwanted as they were, he had to acknowledge his own feelings as well. He didn't simply want Val in his bed. Although he loved the feel of her body, the passion that burned in her, the exquisite joys of touching her and bringing her to a state of wild, trembling need had not been enough. He had not even been content to satisfy her once or twice, he had taken her over and over through the night, until the first edge of dawn had appeared outside the window and they collapsed together, exhausted but still entwined.

Making love to Valence had only intensified the need for all the other things he wanted from her. Listening to her voice, hearing her laugh. Watching her move across a room, so confident and yet so utterly unaware of her own elegant grace. And the less noticeable facets—her inquisitive mind, her dedication to her research, and her deep and abiding respect for the past. Coupled with her empathy and humor, those qualities would have enhanced any man's life.

And then there was Lily.

The child who had unknowingly destroyed his heart had captured Val's completely. He had seen how the two of them had grown closer with each passing day. Until Lily had begun calling Valence

"Mama," he had not realized how deep her emotions ran toward the child. Now he knew Lily was Val's daughter, in every way that counted. And like any mother, she would fight anything to protect her child.

Which is exactly why he had threatened to abandon Lily. It had been an inhuman thing to do, but he was determined to keep Val. Not just for a few weeks or months. Decades wouldn't be long enough to satisfy him now.

Valence had to be his forever.

His cell phone rang, and he answered it, grateful for the distraction. "Yes."

"Aren't you in a good mood," Raven said in a weary voice. "Where are you?"

"On the way to your place."

"Turn around. The feds are there now dusting everything." She sighed. "I need to see you right away. Meet me at Pier Ten in twenty minutes."

Chapter 15

Shikoro left Lily with Val so she could shop for the evening meal. "I make big dinner. Traditional Japanese first night honeymoon dinner."

"We're not having a honeymoon," Val muttered.

The housekeeper patted her cheek. "Have one after dinner, *Okusan*."

When she left, Val brought a pile of brightly colored blocks to the living room and sat on the floor with Lily, stacking them. As soon as a tower began to wobble, the little girl knocked it over and squealed with delight.

Tears stung her eyes as she watched the small smiling face and thought of it pinched and drawn with fear—as her own had been the first week she'd lived and slept on the streets. No child deserved a life like that.

Would it be so hard to stay? He's young, fantastic in bed, and wealthy. He even shares my passion for swords. Lily would be safe, and so would I. In time, maybe he would be able to trust me, and love me.

Someone rang the front doorbell, and Val went to answer it. Through the peephole she saw Dr.

Toyotomi standing outside, carrying his medical case.

With a frown she opened the door. "Hello, Doctor. I didn't expect to see you here."

"Mr. T'ang asked me to come over, to check on Han and Lily." The small man came in and looked around. "Is he at home?"

"No, he went out earlier."

He headed toward the back of the house. "Then I shall speak to Shikoro."

"Um, she's not here either. It's just me and Lily and Han this morning. Han is asleep, I think, but I'll show you to his room."

Val picked up Lily and led the doctor back to the first-floor bedroom that Han occupied. The bodyguard stirred, then sat up with a groan when he saw the doctor.

"What are you doing here?"

"Making sure you have not torn out my stitches." Toyotomi took out a stethoscope and gestured for Han to bare his chest. "Miss St. Charles, while I am examining him, would you dress Lily? We will be driving over to the hospital to have some X rays taken."

"But she's fine," Val said, holding the little girl a bit closer.

"We will be sure of that with the proper X rays." The doctor nodded as he listened to Han's heart, then turned back to reach into his case and remove a prepared syringe. "Your heart rate is rather weak. I will give you an antibiotic shot to speed the healing."

"You haven't looked at my side yet," the bodyguard said.

Toyotomi gave him a faintly exasperated look. "Who is the doctor, *rikishi*, you or I?"

"I do not need a shot, thank you." Han swung his legs over the edge of the bed and grimaced. "Lily will stay here until the master returns."

"You're afraid of a needle, Han? I thought sumo wrestlers had the hearts of dragons." The doctor depressed the plunger, sending a small stream of colorless liquid from the needle into the air. "As for Lily, your master is the one who gave me orders to have her examined."

"We will confirm that when he returns."

Toyotomi, moving so fast that Val barely had time to cry out, plunged the needle into the side of Han's wide neck. The big man grabbed his arms and jerked back, but it was too late. The powerful drug made him reel, then slump over on the bed.

Val turned to run, but at the click of a gun being cocked she froze.

"I will shoot you in front of the child if I have to, Ms. St. Charles. Please do not make that a necessity." Toyotomi left his case and strode over to take her arm. "Shall we go?"

"I'll go with you, wherever you want. Let me leave Lily here. She'll just be in the way."

"Mr. T'ang wants to see his granddaughter as well as you." Toyotomi's glasses glinted as he nodded toward the front door. "Walk slowly. I wouldn't want to think you were trying in any way to escape."

The doctor had parked a familiar-looking rental car in the drive, but he made Val go around to the back and then handed her his keys. "Open the trunk."

When she did, Val gasped. A badly beaten and unconscious Madelaine Pierport lay huddled inside. Lily began to cry.

"Give me the child." Toyotomi took Lily with one arm and kept the gun trained on Val. "Pull her out of there and drag her up to the front doorstep."

"My God, how could you do this?" Val reached in and tried to rouse Madelaine, then had to physically haul her from the trunk. She was heavier than she'd expected, and moaned softly as her legs touched the ground. "Madelaine? Can you hear me?"

The gun nudged her side. "Take her up to the front door and leave her there."

Val gave him an angry look. "She needs medical attention!"

"We have other plans on our afternoon agenda." The doctor smirked. "I have no doubt someone will call an ambulance. Leave her at the door, now."

Jian-Shan saw Raven standing with a tall, silver-haired man at the end of the pier, and hesitated for a moment. Only a decade of trust compelled him to approach the pair. If Raven had meant to betray him to his father, she would have done so a long time ago.

"Cool, isn't she?" Raven said as an old-fashioned steamboat, complete with spinning paddle wheel, drifted slowly past them. "Jay, this is Sean Delaney. The general's fake hit man. Sean, this is my best friend in the whole world, T'ang Jian-Shan."

"I know who he is. He nearly got my wife and me killed," Jian-Shan told her as he leaned against the rail and regarded the older man. "Why is he here, Raven?"

"Well, besides arranging to get me out of the country without attracting more of Kalen's dogs, Sean needs a favor." Raven turned her face, and he saw a large bruise spread over her right cheek. "His favor sort of goes along with your plans." She saw his frown and touched her cheek. "I went a couple of rounds with the ground last night. Our friend the general got me at the airport."

And did worse, he thought, seeing the pain in her eyes. "What do you want, Delaney?"

"I want to take you to see your mother."

Blind fury made him reach past Raven and jerk the other man forward by the shirt. "My mother is dead."

"That's what your father told you after he sold her to his nephew." Sean sounded as angry as he was. "He made her promise to stay away from you, in exchange for your life. And because your father is a cruel son of a bitch who likes hurting women, he knew she'd do it."

"You work for Grady. Why should I believe you?" He released Sean's shirt and took Raven's arm. "Let's go, Sarah. I'll get you back to France."

"Your mother thought you wouldn't believe any-one. She also said you have a birthmark on your right foot, in the center of your instep. It's shaped like a scythe."

Jian-Shan froze, and turned his head to stare at the older man.

"That's not in your file at CID headquarters, Jian-Shan. The general doesn't know about it."

"You're more of a fool than I thought," he

snarled. "My father knows about it. The woman who claims to be my mother works for him."

"I'd be willing to believe that if she hadn't shown me the same mark on her own foot."

The possibility of his mother being alive stunned him, but Jian-Shan kept his expression impassive. "If this woman is who she claims to be, then you must get her out of the city."

"That's not going to be easy." Sean cleared his throat. "She won't go until she knows Po is in custody and that you and the little girl are safe."

Raven pressed his arm. "Listen to him, Jay. He helped Karen before, and he wants to help you."

"He helped Karen." He made a disgusted sound. "He used Karen to get what he wanted. Like he's using this woman who thinks she's my mother." His cell phone rang, and he answered it. Between sobs, Shikoro told him what had happened. He ended the call and looked at Raven. "I have to go."

He took off running for his car.

Jian-Shan found Shikoro and several of their neighbors in the yard, forming a ring around two paramedics. When he saw they were working on Madelaine, he went to Shikoro and took her aside. The housekeeper told him his business manager had been savagely beaten and left on his doorstep, and that Han had also been drugged into unconsciousness.

"I was only gone an hour," Shikoro said in Japanese as she used her sleeve to wipe her tearstained face. "When I returned, I found the neighbors with the Frenchwoman on the front doorstep. They called the ambulance, and said they saw a man take Val-san and Lily away in a car. I found this on the table by Han's bed." She handed him a small scrap of paper with a series of characters on it. "It is not Han's writing."

He recognized the strong, bold hand at once, and closed his eyes for a moment.

Everything you touch dies.

"It is from your father, is it not?" Shikoro asked with genuine terror in her voice.

"Yes." He heard the phone ringing in the house, and gave her a squeeze before striding inside to answer it. "Hello."

"Did you receive my message?" T'ang Po asked.

He gripped the receiver until the plastic began to crack. "Where are they?"

"Safe, for the moment." His father sounded pleased. "Are you ready to return to the tong now, my son?"

"As soon as you release them."

"I have heard such promises from you before. The last time I believed you, it cost me a great deal." His father's voice hardened. "I want the swords back."

"I'll deliver them personally, wherever you want. Just let them go."

"I will take you and the blades in exchange for the American." He paused. "But the child stays with me. Call her insurance for your continued and willing cooperation."

Jian-Shan would have agreed to anything to spare Valence and Lily. But he would never let his father corrupt another child. "Where do we meet?"

"Tonight, at the American's museum. Nine o'clock, in the sword room. Bring the swords and

nothing else," his father told him. "If I see anyone
else but you, I will kill them both."

There was a click, then a dial tone.

Jian-Shan fought back the wave of fear and focused on what had to be done.

"Senpai?" Shikoro hovered anxiously beside him.
"Do you have news of Valence-san and Lily?"

He told her everything, and added, "I will send
Val and Lily back to you. As soon as Han can
travel, leave here and find a safe place to stay. Han
will take care of you all."

As the paramedics passed by him with Madelaine on a gurney, she called out his name and
reached for him.

"She's in a bad way, mister," one of the medics
told him.

"Mr. T'ang . . ." The Frenchwoman's swollen face
turned toward him. "He did this. He took them."

He paused to touch her shoulder. "Don't try to
talk."

"No . . . doctor did this . . . to me. Toyotomi." She
struggled to keep her eyes open. "Heard him talking . . . they mean to . . . kill you . . . tonight." She
coughed. "As soon . . . as you . . . get to . . . the museum."

"You saw him, then," Kuei-fei said as Sean
opened the car door for her. "My son looks well?"

He rubbed his chest. "Your boy's in great shape."

After coaxing the address from Raven, Sean had
stopped by the hotel to pick up Jian-Shan's mother.
Only a face-to-face meeting would convince Po's
son that his mother still lived. Then he could be
persuaded to join their effort.

"You do not like my son," she said as they left hotel row for the Garden District.

"I like him just fine," he said, waiting for a cable car to pass. "Considering what you've told me he's been through, my government should give him a medal."

"They look at him and see the son of a tong leader, nothing more. Jian-Shan is an honorable man, not like his father." She stared out the window.

He sensed her unease. "You can't be nervous about meeting your own son, now."

"I have not held him in my arms since he was a tiny baby." She looked at her hands. "It is still hard to believe he is a man, full grown."

Through the Shandian tong, T'ang Po had been responsible for so many crimes the list seemed endless, but to Sean depriving this gentle woman of her own child ranked among the worst. "We're almost there."

The house was on a quiet street, but a group of people had gathered outside the front gate, and a police officer guarding the entrance stopped them.

"The lady is here to visit her son," Sean told him.

"The guy took off. Housekeeper's inside, if you want to leave a message with her." He turned and knocked on the door, and a middle-aged Japanese woman answered it.

Kuei-fei stepped forward and explained who she was in rapid Chinese. The housekeeper looked troubled, but nodded and replied at length in Japanese.

Sean, whose grasp of both languages was at best

rusty, couldn't follow the exchange. "Where did he go?"

"She says he is meeting Po at the American woman's museum tonight for an exchange." For the first time since Sean had met her, Kuei-fei looked frightened. "Irish, we have to do something quickly. Po will kill them all."

"No. He won't." Sean turned to the housekeeper. "I work for the government, and we can help."

He charmed Shikoro enough to convince her to let them into the house, where he contacted Sarah.

"This has gotten out of hand now, darlin'," he told her bluntly. "Time we called in all the troops."

"I'll come to the house." She sighed. "You'd better call the general and have him meet us there."

Kalen Grady didn't say much when he received Sean's phone call, but the few words he uttered were graphic enough. So was the slam of the phone when he ended the call.

Kuei-fei emerged from her silence as Sean set down the receiver as though it were loaded with nitroglycerin. "Your superior is unhappy with you."

"My superior thought I was retired." He rubbed a hand over the back of his neck. "Should be some fireworks about that later on."

Raven and the general arrived almost simultaneously, but ignored each other and put the length of the room between them. While Shikoro briefed the model, Sean delivered his report to his former boss in succinct sentences.

When he was finished, Kalen Grady asked, "How long have you been mixed up in this, Colonel?"

"I contacted the mother here in the States a few weeks ago. Tried to get to the son through her, but it was a no go." Sean held his gaze. "It was my case, and I wanted to close it."

"What you did was run an unauthorized op and withhold information vital to national security. You also violated a dozen state, federal, and international laws." The general turned away to watch Raven. "When this is done, Colonel, you're to report to D.C. You'll be facing a full court-martial."

Sean had expected nothing less. "Yes, sir."

The tall brunette hugged the housekeeper, and then came over to join them. "We'd better move."

"You're not authorized for this," Kalen told her.

"Shove your authorizations. These are my friends. Besides, Jay doesn't trust anyone but me. You go in there solo, he might cut you to pieces right along with his old man. I'll take care of the girl and Lily—they know me. You two can take down Po."

"I want Kuei-fei to stay here," Sean said. "She's a civilian; I don't want her in the line of fire."

Raven glanced around the room. "You should have mentioned that before now."

Jian-Shan's mother was gone.

Because he had no car seat for Lily, Val strapped the little girl in on her lap. "It's not too late, Doctor. You can take us to the nearest police station and be a hero."

"A hero can't earn twelve percent on his reputation." Toyotomi gave her a sideways smile. "The benefits of an account in the Cayman Islands outweigh just about everything."

Her skin crawled at the smugness in his voice. "But you're a doctor, not a monster. You've sworn an oath to protect people's lives."

"I do protect lives, my dear. My own and that of my employer." He glanced in the rearview mirror as if checking for a tail. "They are both of vital importance to me."

Her heart pounded as she tried to figure a way to escape him. Jumping out of the car, even at a red light, was impossible—he held a gun pressed to her side. There might be an opportunity when they left the car for the museum; she would have to be ready at any moment to take advantage of a distraction and run. But how far and how fast could she go, carrying Lily? What if he started to shoot at them?

"I don't understand." She dropped her head down to rest her cheek against the top of Lily's head. "Jian trusted you completely. How could you turn on him like this?"

"I was sent to him expressly for this purpose." Toyotomi chuckled. "Jian-Shan's father does not tolerate anyone crossing him, especially not his only son."

She thought of Jian's dead wife. "You had something to do with his wife's death, didn't you?"

Now the morose-faced physician laughed out loud. "My dear Miss St. Charles, Po ordered me to murder Karen and then arrange it to appear like a suicide. I personally thought the note was inspired. I was able to use some phrases she'd hurled at him during her labor and delivery to compose it."

She looked down at Lily, and her stomach rolled. "Why did he want you to kill her?"

"To torment his son, I gathered. Although the woman had seduced him away from his preordained place in the tong, and for that she had to die."

Fear and loathing made it hard to speak. "And now you're going to kill him?"

"T'ang Po doesn't want his son dead," Toyotomi told her. "He wants him back under his control. Someday that young man will have more power than any man in China or America. He simply doesn't realize how fortunate he is to have such an understanding and forgiving father." A funeral procession blocked the road, and the doctor swore. "What is this? They carry cadavers in the street here?"

Val wished it was his. "It's a funeral procession."

"I cannot wait for the dead." Toyotomi pulled off onto Bourbon Street and found a space to park. "Get out. Slowly, Ms. St. Charles. Don't forget, I have the gun."

She hitched Lily up in her arms and climbed out of the car. There were a few tourists straggling along, most drinking or near-drunk, but they gave her a small amount of hope. The doctor stayed behind her, occasionally nudging her with the gun when she walked too slowly.

As she'd hoped, a noisy group burst out of a tavern they were passing and separated her from Toyotomi for a few seconds. Val instantly thrust Lily toward one of the soberest-looking women and whispered, "Take her. Hurry. The man with me has a gun."

As soon as the startled woman tried to take the child, Lily began to scream, "No, Mama! Mama!"

and hurled herself back at Val, clutching tightly at her neck.

Toyotomi grabbed Val and forced her and Lily away from the group. "If you try that again, I'll shoot the child in the leg. Then we'll see who wants to take her from you."

Impatience made Jian-Shan drive up on the sidewalk to avoid the funeral procession, which caused several pedestrians to jump out of the way. Angry shouts followed him, but he couldn't wait for the honored dead or the grieving family. Not when the two people he loved were in danger.

The thought was so involuntary that it hung in his mind, startling and clear.

The two people I love. My woman. My daughter. I have to save them both.

As he negotiated his way around a trumpet player performing to a scant group on a street corner and bumped over the curb to rejoin the flow of traffic, he felt the emotions he had locked away for years flow through him.

He allowed himself to feel what he had sworn to resist at all costs. Love for a woman, and love for his daughter. His love for Karen had been a thing born of pity and protectiveness, yet she had loved him enough to free him from the dismal horror of his life. And she had paid for that love dearly. Even as he knew he couldn't allow the past to repeat itself, he could accept Val's love now. For he would not allow it to be sullied by his father's relentless pursuit of him.

Tonight. It ends here, tonight.

Val wasn't his wife, and Lily wasn't his daughter,

but those were only circumstances to be changed. He loved them both, too much to allow his father's hatred and obsession ever to touch them again. He would save them. He had to save them, because there would be no point in living otherwise.

He would give his father whatever he wanted. His loyalty, his legacy, even his life if that was what it took to settle the score between them. But somehow Val was going to walk out of the museum with his daughter and live freely.

If they weren't dead already.

The museum closed at nine p.m., but the security guard at the door recognized Val. "Ms. St. Charles. I didn't expect to see you back here."

"I need to get some personal things from my office." She directed a frozen smile at Toyotomi, who had his arm around her waist. "My friend came to help me carry things."

"I didn't know you had such a pretty little girl." The guard smiled down at Lily's tearstained face. "Tired, is she?"

"Yes, it's way past her bedtime." Val held her breath as the guard hesitated, then unlocked the front entrance door for them. "Thanks. I really appreciate it."

"No problem, Ms. St. Charles. You have a good night, you hear?"

Toyotomi told her to take him to the administrative offices, where most of the office lights were out. He nodded toward Drake Scribner's door. "In there."

Val walked in to find her former boss in an extremely compromising position with one of the middle-aged tour guides. The woman jumped off his desk and jerked her skirt down as she fled from the room.

Scribner merely zipped up his trousers. "This had better be good, Ms. St. Charles, or I'm pressing harassment charges."

Val suppressed a groan. "You should leave, Mr. Scribner. Right away."

"Leave my own office? For you? I don't think so."

Toyotomi made an impatient sound and shot the museum director in the chest. Lily shrieked even as Val turned her little face against her chest. With a look of disbelief, Drake sagged forward and collapsed on top of his desk.

"You will stay here now." Toyotomi quickly searched the office and took Scribner's keys from his pocket before exiting and locking the door from the outside.

Val set Lily down long enough to check Scribner, but found no pulse. Then she scooped up the little girl and went to the window. It was locked down tight.

She sat as far away from the body as she could and tried to comfort Lily. "I know this is scaring you, *bebe*, but I promise I'll get you out of here. I promise."

"Mama." Lily buried her face against Val's neck. "Da."

"Daddy'll be coming soon." She hoped not. She prayed Jian-Shan would stay as far away from the museum as possible. For she knew with eerie certainty that his father had no intention of letting anyone escape alive. Not her, not Lily, and definitely not the son who had defied him.

She had just begun looking for a place to hide Lily when the doorknob turned. Without thinking, she put Lily down, grabbed one of Scribner's heavier football trophies, and positioned herself by the door.

The person who came in looked up and stopped Val from crushing her skull by saying in a calm voice, "I am Jian-Shan's mother, Kuei-fei. You must be Valence."

"Why should I believe you?"

"He has a birthmark on the inside of his foot." The petite woman slipped off her shoe and displayed an identical mark on hers. "Exactly like this."

Val weighed the information for a split second before deciding to trust the stranger. "Nice to meet you." She put the trophy down and grabbed Lily. "I need you to take her and get out of here, right away. They're going to kill Jian-Shan and us."

Kuei-fei took her granddaughter in her arms and smiled. "I have never seen her before."

"Then you'll have plenty of time to get acquainted." Val snatched a letter opener from Drake's desk and paused to touch the older woman's arm. "I'm going to him now. Promise me you'll take care of her if we don't make it out of here."

"I promise."

Val kissed the little girl and ran out into the hallway and almost directly into a tall, silver-haired man. "Out of the way."

"You'd be Val," the man said, and pulled out an

ID folder. "Colonel Delaney, army CID. I'm here to help."

"They need you in there." She nodded toward Drake's office and went around him.

"We have men here to take care of Jian-Shan," he said, coming after her. "It's best you stay out of it."

"The hell I will." She ran toward the sword room. Nothing was going to keep her from going to the man she loved. Not the army, not T'ang Po, not even God Himself.

Jian-Shan had been prepared to shoot out the front glass doors to the museum to gain access, not walk through one left propped open. The utter silence and lack of security in the main lobby didn't concern him. Nothing concerned him but finding Val and Lily and finishing the game with his father.

He wouldn't have killed them yet. He'd want to do it in front of me.

He knew the exact location of the sword room; Val had reviewed the plan of the entire floor when they had discussed promotion for the collection back in Provence. That his father chose the same spot for their reunion only added to the inevitability of the confrontation.

Lights flickered in the corridors as he mounted the steps to the second level; then they winked out. He continued steadily toward his goal, watching for any sign of ambush. The only light on the floor spilled out of the sword room, and as he turned the corner he saw his father waiting in the center of the room with a black sword in his hand.

The night dragon blade.

He stepped inside, and then caught the man who

lunged at him from a hidden spot at his right and used that momentum to throw him headfirst into a display case. Glass shattered and a fourteenth-century rapier clattered to the highly polished floor.

T'ang Po inclined his head. "Your reflexes are still superior."

"*Otousan.*" The heavy, pounding rage inside him bloomed, black and malignant, but Jian-Shan shoved it back. "We were to meet alone."

"I thought a small test of your abilities was in order. It has been two years since I saw you last, my son." T'ang Po eyed the scabbard strapped to his back. "I see you brought one of my blades. Where are the rest?"

"You will have them as soon as you release my women." He drew the phoenix blade out and held it with the tip pointing to the ground—a stance of confidence. "Tell whoever is in the corner to my left to either attack or leave."

Dr. Toyotomi stepped out of the shadows to Jian-Shan's left, but held up his hands. "I am unarmed." He approached T'ang Po, bowing slightly before turning to face Jian-Shan. "You do not honor your father, Jian-Shan. Put the sword away so we can discuss this matter as civilized men."

He thought of how the physician had repeatedly treated both Val and Lily, and how often he could have killed either or both of them. His blood chilled, and a slight humming began in his ears. "What did he promise you to betray me, Toyotomi? Money? Power?"

"Both, actually." The doctor smiled. "But you are confused on the other count, T'ang-san. In order to betray you, I would have had to be loyal to you in the first place. I never was."

"Toyotami has no loyalties, my son." T'ang Po stepped forward and lifted his blade. With a single stroke, he decapitated the doctor. "And men incapable of loyalty quickly outlast their usefulness."

Jian-Shan watched the doctor's head roll off to one side as the body convulsed and fell over. "Will you skin off his face and have it hung in your conference room?"

"I've always found it an effective management tool." The older man circled the pool of blood, angling for a better position. Jian-Shan matched his movements. "Shall we speak of the future?"

"You have no future."

"You are wrong. With the alliances I have made, the Shandian tong will be three times as powerful as it was before. You will become my second-in-command over the unified triad."

"You raised me to be your personal enforcer," he said, watching his father's flat expression. "Why offer me a promotion?"

"Never fear, being my second-in-command will constantly require your particular skills. More important, you will ensure the future of our bloodline when I am gone." He stroked a hand down the bloody length of the black blade. "You know that whoever possesses the White Tiger blades retains absolute power over the tong. And when the tong unifies the triad, it will all belong under the rule of the T'ang alone."

"The other triad leaders are challenging you for control, aren't they?" Jian-Shan felt disgusted. "Is that why you pursued me? Only to repossess your precious swords and secure your own position?"

"You are my son. You are T'ang." His father smiled. "You belong to me."

"I belong to no one. I turned my back on you when I left China." He felt sick, thinking of how hard he had tried to please this man most of his life. "Do you realize that if you had let me go, you would still have your precious swords? But you could not."

His father laughed. "I know you want the power. Why else would you take them?"

"To humiliate you."

T'ang Po's expression darkened. "Yes, you did that as well. I have punished you for it accordingly."

He lifted the phoenix blade. "You've done nothing to me but make empty threats. Come and meet me like a man, *otousan*."

They squared off, closing in on each other and circling as the distance between them shrank. "So the son finally challenges the father. I had not thought it would come to this."

Jian-Shan watched the dark glimmer of the black blade as it moved in front of him. "I challenged you two years ago. You had your men hold me so you could beat me unconscious."

"I also had Toyotomi murder the senator's wife. Her name was Karen, was it not?"

For a moment his concentration broke. "My wife committed suicide."

"Your wife was hung from a hook like a roast duck on market day. The doctor said she struggled a great deal for a woman who had just given birth to a dead child." His father went to the left, measuring Jian-Shan's guard. "Imagine my surprise to learn the child lived. I enjoyed my time with my granddaughter, such as it was."

Whatever humanity he had left withered and died inside him. "You killed my daughter."

"Yes, I did. She did not die as slowly or as painfully as your woman, but she suffered." T'ang Po gave him a ghastly smile. "Your mewling females are all gone now, Jian-Shan. I dispatched them, and I am all you have left once again."

"No." He knew his heart had shattered, and something dark and hopeless seeped from it. "Now you will join them."

Val heard shouts as she raced with Sean up the stairs—Raven's voice, and another, deeper one. A man, repeating Jian-Shan's name.

"Jay!" The model was nearly screaming. "Don't do it!"

The grisly tableau that met her eyes when she skidded into the sword room shocked her. There were men with guns all around the room. Raven and a red-haired man stood in the center, near Jian-Shan, who was standing over a man bleeding on the floor. He held the phoenix blade high in the air.

Val recognized the man on the floor as the dealer she had known as Li Shen.

"If you kill him, it's murder one," the red-haired man said. He held a gun trained on Jian-Shan.

"He had my wife murdered. And my daughter, and Valence." Jian-Shan's voice held no emotion, but there were tears running unheeded down his face. "He killed the woman I love. This is justice."

"No, *cher*. Karen wouldn't want you to do this." Val kept her voice soft and low as she moved forward slowly. The letter opener fell from her nerveless fingers, and the sound made Raven whirl around. "Please, Jian, think of Lily. She needs you."

"Valence?"

She tried to smile as she drew closer, but the despair and hope in the way he said her name nearly sent her to her knees. "I'm right here, Jian-Shan. Lily is fine. I'm so sorry about Karen, but please, don't do this."

The sword in Jian-Shan's hands slowly began to lower.

"That's it, boyo. Everyone's going to get out of here alive." Sean gestured at the men around the room to put down their guns.

"I thought you were dead," Jian-Shan said to her, and life began flooding back into his deathly pale face. "I thought he had taken my last hope away from me forever."

"Oh, *cher*. You can't get rid of me that easy," she said, smiling through her own tears.

Without warning, the man on the floor jumped up and knocked the sword from Jian-Shan's hand. The phoenix blade hit the floor and slid to the other side of the room as T'ang Po dragged his son back, holding out the black sword.

Val ran, but someone rushed from behind her and pushed her off balance. She collided with Raven, who was also trying to reach the men.

"Now you will die for me." The man lifted his own, black blade and thrust it toward Jian-Shan's heart. Val's eyes widened as a small woman stepped between them to take the sword in her chest. "No!"

The red-haired man, who had already retrieved the phoenix blade, thrust it into the killer's back. He half-turned, his face ugly with rage, and then he toppled over.

Jian-Shan had Kuei-fei in his arms and was gently lowering her to the floor. She smiled up at him as though nothing had happened. Val knelt on her other side and took her hand.

"You are . . . as beautiful to me . . . as the day . . . you were born," his mother whispered, and lifted her hand to his face. "It is good . . . to see you again . . . my son."

"Mother," he breathed.

She smiled one last time, then her eyes closed and never opened again.

They left the museum together, driving through the night to the house in the Garden District. Lily, whom Kuei-fei had left with a CID agent, slept peacefully in her car seat behind them, unaware of the terrible events they had endured.

"The general asked if we would meet with him tomorrow," Val said quietly. "There are some things to clear up before he goes back to Washington."

"I know." He glanced at her. "He will ask me to go to Washington, to help with his investigation of Shandian."

"I can stay with Lily here, while you're gone."

"If I go anywhere, you and Lily are coming with me."

Before she could respond to that, he pulled up through the gate and parked the car. Easing Lily out of her car seat without waking her was easy; the child was exhausted. "I'll take her up to bed."

He went with her, and helped change and dress Lily in her nightclothes. Shikoro brought a warm bottle, but it was Jian-Shan who asked if he could give it to her.

"Of course you can." Val smiled at the tender picture of the little girl cradled in his arms. "She's your daughter."

"Yes." He eased down into the rocking chair and stroked Lily's head as she fed. "She is."

Val left them alone and joined Shikoro in the kitchen to make tea and fill her in on what had happened. Han had come out of his drug-induced sleep several hours earlier, and the housekeeper had had her hands full trying to keep him from going after them.

"Terrible thing, lose mother, father." The Japanese woman shook her head. "Master need you now, *Okusan.*"

"He says I'm not going anywhere." And she wouldn't, no matter what was decided between them.

Shikoro excused herself to return to her husband, and Val went back upstairs. Jian-Shan was not in Lily's room or his, so she went to hers.

He was standing looking down at the garden through the window. "Is Han well?"

"The drugs are wearing off." Silently she closed the door. "How are you feeling?"

"A little lost."

She went to him, and on impulse slid her arms around his waist from behind. "I don't know what to say. I can't believe your father pretended to be an art dealer and drove me to my hotel that night in Paris."

"Had you stayed there that night, his men would have tortured and killed you." Jian-Shan covered her hands with his.

"The way he killed Karen." She rested her cheek against his strong back. "I'm so sorry he did that to you, Jian. I know how much you loved her, and I don't think anyone would have blamed you for killing him."

"When I spoke of the woman I loved to my father, I did not mean Karen." He turned in her arms and pulled her up against him. "I meant you, *xia*."

She cradled his face between her palms. "You love me?"

"I didn't know I could, until I discovered he had taken you. And then life meant nothing to me without you." He sounded as if he were in terrible pain. "Valence, what happened tonight was like reliving a nightmare, but it must have been much worse for you. I don't know if you can forgive me for what I have done, and what my father has done, but it would mean a great deal to me if you would try."

"There's nothing to forgive. Oh, Jian, don't you understand? I would die for you." The kiss she gave him was soft and tender and edged with tears. "I love you."

This time she drew him to her bed, and pushed him down, and stripped off his clothes. Somehow hers ended up piled on the floor with his. It didn't matter. Nothing mattered but slipping into his arms and feeling him warm and alive under her hands.

He held back when she tried to kiss him again. "And if I ask you to stay with me and Lily?"

She tried to tease him. "Are you asking this time?"

"No. I'm begging," he said simply.

"*Cher*, you couldn't beat me away with a stick." She rolled until he was on top of her, and her expression grew serious. "If I stay, Jian-Shan, I stay for good."

"Then stay, Valence."

The gentle tenderness of his lovemaking nearly broke Val's heart. He handled her like some precious, fragile thing to be worshiped and protected. His hands whispered over her skin as he stroked her, from her narrow heels all the way up to her tangled hair. And along the way, he loved every inch in between.

Her breathing had gone raspy, and her body hummed with aching need by the time he moved to his side and urged her thigh up over his hip. Feeling him nudging her made her bite her lip and reach for him, as much to curl her fingers around his hard shaft as to seat the full, heavy crown where it belonged.

He covered her fingers with his. "I haven't protected you."

"I don't want protecting." She shifted, sliding down to take the first inch of him into her body. "I've never been truly naked with a man. I want you to be the first. All of you, Jian-Shan. Nothing between us anymore."

Without the barrier of a condom, she could feel every ridge, every contour, every satiny smooth inch of him as he slowly pressed into her.

"Do you feel it?" she whispered.

His eyes had gone so dark they looked beyond midnight. "I feel you, Valence. So soft and wet." He made a low sound as the tip of his penis touched her womb. "You hold me like your hand does."

"I like you better here." She threaded her fingers in his hair. "We might make a baby tonight. You know that."

He gripped her waist with his strong hand. "And if we do?"

"Lily would love to have a baby brother or sister." She released a breath as he slid out, then back into her. "Would you mind?"

"Only if you don't marry me." He watched her face as he stroked her hip in time with his movements between her thighs. "Our children will need a mother, but I want a wife."

"Then marry me, Jian-Shan." She kissed him. "And we will both have everything we want."

Turn the page for a look
at the next book in
Jessica Hall's thrilling trilogy—

THE
STEEL CARESS

Coming from Signet in May 2003

General Kalen Grady had spent the previous thirty-six hours pulling together the people, resources, and paperwork required to initiate the Dai operation, and three of the last four hours on the Concorde justifying the expenditures and his own involvement to everyone from the Chief of Accounting to his own boss.

Everything was in place, except for the bait.

Even knowing there was no other woman suitable for the job, he'd argued with himself. *You agreed to stay away from her. She agreed to stay in Europe. After that night in New Orleans—*

He could justify breaking his word to her—what had happened between them last fall didn't matter now. The violence was spreading daily, erupting in formerly peaceful neighborhoods as the tongs took their war to the streets. He had no choice but to recruit the last woman on earth he wanted involved in one of his operations. And to add insult to injury, the only way he could contact her was by staking out a goddamned fashion show.

So far sixteen stunning young women had strolled out onto the stage, wearing what looked like fancy negligees. All of them were magnificent, like young sirens out to lure any man to his doom. Not one of them was the woman he needed.

Kalen was beginning to wonder if she'd show when silence fell over the room, and a woman wrapped in mist stepped onto the stage.

"*Le Corbeau,*" a reporter beside him said in a reverent whisper before bringing his camera up and focusing. "*Le Bon Corbeau.*"

Raven.

For a moment, he saw a haunting image superimposed over the elegant, veiled form walking down the runway. The ghost was just as tall and lean, but wore her mouse-brown hair in a ponytail. Her face had been average, ordinary, nothing special. She'd had bright, dark eyes, and a saucy mouth, but otherwise, a totally forgettable face.

Which was why she'd been such an effective agent.

Captain Ravenowitz, reporting for duty, sir, the ghost had said, the first time they'd met. Sarah had been straight-faced and standing at attention, her expression pure business—and still he'd seen trouble written all over her.

Slim fingers reached up to tug the veil back, and the ghost vanished.

There were reasons a woman became a legend. Some said Raven had the most perfectly proportioned face ever captured by the camera—utterly faultless from the graceful wings of her dark brows to the balanced perfection of her full lips.

Sarah's mouth had been a little crooked on one side, he recalled, and she suffered with chapped lips every time the temperature changed.

Other critics, baffled by Raven's instant and enduring popularity, blamed her slightly slanted, turbary brown eyes—*as deep and mysterious as the mist-shrouded moors of Ireland,* one wrote, trying to pin down the elusive star quality.

How can I look tough when I had these puppy dog eyes, Sarah called them, pointing at her reflection. When Kalen had told her she resembled a dog as much as he resembled a jackass, she'd laughed, then demanded, *Okay, wise guy, what else do you call it when they droop down at the corners like this?*

Dozens of skin cosmetic manufacturers fought for contracts to use her smooth, alabaster skin as a showcase for their products. Raven, it was rumored, had her own special face cream made for her in some remote village in the Alps. She'd been offered several fortunes for the formula, but had always denied it even existed.

Kalen saw the ghost again—a ghost with freckles scattered across her too-long nose, and a small, velvety mole under her right eye.

If you want Mati Hari, Colonel, you'd better transfer me back to Armament Division, the ghost had said to him once. *But if you want someone who knows how to plant a tracer, tail a target, or blow up a bridge without getting caught, well then, I'm your girl.*

Raven's body shouldn't have matched the perfection of her face, but it, too, seemed to have been sculpted by the gods. Gods who defied the anorexic standards of fashion and created tall women with taut, toned muscles, high, full breasts and incredibly long, shapely legs.

Kalen knew *Playboy* had offered Raven a million dollars to pose nude for a special anniversary issue, and she had turned them down flat. He often wondered why she drew the line at outright nudity—she'd already paraded everything else she possessed before the entire world, had taken a dozen celebrity lovers, and did exactly as she pleased.

An ugly heat surged inside him as he thought of her many, public affairs. *That was to rub my nose in it. Like everything else.*

Raven let the filmy fabric float from her hand and continued her walk down the runway. She ignored the snapping lights and the voices that swelled with every step she took. Her movements were so liquid and effortless she seemed to glide through the air. By the time she reached the end of the runway, every man and woman in the room were on their feet, calling her name. She paused, scanned the room as if inspecting the audience for flaws, then allowed her legendary smile to slowly appear.

The face and hair and the mouth had changed, but the smile hadn't. It was warm, generous, and contagious—just as it had been six years ago, when he'd sent her off on her last mission.

I love you, Kalen. I want a house, and ring, and you, naked, on my grandmother's quilt, waiting for me when I get back.

He kissed her good-bye. *When you get back, we'll talk about it.*

And that not only stuck the knife in his ribs, but turned it. A small shred of Sarah Jane still existed behind that gorgeous, stranger's face, and he saw it in every smile she sent to the camera.

Raven's gaze swept past him, then darted back and locked on his face.

She shouldn't have recognized him. He'd grown out his hair and beard, then bleached them. He wore contacts that concealed the vivid color of his eyes. And still her lips parted and soundlessly shaped his name.

Kalen.

He nodded.

Her gaze went flat, and her expression iced over as she mouthed another word. *No.*

He only had a couple of seconds before she would stroll off stage, disappear, and the mission would be over before it ever got off the ground. Kalen couldn't allow that to happen. He pushed forward to the edge of the stage, moving rapidly, willing her to keep her eyes on him. *That's it; keep watching me. Don't run away yet.*

As if she'd guessed his intent, she pivoted on her heel.

He planted a hand, vaulted up on the stage before a nearby security guard could react, and caught her by the arms from behind.

"Hello, Raven." Then he lifted a hand and pushed the pressure dart concealed in his palm against her jugular vein. The drug inside the dart entered her bloodstream at once and efficiently went to work.

She whirled, her eyes wide. "You . . ." Her hands came up against his chest, then she abruptly went limp.

Pretending it was part of a planned finale, Kalen swept her up in his arms and carried her back down the runway, amid laughter and cheers from the thrilled crowd.

New York Times **Bestselling Author**

JUDITH GOULD